FRAGRANCE OF FORGOTTEN TRUTHS

A Serenity Falls Cozy Mystery

Iris Applewood

ALSO BY IRIS APPLEWOOD

Serenity Falls

Keeper of Lost Loves: A Serenity Falls Cozy Romance

Enchanted Owl

enchantedowlpublishing.com

Book cover by Angie Andriot

First edition 2025

CONTENTS

CHAPTER ONE

HOMECOMING

I rolled down my window to get a better view as my Uber turned onto Serenity Falls' historic Main Street. The car wove past The Purple Pantry, with its purple-and-white striped awning. A few doors down, the open door of The Cozy Cup beckoned, letting the aroma of fresh coffee spill onto the street. It was a scene from a storybook. Albeit, one penned by an author with an affinity for cobblestones and an aversion to modern architecture. It was also a scene I hadn't seen in almost a year. Too long. I should have—

No. The past was the past. No sense dwelling.

"Pretty different from the city, I reckon?" Roger glanced at me through the rearview mirror. His voice carried the lilt of someone who had spent years driving these streets, narrating the town's tales to anyone who would listen.

"Oh, absolutely. Less honking, more ... honking?" I replied, as a gaggle of geese strutted past The Enchanted Oven.

Roger's laughter filled the car. "That's Serenity Falls for you. Swapping traffic jams for goose parades. These birds think they own the town, and frankly, they might be right."

I didn't tell him I grew up here; my family's reputation often invited more whispers than welcomes. Anyway, surely he saw my last name when he accepted my ride request.

As we crossed through an opening in the flood wall, a panoramic view of Riverside Park spread before me, bursting with spring greenery. The cherry trees were ripe with buds, and daffodils lined the meandering paths. Whisperwind River twinkled under the afternoon sun. And there was the Whisperwind Bridge, where, legend had it, you could trade a secret for a wish. At least that's what my grandmother used to say, usually followed by a wink.

I whispered a secret there once. I was still waiting for that wish to be fulfilled.

The road wove between the flood wall and the park before transitioning into a narrow gravel lane. People seldom frequented this part of town since the construction of the flood wall. There wasn't much to see back here anymore, other than the house everyone avoided, occupied by the family everyone shunned.

"This it?" Roger slowed the car as we approached the house at the end of the road. His eyes lingered on the structure. "The Attar residence, isn't it?"

An old Victorian house loomed. The house's once-vibrant yellow paint now flaked and curled, peeling away like sunburnt skin. Despite the wear, it stood proud amidst the wild embrace of overgrown gardens and the dense Serenity Forest looming at its back.

"That's the one." I side-eyed the turret as I opened the door. It seemed to frown down at me.

After a moment's pause, Roger unbuckled his seatbelt and stepped out of the car with a friendly yet reserved demeanor. "Let me get those bags for you."

I nodded. Good. He wasn't going to say anything.

As Roger drove off, I stood before my family's ancestral home, taking it all in. The front garden had given over even more to nature's whim than when I had last seen it. Flowers tangled with creeping ivy, creating lush greenery that climbed up the walls of the house.

I'd have to do something about that.

With a deep breath that tasted like childhood, I lugged my suitcase down the stone path. My wheels clicked against the porch steps, a soft counterpoint to the birdsong overhead. I paused before the blue front door and pressed the doorbell.

After all this time away, it would feel odd to just waltz right in.

The door swung open, and there stood Emilia, auburn hair in a messy bun, wearing sweats and a t-shirt that read *Murder Shows and Comfy Clothes*. "Anna! You do exist outside of a Zoom screen!"

I stepped into the embrace of my little sister. Though at twenty-six, she was not so little anymore. "Confirmed. I'm not just a sophisticated AI after all."

Emilia pulled back, scanning me with playful scrutiny. "Well, if you were, I'd have to ask for a refund. The sister algorithm seems a bit off."

I self-consciously brushed a hand through my usually neat hair, which now felt like it had surrendered to a bout of turbulence. And I could only imagine the state of my makeup. Anyway, I had nothing to dress up for now. "Travel chic?"

Emilia laughed. "You do look like someone who's just survived a three-hour tribute to the wonders of commercial aviation. But don't worry, you're in Serenity Falls now. Here, the dress code strictly enforces comfort over couture."

She gave me a reassuring pat on the shoulder. "It's good to see you without all the city polish. I am sorry about your job, though."

"Thanks." I offered a strained smile. "Makes the city polish less necessary now."

That research job had consumed so much of my life. The long hours and missed family moments, all sacrificed at the altar of corporate ambition. I had barely even managed to escape for a few days to attend Mom's funeral last year, as it happened to overlap with a big client meeting that "only you can handle, Anna." And my repayment? A terse meeting, cold handshakes, and a severance check meant to erase years of toil and loyalty.

"Six weeks' severance for six years of everything I had," I muttered.

"Did you say something?" Emilia grabbed my suitcase out of my hand.

"No, nothing." I allowed Emilia to take the suitcase. "But what was the point of it all? I'd been with that company since graduation. Where's the appreciation?" I was teetering on the edge of a rant. With a conscious effort, I reined in my emotions.

Emilia put a hand on my arm. "It's okay. You're here now."

I swallowed my anger and stepped inside. *Whoa.* The foyer, which had once been a warm hug of family memories, greeted me now with a ... different ... ambiance. Gone were the familiar rows of family photos. These walls bore a more contemporary look, adorned with abstract art that brought a modern vibe to the space. The floral wallpaper, a hallmark of our mother's classic taste, had been replaced with gray paint.

As Emilia set my suitcase by the winding wooden staircase, I wandered into the living room. It, too, had transformed under Emilia's hand. Shelves of true crime thrillers now stood where Mom's delicate china used to be displayed. Emilia had moved Gran's armchair to face the floor-to-ceiling window overlooking Serenity Forest. It was like a different house.

"I've been making some changes," Emilia said, a note of understatement in her voice.

I felt a pang for Mom's past that once filled these walls, now giving way to Emilia's present. But it was nice to see my sister find her footing. Really, who could blame her for wanting to make the home her own now?

"It's different, I know."

Say something nice, Anna. "It's ... good." I offered what I hoped was a supportive smile. "Mom would have liked seeing it loved and lived in."

Emilia's eyes brightened. "I hope so. And Gran, she's okay with it, you know. In her own way."

She hesitated, then added, "I haven't touched Gran's suite, though. I just ..." She trailed off, shaking her head as if brushing away a thought too fragile to voice. "I keep thinking she'll come back to it, that she'll need it just as it was."

I swallowed hard. Hope was a stubborn thing.

Instead of pressing, I simply nodded.

The appearance of a plush gray cat interrupted our conversation. He leaped gracefully from the top of a bookcase that now occupied the space where our mother's cherished curio cabinet once stood. The cat wound himself around my legs.

"And this little guy showed up on my doorstep a few days ago. When I opened the door, he rushed inside and has refused to leave since. I've posted an ad on the neighborhood app, but no one seems to be missing a cat. I've decided to call him Watson."

"You named him after Sherlock's sidekick." I crouched down to give the cat a hello and a scratch behind its ears. Then I gazed up at my sister, nodding pointedly at her shirt. "So, you're still into all that true crime stuff."

"You could say that." Emilia gave a sheepish grin, motioning for me to follow her. We left the living room and navigated into the kitchen. The window over the sink bathed the room in natural light, highlighting the massive cork board that dominated the wall where mom's pots and pans used to hang. This board was cluttered, not with recipes or cooking notes, but with newspaper clippings, photos, and notes about unsolved mysteries and true crime.

"A murder board?" I raised an eyebrow. "Where did the pots and pans go? How do you even have room to cook with all this?"

"Cook? What strange magic is that?" Emilia grabbed a box of chicken crackers and a can of spray cheese and set them on the counter between us. "I DoorDash like a civilized person."

She opened the box and pulled out two crackers, then sprayed cheese in waves to cover the top of hers. She handed the cheese can to me, then gestured towards the board. "This is for the series I'm watching. I like to try to figure out the killer before the detective does."

"Of course." I carefully sprayed my cheese into a flower shape on my cracker and popped it into my mouth whole, then examined the murder board. This murder hobby couldn't possibly help my sister's reclusive tendencies.

Thirsty, I opened the fridge to get a soda. There was a distinct lack of groceries within. Finally, a problem I could solve. Grabbing a soda from the vegetable drawer, I said, "I'm not really into solving murder mysteries, but maybe I'll do some cooking while I'm here. It could be a nice change of pace. Help get my mind off things."

"I'm so glad you're here, Anna. This house has been too quiet without you."

I froze, can halfway to my lips. *She* could have come to visit *me*. In the ten years since I'd left for college, not once had Emilia made the trip. After Danny, she'd pulled the curtains tight on the world. Mom and Gran had tried to coax her back, even lined up a therapist. But Emilia dug in, even landing a remote job as an import logistics coordinator. Aside from not going out, she appeared perfectly fine. Content, even. Like she'd taken up residence in the eye of a storm no one else could see.

But I caught myself. A weight settled in my chest. "I should have come back sooner. After the funeral, and everything ... I just got caught up in my own world."

With me living so far away, Emilia had been left to shoulder the responsibility of Gran's deterioration after Mom's death. And the fact that my sister did it with no attempt to make me feel guilty about it only intensified my guilt.

Emilia reached across the kitchen table, her fingers squeezing my hand. "You're here now, and that's what matters. Let's make the most of it, right?" Her voice was encouraging, yet I could sense the underlying strength that Emilia had cultivated over the difficult months.

"Right." I nodded, making a silent promise to myself to be more present, to share the weight that my sister had been carrying alone.

I carried my suitcase upstairs into my old bedroom. What a blast from the past! Posters of my favorite bands from high school still adorned the walls. Well-thumbed novels and diaries lined my bookshelf, exactly as I had left them. Even the bedding, with its retro floral pattern, remained unchanged. The room was a monument to my teenage self.

This would have to change. Surely Emilia still had some of Mom's, or even Gran's, old stuff lying around that I could pick through to find more ... ahem ... adult decorations.

I walked over to my mirror, still bordered with photos. There I was in my science fair glory, standing proudly next to my aromatherapy study from eighth grade—charts of lavender's effects on stress levels. Beside it, Emilia and I grinned with gap-toothed smiles and ice cream-smeared cheeks, maybe nine or ten years old, our arms thrown around each other's shoulders on what must have been someone's birthday.

My eyes lingered on the sole photo of my dad. He was leaning against his old Chevy, sunlight catching in his hair the same way it sometimes did in mine, his eyes crinkling at the corners as he looked at something beyond the camera's frame. Something about his stance suggested he was already halfway gone, even then.

As I ran my fingers over a photo of my teenage self, arm draped over the shoulder of my old bestie Vee at a long-forgotten concert, a bittersweet smile formed on my lips. Despite the town's cool reception towards my family, there had been pockets of warmth and joy to be found.

My family, with our unorthodox ways and an old, enigmatic house straight out of a horror novel, had always been the subject of whispers and sidelong glances. Heck, the distinct lack of Attar men was enough to set the more old-fashioned townsfolk gossiping. Like seriously, there was no mystery there. Grandpa died of cancer, Dad ran off, and Emilia and I ... well, we just haven't found our forever people yet. But then again, our town was not known for their logic. Some have even gone so far as to blame us for a fifty-year old flood.

Us. Not bad zoning or poor infrastructure. Not the fact that the town had ignored years of warnings from actual engineers. Nope. It was the Attar women, with our herb gardens and odd hours, calling down storms like biblical plagues.

Yet, within these walls and among these photos, I could remember the good times—the laughter, the unshakable kinship that defied the town's wary glances. It was a strange kind of comfort, clinging to these memories, especially as I stood in front of the mirror now, staring at the space between past and present.

The girl in the photo, with her bright, expectant eyes, was nothing like the woman staring back at me now. My hair, once an unruly mass of auburn curls, was now straightened into submission, a misguided attempt at looking 'professional.' My features were sharper, my blue eyes carried the weight of things learned the hard way.

Was it a good change?

The realities of adulthood had tempered the carefree girl I used to be. Had I lost something in the process? The part of me that laughed too loudly, dreamed too recklessly, believed in magic without hesitation?

Nah. I'd grown up, that's all.

The city, the corporate grind, the relentless pursuit of success had sculpted me, honed me, turned me into the unstoppable force I was today.

The unemployed force.

I sighed, then heaved my suitcase onto the bed. As I placed my belongings in my old dresser, a small, dusty bottle caught my eye. I picked it up. It was my favorite perfume, a concoction Emilia and I had created under Gran's guidance. We thought this perfume was going to solve all our problems. A magical perfume to transform us into the prettiest, most popular girls in school. It hadn't worked, of course. But we wore that perfume religiously, anyway.

The label, faded but still legible, bore the name Whisperwind Whimsy.

Memories of my grandmother flooded through me, vivid and warm. We were back in the kitchen, laughter mingling with the scents of herbs and flowers.

"A dash of lavender for a calm mind, and a hint of rosemary for remembrance." Gran's hands had expertly maneuvered the array of herbs and flowers on the table. She crushed the lavender in a mortar, the fragrance intensifying with each grind. "You must treat each herb with respect; understand its nature." She poured pure alcohol over the crushed herbs. "Remember, Anna, every scent tells a story. It's not just about the fragrance; it's about the feelings it evokes, the memories it awakens."

Coming back to the present, a sigh escaped my lips. How simple life had seemed then. What I wouldn't give to go back to that time, when my grandmother was still lucid. When mom was alive. When dreams were just a scent away.

Chapter Two

THE PERFUMER'S ORGAN

A few days into my stay, the novelty of movie marathons and couch lounging had worn thin. As much as I loved the comfort of Emilia's L-shaped couch, fluffy enough to lose a shoe in and lined with an army of throw pillows in varying shades of 'calm blush' and 'intentional gray,' a restless energy had begun to bubble within me.

Emilia had taken the week off in an act of sisterly solidarity that I genuinely appreciated. This time together was fantastic, but the constant inactivity was grating on me. It was so unlike my usual pace—on the move, days filled with tasks and challenges. Now, in the lazy lull of Emilia's living room, all sunlight and softness, I was going mad with boredom.

I stretched my arms above my head. "I was thinking. I should grab a few things from Gran's room to make my bedroom feel less like a sad, leftover dorm."

Emilia arched a brow. "You mean pillage Gran's suite?"

I rolled my eyes. "It's not pillaging if she'd want me to have it."

Emilia looked unconvinced but made no move to protest. Instead, she gestured at her lap. "Unfortunately, I can't. I have a cat on my lap."

"Oh, come on! I'll cook your favorite meal tonight—Marry Me Chicken."

At the word *chicken*, Watson's ears perked up. He stretched luxuriously before hopping off Emilia's lap, purring with what I could only describe as opportunistic affection.

A smirk played on Emilia's lips as she stood. "Okay, fine. I'm obviously outnumbered. But just so we're clear, I'm never going to marry you."

"Are you kidding? I'm never leaving this place. We'll be the batty old sisters in the weird house that everyone whispers about and avoids."

Emilia laughed, hooking my arm as we headed down the hallway to Gran's suite. "Works for me. Maybe there's some nice floppy hats in Gran's closet to complete the look."

The door to Gran's bedroom groaned as I pushed it open, releasing a familiar scent of cedar sachets and old books. Just as Emilia had promised, Gran's room remained frozen, untouched and waiting.

A heavy four-poster bed dominated the space, draped in a quilted floral bedspread that Gran had sewn herself. Its pale blues and greens were patterned with lavender sprigs and roses, the very flowers she once taught me to enfleurage. The matching lamps on the nightstands had pleated shades that cast a soft golden glow when lit, though one was slightly crooked, a little off-kilter like everything else in here.

My fingers skimmed the soft quilt as my gaze drifted to the old Tiffany-style lamp by the window. This would look perfect on my nightstand.

Nostalgia tugged me deeper into Gran's suite. While the bedroom radiated her essence, it was the perfume studio beyond that held the real magic.

The moment I pushed open the door, the air shifted. Scents wrapped around me like a familiar hug. I paused, eyes closed, letting the layers wash over me: lavender, earthy sandalwood, the sweet whisper of jasmine, and beneath it all, that unmistakable blend that was pure Gran.

As much as Gran made perfumes, she rarely wore any herself. She didn't need to. Her creations had always seemed to be baked into her skin.

I wandered deeper into the room. Glass-fronted cabinets still lined the walls. A long worktable stretched beneath the window, bare except for a few stray pipettes and a forgotten notebook. And then, in the farthest corner, was Gran's perfumer's organ.

The wooden frame, once polished to a warm shine, now bore the patina of age. Rows upon rows of tiny shelves cascaded in a semi-circle, designed to hold an array of scent bottles. The central workstation, with its faded marble top, spoke of countless hours spent blending and creating.

Emilia's footsteps echoed behind me.

"Gran's perfume organ," I said almost reverently as she approached.

Emilia smiled and caressed the vacant tiers of the organ. "I remember being so befuddled as a kid, expecting it to play music. I'd even try to press the shelves like piano keys."

"In a way, it does play music. Perfume is like a symphony. That's why the language of perfume draws from music—notes, accords, harmonies. Each scent is a note, each blend a chord, all coming together to create something as moving and memorable as a concert."

Emilia leaned against the organ, her expression turning reflective. "You spent so much time with her, learning the craft. I never had the patience. To be honest, I never understood why you ran off to college instead of apprenticing in Gran's shop."

Ignoring her comment, I ran my hand along the smooth surface, feeling the grooves and dips worn into the wood by my grandmother's diligent work. My heart ached at the thought of Gran, now in the facility, devoid of the scents that were so much a part of her soul.

"We should make her a perfume," I said suddenly. "Take a little bit of her world to her."

To my surprise, Emilia nodded in agreement. "Let's do it. But first, you promised me dinner."

The morning sun spilled into the dining room in soft, golden streaks. The wide windows, framed in pale gauzy curtains, offered a view of Serenity Forest just beyond the backyard. The quiet hush of green somehow made the room feel sacred.

Emilia and I set about our task in near silence. Watson perched atop the sideboard like a feline overseer, his tail flicking in even, contemplative arcs.

I spread out the perfume-making tools on the large, sturdy dining table—a piece of furniture so well-loved its nicks and scratches formed a kind of secret family language. It had borne birthday cakes and report cards, holiday roasts and heated debates. Now, it bore the quiet potential of something new. It would serve as my makeshift workstation.

Gran's perfume organ remained untouched in her suite. I could have used it. Maybe I should have. But even the thought made my stomach knot. Every worn groove in the wood, every lingering trace of scent, was hers. The idea of disturbing it felt like cracking open a diary I hadn't been invited to read.

I wasn't a real perfumer. Not like her.

So instead, I set up in the dining room, where things felt less permanent. Less like I was trespassing. Here, the air still smelled faintly of cinnamon and citrus, the ghosts of past dinners mingling with the sharp, fresh clarity of essential oils.

With deliberate care, I placed slender vials in a neat row on one side of the table. The glass caught the light and threw tiny rainbows onto the wood grain.

Watson tilted his head, as if assessing the symmetry of my arrangement with the seriousness of a sommelier evaluating wine. There was a faint tingling in the air, like static before a storm or the soft press of possibility.

Turning my attention to the squat, round bottles, I set them apart for storing final test blends, then laid out the pipettes and test strips, zeroed the scale, and gathered my materials. With everything in place, I felt a sense of reverence for the process about to unfold, a ritual handed down through generations, now resting in my hands.

"But you're missing the most important piece," Emilia said, a hint of excitement in her voice. She arose and opened a drawer in the curio cabinet, then returned holding out a leather-bound tome.

"Gran's perfume recipe book." I reverently accepted the book. The brown leather felt soft and supple under my fingers, the pages within yellowed with age but still intact. I opened it to the first page, where my grandmother's elegant handwriting chronicled the beginning of her journey into the world of perfumery. It was a treasure trove of information—notes on scent combinations, observations on how different oils interacted, and personal anecdotes about what inspired each fragrance.

"Her grimoire," said Emilia, evoking Gan's whimsical name for her book.

"Except this is more practical than magic." I flipped through another page. "Gran's talk of grimoires and the healing properties of perfumes only fueled the town's whispers. Magic isn't real."

As Emilia and I admired the aged illustrations, the pages quivered, as though stirred by a gentle breeze that had found its way into the room. Suddenly, the book fluttered open. The pages turned as if guided by an unseen hand, flipping with a graceful yet deliberate motion. It was as though the book itself were eager to reveal its secrets, to share a particular piece of wisdom hidden within its depths.

Which was just plain silly.

Watson, however, seemed less skeptical. His body tensed as if ready to pounce on any further anomalies.

"Whoa, you sure about that?" Emilia backed away from the book as if it might bite her.

"Clearly there was a breeze." I peered at the perfume recipe the book had opened to. *Evoko*. The formula was described as a memory perfume.

Emilia reluctantly returned to her seat. But not without side-eying the page. "A breeze that just happened to land on the perfect perfume for Gran?"

"It's probably just how the spine has settled over the years."

"*Clearly* the Universe wants us to make this one. And who knows? Maybe it will cure Gran's dementia!"

I smiled at my sister's whimsy. "Well, it can't hurt to try."

I arranged the ingredients, starting with the top notes. "Could you pass me the rosemary and peppermint oils?"

Emilia handed me the vials. "Peppermint, huh? Never thought of it as a memory aid."

I nodded, carefully measuring the oils. "It invigorates the mind. And sweet orange is for that immediate impact. It's an immunity booster, and helps alleviate depression and anxiety." The citrus's bright aroma filled the room as I carefully measured it out.

Emilia gave me a sly look. "You say you don't believe in magic, eh?"

I stiffened. "Aromatherapy is science, not magic."

"Suuuuuurre. Whatever you say."

"Moving on. Let's mix the heart notes." I reached out for more vials. "Now jasmine, for its connection to romantic memories, and sage for wisdom." I paused, inhaling the heady fragrance. "Can you find the rose oil? It adds an elegant touch, tied to love and beauty. And it releases endorphins."

As Emilia looked for the rose, I focused on the base notes. Frankincense for grounding, often linked to spiritual memories. Sandalwood for a sense of calmness and serenity, and vanilla's warm, comforting scent evokes nostalgia.

I smiled as I finished the formula, then closed the bottle and shook it. The golden-pink liquid shimmered in the light. I uncapped the bottle and inserted a test strip, which I then held to my nose, inhaling deeply.

With a nod of satisfaction, I extended the small vial to Emilia. "Here, give it a try."

She leaned forward, taking the bottle from my hand. Carefully, she dabbed a drop onto the inside of her wrist, then closed her eyes as she brought it to her nose. Watson, ever curious, twitched his whiskers and craned his neck, inching closer as if he, too, wanted to test this newfound creation.

"Anna, this is amazing," Emilia said, a smile spreading across her face as she breathed in the complex aroma. "You should sell these at the farmer's market. It'd give you something to do. And be a way to make some extra money."

I considered the idea. The bottle of homemade perfume glistened in my hand. It was a far cry from the corporate world I had known, but maybe it was exactly what I needed to get me through these next few weeks. A project that connected me to my roots and sparked a joy I hadn't felt in years.

"I'll think about it. But first, let's take one to Gran."

CHAPTER THREE

A VISIT TO GRAN

"Looks like Serenity Falls is going futuristic." I shielded my eyes against the bright morning sunlight that washed over the angular silhouette of Golden Pines Assisted Living. The building shimmered with sleek glass, neutral panels, and neat edges.

I shifted my bag on my shoulder, the weight of the perfume bottle inside suddenly enormous. I'd blended it with the hope it might stir something familiar in Gran. Something comforting. But what if it didn't? What if she didn't recognize me at all?

Or worse, what if Emilia had pinned all her hopes on some kind of miracle?

"This building has to be from, what, the eighties?" I asked, more to distract myself than anything else.

Emilia laughed. "I bet our favorite town historian nearly fainted when he saw the plans. He probably thought it was an alien invasion."

I smiled, grateful for the familiar rhythm of our banter. "Harold Jenkins? Faint? That'd be the day. He's more likely to chase aliens off with his cane while grumbling about the good old days of architecture." I glanced up again at the building, trying to picture Gran inside. "He must be in his eighties by now, eh? Heck, maybe he lives here."

"He turned eighty last year, actually. Trust me, he's still in his old house, guarding it like a fortress." Emilia led the way down the path. "But get this—he has a *girlfriend.* And you'll never guess who it is."

"Who?" I hated guessing games.

Emilia leveled her gaze at me. "Doris Fletcher."

My jaw dropped. "The town curmudgeon and the town busybody are *dating*?"

Emilia grinned. "I'll tell you the whole story later. It's a doozy."

We strolled past the tranquil gardens toward the glass entrance. I adjusted the strap of my bag as we passed a bench tucked beneath a cherry tree, where an elderly couple sat hand-in-hand, their heads bowed together in quiet conversation. My heart twinged. I was turning thirty in a few months, and nowhere near finding my love. Not that I hadn't tried. I'd gone through my share of fleeting relationships that never quite ignited the spark I longed for. There was Mark, the charming graphic designer who ghosted me after two months, and Jennifer, who said I was "too focused on chasing other people's dreams."

Maybe they were right. My life was a patchwork of busy days and restless nights, with no room left for the kind of connection that left people holding hands on park benches after fifty years. Or, at least, it used to be. I let out a sigh as we approached the entrance, pushing the wistful thought aside.

Inside, the reception area was bright, with comfortable seating in cozy arrangements. I followed Emilia to the registration desk, observing the familiarity with which she navigated the space. It was clear that visits such as this had become a routine part of Emilia's life. And it was nice to know that my sister got out of the house at least once a week.

A pang of guilt tugged at my heart. Gran had been here for almost a year, and this was the first time I'd set foot in the place. Well, that would change, starting now.

As we approached the reception desk, an older woman in crisp nurse's scrubs bustled toward us, her short, curled hair bouncing with each quick, purposeful step. She moved as though propelled by an endless well of enthusiasm.

"Emilia!" she sang out, wrapping my sister in a tight squeeze before Emilia had fully turned toward her. "Ah, look at you. Just as beautiful as ever!"

Then she spun to me, her round face glowing with excitement, the fluorescent light catching the warm olive tone of her skin. "And you must be Anna!" She grabbed my hand, sandwiching it between both of hers in a grip that was both chilly and oddly clammy. "You've got your mother's eyes. It's wonderful to finally meet you!"

Oh. She's a hugger.

And a hand-clasper.

And a shoulder-patter. Right. This is happening.

"Uh, yes," I managed.

"Susan Eldridge!" she declared as if announcing herself to a grand ballroom. "Head nurse."

"Susan's been an absolute angel with Gran," Emilia said.

"Oh, pish," Susan waved off the compliment, though her extra chin wobbled with pleasure. "It's the least I can do. Your mom and I were thick as thieves as kids. And your nonna—what a woman! Kind as anything, but sharp as a tack. Just the other day she had us in stitches telling the story of her trip to Hollywood! Swears a casting director called her 'the next big thing.'"

I blinked. "Gran hates driving more than ten miles from home."

Susan gasped, pressing a hand to her chest. "Oh, I know, but you just have to hear her tell it! The way she describes the whole adventure? Just magical! And that's what matters, you see. Here, we use validation therapy—meeting our residents where they are rather than dragging them back to where we think they should be."

Emilia nodded, her voice gentler. "She gets upset when we correct her, so we just go along with it. It keeps her calm."

"Exactly!" Susan tapped my arm with an encouraging pat-pat-pat. "And you'll catch on so fast. I can tell! Don't you worry a bit! We're all about family here!"

Before I could respond, she bustled away, calling over her shoulder, "I'll let Nurse Helen know you're here! Don't you worry, dear, we've got everything handled!"

As she disappeared around the corner, I let out a breath. The air felt oddly still in her absence, as though someone had just switched off an industrial fan.

I glanced at Emilia, who was practically glowing.

"She seems ... nice," I ventured.

Emilia nodded enthusiastically. "Oh, she's been a godsend. You'll see."

I mustered a small smile, already feeling the need to locate the nearest quiet corner to recharge. If this was just the welcome committee, I was in for a long visit.

As if on cue, another nurse approached. "Emilia, so good to see you again." Her gaze shifted to me, warm but not overwhelming. "You must be Anna. I'm Helen Hevel. I've heard so much about you."

Helen carried herself with a quiet confidence. Like Susan, she also appeared to be about the same age as Mom would have been, with soft brown hair pulled into a low ponytail, strands of silver weaving through it like reminders of wisdom earned. A silver pendant in the shape of a tree hung from her neck, catching the light as she moved.

"Yes, this is my sister. We're here to visit Gran," Emilia confirmed.

Helen nodded, her gaze lingered on me for a moment longer than comfortable. It felt almost judgmental.

If that was Helen's goal, it worked. I felt a rush of regret. Had my lack of visits been noted and discussed among the staff? I pushed the feeling aside, reminding myself of the purpose of our visit. I extended my hand to Helen. "It's nice to meet you. I hear you're taking great care of our Gran."

Helen's shoulders relaxed. "I'll walk with you. I'm headed that way myself."

As we rounded a corner, we approached a set of closed double doors. Above them hung a wooden sign with 'Silverleaf Crossing' painted in silver letters against a dark green background. The sign was framed by an arch of ivy painted on the wall.

"Silverleaf Crossing?" I asked, pausing. "That's creative for a memory care unit."

Helen smiled as she reached into her pocket for a small badge. "We wanted something that felt less clinical. For our residents, this is their neighborhood, their home. The name is part of creating that sense of belonging."

She swiped the badge against a panel, and the doors clicked open, revealing a world unlike anything I'd expected. As we stepped inside, the modern feel of the main space gave way to the charm of a small town. The ceiling was painted a soft blue with white, fluffy clouds, and warm, ambient lighting mimicked sunshine. The floor resembled cobblestone streets, winding through a carefully designed space that felt like stepping into a 1950s neighborhood.

On either side of the 'street,' small houses with pastel-painted shutters and cheerful flower boxes served as the residents' rooms. Each door had a nameplate and the occasional decoration—wreath, photos, or flags—that gave them personality.

"You really went all out," I said.

Helen's smile widened. "We're trying to create an environment that feels familiar. For many of our residents, these are the places they grew up with, places they remember fondly. Familiarity helps keep them calm and engaged."

A small group of residents strolled past, chatting as they window-shopped in front of the candy store. Another resident sat in a chair just outside the barber shop, engrossed in a crossword puzzle.

"Do they actually use all of this?" I asked, gesturing to the storefronts.

"Oh, absolutely," Helen said. "The barber shop is open twice a week, and the general store is stocked with snacks and simple supplies they can purchase with tokens. The spaces also encourage residents to socialize and explore. It's a way to give them independence, even within the structure of care."

We rounded another corner and stood facing a charming 1950s diner. Residents sat at red pleather booths with checkerboard-patterned tabletops, sipping from tall glasses filled with what I assumed were milkshakes or malts. A few were playing cards at one of the tables, while others chatted animatedly, their laughter ringing out over the soft hum of Elvis Presley crooning from the jukebox.

A woman in a waitress's uniform, complete with a pink dress and white apron, moved among the tables, handing out trays of snacks and drinks with a smile. The residents greeted her warmly, a few even calling her by name.

"It's like stepping into another time," I murmured, glancing at Emilia, who was beaming.

A resident seated at the counter swirled his straw in his glass, leaning over to his neighbor and pointing at the jukebox. "Remember this one? 1966, summer on the boardwalk..."

Helen's walkie-talkie crackled at her hip. She paused, listening.

"Helen?" a voice came through, slightly tinny. "Can you come over to the general store? We've got a resident who's confused about the tokens again."

Helen smiled apologetically. "Excuse me a moment," she said. "I'm just over there if you need anything." She gestured toward the small general store down the street and moved briskly away, weaving through the tables with practiced ease.

Emilia tugged gently on my sleeve, steering me toward a booth tucked beneath a mural of a drive-in theater. My breath hitched. Gran.

It had been a year since I'd last seen her. Since we'd all stood together at my mother's funeral, Gran's hand trembling in mine as we whispered our goodbyes. Even then, the signs of her slipping memory had been there—the confusion in her eyes when she forgot names, the way she'd paused mid-sentence, lost in the fog of her own mind.

As she looked up from her crossword, my heart clenched. Her silver curls framed a face that lit up as she filled in a line on her crossword puzzle. A nearly empty glass sat beside her, a smudge of whipped cream lingering on the rim. She wore a light blue cardigan that complemented the sparkle in her eyes.

She looked happy.

Gran turned to us with a bright, welcoming smile. "Oh, we have visitors!" Her hands fluttering up as if she might cup our faces but stopping just short, as if uncertain whether she should.

Tears burned the backs of my eyes. I had clung to the idea that she was still the same. That even if she forgot small things, she'd still be my Gran.

I approached my grandmother and was enveloped in a wave of familiar scents. The complex, earthy aroma of clary sage greeted me first, evoking memories of Gran's tales about its use in soothing concoctions. Then came the almost mystical scent of mugwort, a fragrance that reminded me of Gran's dream tonics. Finally, I discerned the subtlest hint of a more pungent, slightly bitter aroma—wormwood, a hallmark of Gran's more potent blends. Together, these essences seemed woven into the very fabric of Gran's being, as if years of crafting with them had imbued her presence with their distinct characters.

"You are so beautiful," Gran murmured, her gaze moving between us with warm curiosity. "My name is Margaret."

Emilia stepped in, taking Gran's hand. "Hello, Margaret. My name is Emilia, and this is Anna."

Gran beamed up at us, her voice lilting. "Emilia and Anna, what delightful names! It's such a pleasure to meet you both."

"It's a pleasure to meet you, too." I forced a smile, even as my heart screamed, *It's me, Gran! Your granddaughter. Don't you remember me?*

"And what brings you lovely young ladies to Silverleaf?"

"We heard this place was full of wonderful people and stories," I said. "We just had to come and see for ourselves."

Gran clapped her hands. "Oh, you've come to the right place! Everyone's so friendly here, and there's never a dull moment." Her eyes sparkled with contentment.

I felt a tug in my heart. At least Gran liked it here.

Emilia guided Gran's hand back to her lap. "Margaret, may we join you? Perhaps share a milkshake?"

Gran's eyes lit up, and she nodded with a cheerful smile. "Oh, that sounds lovely, dear. I haven't had a proper milkshake in ages."

Emilia and I slid into the booth opposite Gran. She set her crossword aside.

We asked Gran questions about her life, and Gran asked the same of us. As the conversation ebbed, I knew the moment had come to present my special creation. I reached into my bag and pulled out a small, elegantly crafted bottle filled with my homemade perfume blend, Evoko. The liquid inside shimmered.

"Gra ... Margaret, we wanted to bring you something special." I held the bottle out to my grandmother, watching as the light caught the contours of the glass. Maybe this perfume really would pierce through Gran's fog.

I shook off the thought. Best not to harbor unrealistic expectations.

Gran's eyes lit up as she accepted the bottle. She studied it, her fingers tracing the design on the glass. "Oh, I love perfume!"

Emilia chimed in. "We made it just for you. We thought you might enjoy it."

Gran opened the bottle and dabbed a bit of the perfume on the inside of her wrists. She took a moment to inhale the fragrance. "Mmm, it's lovely. I can smell the frankincense, the orange, the rose..." Her nostrils flared. "And peppermint, too. That's quite a bold choice for this blend."

Even in her current state, Gran's senses remained keen, and there was a shadow of the skilled professional she used to be. My throat burned and I struggled to hold back tears.

Gran beamed. "Thank you both. This is such a thoughtful gift. It makes me feel like a queen." She brought her wrist to her nose and sniffed. Her eyes sharpened. "You know, I used to make perfumes. Back in the day."

"You did?" Emilia eyed me and mouthed, *It's working*!

Gran nodded, a wistful smile playing on her lips. "Yes, dear. It was a long time ago. I had my own little shop called Charm & Petal, and people from all around used to come to me for custom fragrances."

Emilia reached out and squeezed Gran's hand. "It sounds like it was wonderful."

Gran's smile brightened. "Oh, it was."

It felt so weird talking to Gran as though she were a stranger. But if it kept her happy, if it brought her even a sliver of the joy she used to know, then it was worth it.

I patted Gran's knee. "I used to blend perfumes with my grandmother. This is actually one of her formulas."

Gran dabbed more perfume on her wrists, then rubbed some into the pulse points on her neck. "Oh!" Her eyes widened with recognition. "I remember this scent. Evoko."

Tears welled up in my eyes as I nodded. I choked back the hope. Was Gran coming back? Aromatherapy was one thing, but if perfumes really could cure dementia, one would think that would have made the news.

A look of realization and warmth washed over Gran's face. "Anna? Emilia?" Her eyes brightened even more. "My sweet granddaughters. It's you!"

Emilia and I exchanged tearful smiles as we embraced our grandmother.

But as quickly as it had come, the clarity faded.

Gran's expression changed, her brow knitting with alarm. She stiffened, her grip on Emilia's arms tightening until her knuckles whitened. Her eyes held a hard, anxious look. Voice trembling, she asked, "Did they catch the killer?"

Emilia drew back, a look of bewilderment on her face. "What killer, Gran? Who are you talking about?"

My heart sank as the serene moment shattered.

Gran pulled herself from the booth with a sudden energy. Emilia stood and steadied Gran by the arms. "Gran, are you talking about that mystery show we watched together? The one we couldn't finish because...?"

She didn't finish the sentence.

Gran's breathing quickened, her chest rising and falling as panic took hold. She glanced wildly around the diner, muttering fragmented phrases. "No one listened ... I told them, but they wouldn't believe..." Her voice grew louder, drawing the attention of nearby residents. "They're all in danger! You have to understand!"

Chairs scraped as residents shifted uneasily, a low murmur spreading. A man across the room stood, frowning in confusion, while a woman near the window gasped and clutched her napkin.

Helen dashed in, eyes sharp with concern as she took in the scene. Her skilled hands rested firmly on Gran's shoulders, trying to ground her. Susan was quick to follow, pushing a wheelchair with practiced urgency. "We need to get her back to her room."

The nurses worked efficiently to limit Gran's frantic thrashing. Emilia and I exchanged worried glances. As Gran was wheeled away, she turned and cried out, "My daughter! Did they catch her killer?"

I sat with Emilia, now alone in the red vinyl booths in the Silverleaf Diner, the checkerboard tabletop between us dotted with water rings from our untouched glasses. Each of us absentmindedly twirled the straws in our milkshakes. The jukebox played in the background, but the cheerful tunes couldn't quite dispel the unease that settled between us.

The diner buzzed quietly with life. A few residents chatting over their meals, a group playing cards at one of the round tables. A staff member in a pastel pink uniform passed by, offering a tray of cookies to a couple seated at the counter. It was all so idyllic, but neither of us seemed able to sink into the charm.

The hum of conversation and soft clinking of silverware was interrupted as Susan approached our booth, her face etched with concern. "How are you two holding up?" She slipped into the seat across from us without preamble, her earlier cheerfulness muted. "Helen's finishing up with your grandmother now."

I nodded. "We're managing. Is everything okay with Gran?"

Susan's smile tightened. "Oh, don't you worry. I know what Margaret said must have sounded alarming, but outbursts like that are quite common with dementia patients. They often get confused, mix up memories."

"Ah yes, the old 'did they catch the killer?' classic," I quipped.

Susan chuckled nervously. "Well, you'd be surprised how often we hear things like that. These episodes pass quickly."

Oh, sure. Next, she'd tell us Gran was merely auditioning for a retirement home production of *Murder, She Wrote*. But I was not some child that needed placating. If Gran's condition was worsening, I needed to know.

"Gran seemed so agitated," I pressed. "Should we be concerned?"

"Not at all, dear," Susan said, patting my hand. "Margaret is in good hands."

As Susan bustled away, Emilia and I exchanged glances. The nurse's words were meant to comfort, but they left me with a nagging sense of unease. I leaned in closer to Emilia, lowering my voice. "Is it just me, or was Susan trying way too hard to make Gran's outburst seem normal? It's like she thinks we can't handle the truth about how bad Gran's condition might be getting."

Emilia shook her head. "Susan wouldn't do that. She's always been forthright with me."

"Really? Because I half-expected her to pat us on the heads and offer us lollipops for being such brave little visitors."

"Susan just doesn't understand." Emilia's eyes were earnest and hopeful. "Gran broke through. The perfume worked. Gran was agitated because she was trying to tell us something important."

I shook my head, my gaze fixed on my untouched milkshake. "You're reading too much into it. You're conditioned by those crime documentaries to see a murder around every corner."

Emilia's fingers tightened around her cup. "But why 'the killer'? Why would she say that?"

I sighed, feeling the weight of our predicament. I looked around the hall. The oblivious contentment of others only deepened my sense of isolation. "I don't know. Maybe Gran got mixed up. I mean, weren't all three of you watching that murder mystery show when mom had her heart attack?"

Emilia leaned back, the chair creaking slightly under the shift of her weight. "Yeah, you're probably right. It's not like someone could murder a person while they're surrounded by family at home."

A resigned sigh escaped her lips. "Maybe the perfume doesn't work, after all."

A pang of guilt washed over me. I felt bad for quashing Emilia's hope, but the truth was the truth, however unpalatable. "Should we go to Gran's room?"

Emilia nodded, her eyes briefly meeting mine. We both stood, our chairs scraping against the floor. We left our untouched sodas behind. Unanswered questions and unspoken fears followed us out of the diner. The street was quiet, the only sound the faint hum of an air vent and our footsteps echoing on the faux sidewalk.

Gran's room was small but homey, painted in soft, calming colors. Her belongings were neatly arranged, giving the room a personal touch. Photos of family, including one of a much younger me and Emilia, smiled down from the walls. A small vase of fresh flowers sat on the bedside table, adding a splash of color. The room, however, smelled sterile, with a strong overtone of ethanol.

Gran lay in bed, propped up by pillows. The sight of her, so fragile, tugged at my heartstrings.

Helen, who had been sitting in a chair beside the bed, stood. She held out the perfume bottle to me with an apologetic look. "I'm sorry, but we can't allow fragrances. Some residents have allergies."

I took the bottle, a lump forming in my throat. Perhaps it's for the best. The perfume seemed to upset Gran more than anything.

Gran, meanwhile, turned towards us, her face lighting up with absolute delight. "Oh, I have visitors! How lovely. And such beautiful ladies, too. My name is Margaret."

I mustered a smile, determined to make the most of the rest of our time together, even if Gran didn't remember who we were.

Chapter Four

Farmers Market

That next Saturday, the Serenity Falls Farmer's Market was bustling with activity. Cobbled streets, worn smooth by time, led to the market's heart in the town square, where a wooden pavilion stretched around the market's heart. Vendors set up their displays beneath this rustic structure.

The market had grown since I was last here. Now, vendors spilled out from under the pavilion onto Willow Street, as well. This side street was cordoned off to make space for people to safely explore the booths, which overflowed with everything from crusty artisan bread to homemade soaps.

Emilia placed the last of the perfume bottles on the table, then swept her gaze across the bustling scene. "You know, you really lucked out with this spot. I still can't believe they had a last-minute opening."

I snorted. "You know I don't believe in fate."

"Pshaw." She flicked a hand dismissively. "And let's not forget my entire week of … ahem … *gentle nudging*. That's what really got you to sign up."

I shot her a look. "*Gentle nudging*? That was a full-blown campaign. I'm surprised you didn't start handing out flyers."

Emilia grinned, unrepentant. "Well, it worked, didn't it?"

I sighed, shaking my head. "Unfortunately, yes." Once Emilia had agreed to come with me, I felt I had to, for her sake.

Emilia's bright laughter mixed with the sounds of early shoppers. "You've been concocting these perfumes nonstop all week. It only made sense to bring them here. The house can only hold so much of your creative output, after all."

"It was a soothing way to get my mind off everything." I took in a deep breath of the crisp morning air. The aroma of lavender and rose blended with the earthy smell of fresh produce and the comforting warmth of freshly baked bread from the neighboring stall.

Then my eyes landed on the Cozy Cup café in the distance. Its inviting façade beckoned me. A breeze wafted over, carrying with it the rich, inviting aroma of freshly brewed coffee. *Mmm. Coffee.* The smell alone was enough to stir a sense of comfort and warmth within me. Perhaps I could capture this essence in a bottle. A coffee-scented perfume. The idea of blending the deep, roasted notes of coffee beans with other complementary scents flickered through my mind.

"Daydreaming about coffee?" Emilia's voice was laced with amusement.

I snapped back to the present, chuckling. "I was actually thinking about a coffee-scented perfume. I could call it 'Cozy Cup' or something. Maybe even collaborate with the café's owner."

"Ah, merging business with pleasure, I see." Emilia playfully nudged me. "Strategic and aromatic genius!"

"Thanks! It's all about proximity to inspiration."

"Well, in that case, shall I venture into the wilds of Serenity Falls and procure us some lattes? For market research, of course."

"Would you? That'd be amazing. Just try not to get lost in the perilous two-minute walk."

Emilia feigned a dramatic sigh. "The things I do for you. If I'm not back in ten minutes, send a search party."

I smiled as my sister wandered toward the Cozy Cup, waving at passers-by. It was good to see Emilia so engaged. And outside the confines of her home. Especially after what happened with Gran at Golden Pines. Though Emilia didn't talk about it, I could tell that Gran's behavior and words still bothered her. It bothered me too, to be honest. Gran's dementia seemed to be getting worse. But here, in the midst of the bustling farmer's market, surrounded by the fruits of my labor and Emilia's unwavering support, I felt a sense of calm and purpose.

I stepped back, surveying my setup with a critical eye. The booth was a harmonious blend of the old and the new. At its heart was the old Charm & Petal signage, a relic from Gran's shop. The sign's elegant, swirling font and faded pastel colors spoke of a bygone era, lending a vintage vibe to our space. Its edges were slightly worn, and the paint had chipped in places, but these imperfections only added to its authenticity and allure.

The table beneath the sign was draped in a cream-colored cloth. On it, I showcased my perfumes like precious gems. Each unique bottle captured the light, casting delicate prisms across the table. To the side, a small, neatly arranged stack of blotter squares invited customers to experience the scents.

Among the bottles, I had carefully placed Gran's recipe book, opened to one of her most enchanting pages. The intricate hand-drawn illustration depicted jasmine blossoms winding around a glass bottle, their delicate petals almost seeming to flutter on the page.

It was a risk bringing out so precious an heirloom, but I just couldn't resist. The book added a touch of mystique to the display, drawing curious glances from passersby and grounding my work in its rich, storied heritage.

I adjusted the angle of the signage, tilting it toward the entrance of the market. This small change seemed to open up the booth even more, making it more welcoming. With the book glowing softly in the sunlight, the entire booth felt alive. It was a fusion of Gran's legacy and my vision for the future.

Just as I perfected the setup, a gust of wind swept through the market aisles. It caught the stack of blotter squares, scattering them like petals in a spring breeze. I lunged forward, attempting to catch the fluttering papers as they danced away. The wind seemed to tease me as I weaved through the aisle, my hands grasping at the elusive sheets.

My pursuit of the wayward blotters took on a life of its own as I darted between stalls and onlookers, my focus solely on the escaping paper. Just as I reached for the last runaway square, my path intersected with someone else's. With a soft thud, we collided, both reaching for the same elusive piece.

"Sorry!" I exclaimed as I straightened up.

At the same moment, a deep, resonant voice also offered an apology. My eyes traveled upward, and my heart skipped a beat.

The man standing before me was ... picturesque, to say the least. Towering in height, he had broad shoulders and hands that spoke of manual skill and dedication. His chestnut brown hair was casually tousled, as though he frequently ran his fingers through it. Jeans dusted with sawdust and wearing shirt that hugged his frame in just the right way, he exuded a comfortable, unpretentious charm.

Holding the runaway paper with care, he offered it to me with a warm, humorous glint in his eyes. "Looks like we both have a knack for catching runaway things." His smile was as inviting as his voice.

The bustling sounds of the market receded into the background. The striking green of his eyes reminded me of the dense forests behind my house. As I reached to take the paper, our fingers brushed, sending a thrill through me that echoed louder than the surrounding market noise. "Thank you," I managed to say.

"I'm Parker Ekstrom." He pointed diagonally across from my setup. "My booth is just over there."

His booth was an eclectic collection of woodwork, from elegantly carved bowls to intricate picture frames.

Parker walked with me back to my booth. "You've got quite a setup here."

I tried not to ogle his hands as he set upright the overturned sign that read *Evoko* in elegant script.

"These are all homemade?"

Feeling a surge of pride, I nodded. "Yes, they are. It's a bit of a passion project."

I picked up a bottle and offered it to Parker, watching his reaction as he took a whiff.

A young girl darted to the booth, her face lighting up with awe. "Look, Mommy, they're so pretty!" Her small fingers reached out in fascination.

Her mother rushed up behind her, expression taut with disapproval. Without giving the booth more than a cursory glance, she grasped the girl's arm. "We don't need any of that nonsense," she said in a sharp tone, pulling the girl back. "Stay away from that booth, dear. You know how we feel about such things."

My heart sank. The mother's words cast a shadow over the bright morning. I turned back to Parker, forcing a smile, but couldn't help feeling a sting from the woman's judgment.

"Afraid of perfume? That's a new one." Parker raised an eyebrow at the departing pair.

I forced a chuckle. His comment, however, stirred a distant memory in me.

I found myself transported back to a time when I was a little girl playing behind the counter at Charm & Petal. The memory was vivid—the scent of herbs and flowers mingling in the air, the colorful bottles lining the shelves.

The door had burst open, an angry customer storming in, her face twisted with accusation. "You've cursed me!" she yelled at Gran, who stood behind the counter, a picture of calm and patience. "Ever since I bought your perfume, or should I say *potion,* strange things have been happening to me."

Gran had tried to calm the woman, explaining that her perfumes were crafted with love and care, with no ill intent. But the woman was inconsolable, convinced that Gran had bewitched her with her fragrances.

I shook off the memory as I watched the mother and daughter disappear into the crowd. How little things seemed to have changed. I had hoped that over the last decade, Serenity Falls would have become more open-minded, especially about something as benign and therapeutic as aromatherapy. Yet, it appeared that some remnants of suspicion and misunderstanding still clung to the town like morning fog.

A sigh slipped from me before I turned back to Parker, who was watching me carefully. "Guess some people still think scent has ... more power than it should."

"Or maybe they're just scared of what they don't understand," he mused. His gaze lingered on me for a moment, something thoughtful flickering behind his eyes.

I swallowed, then forced a lighter tone. "Well, thanks for rescuing my rogue blotters."

Parker grinned. "Anytime. But if the wind carries them off again, I expect a finder's fee. Maybe a sample?"

A laugh bubbled up despite the lingering ache in my chest. "Deal."

He gave me a small salute before heading back to his booth, leaving behind the faintest trace of cedar and sawdust in his wake.

I watched him go, exhaling slowly.
Maybe some things hadn't changed in Serenity Falls.
But maybe, just maybe, some things had.

Chapter Five

PATTERN RECOGNITION

Emilia and I sat at the Farmer's Market booth sipping lattes, the warm comfort of the drinks contrasting with the cool morning air. We watched the ebb and flow of shoppers as they strolled past. My eyes widened as I spotted two familiar figures walking hand in hand. I nudged Emilia, barely able to contain my excitement. "Look, it's Doris Fletcher and Harold Jenkins! Together!"

Doris, wearing a cardigan as colorful as the market itself, leaned into Harold, her eyes twinkling with affection. Harold, usually so reserved, had a boyish grin on his face. They looked like teenagers in love, oblivious to the world around them. It warmed my heart in a way I hadn't expected.

Sitting there, I found myself in an entire sea of familiar faces and half-remembered names. My eyes darted towards another figure approaching the strawberry stall. I nudged Emilia, my voice dropping to a hushed, conspiratorial whisper. "Look. Over by the strawberries. Blue jacket. Sleek hair. Stupid perfect butt. Is that Lisa Marconi?"

Emilia leaned in, her eyes following my discreet gesture. "The high school queen bee herself? No way!"

I giggled, keeping my voice low. "Shh, don't let her hear you. She was the ultimate mean girl in my class. Remember how she used to call me 'Antenna Anna' because of my hair?"

Emilia snorted with laughter, covering her mouth quickly. "Oh, I remember. And now she's just here, casually picking strawberries like a normal human being. Who would've thought?"

"Right? I half-expected her to be hand-fed grapes by a flock of admirers."

Emilia grinned mischievously. "Dare you to go say hi."

"Oh, sure. And bring up old antenna days? I'll pass. Let's just spy from here. Like mature adults."

We both giggled, ducking to hide from Lisa. But as the laughter faded, my gaze returned to our booth, and the reality of our present situation settled back in. I watched as people meandered by, some pausing to admire the perfume bottles, their intricate designs catching the sunlight. Yet, admiration was not translating to sales. I had thought today would be different. How could people be so closed-minded?

A woman scooched past, side-eyeing the bottles.

I shouted at the woman's retreating backside. "For crying out loud, they're just perfumes!"

Emilia placed her latte down and turned to me. "Hey, why don't you take a break? Walk around a bit. I've got this covered."

I hesitated, my gaze sweeping over our carefully arranged booth. "Are you sure? You know how to handle the credit card orders, right?"

Emilia rolled her eyes. "Yes, yes, I'm not completely hopeless, you know. Go on, take a breather. Enjoy the market."

Reassured, I stood, stretching my legs and feeling the tension of the morning ease from my shoulders. I cast one last glance at the booth. My creations laid out for the world to see.

My work as a research analyst had been defined by data, statistics, and cold, hard facts. There was a certain comfort in the predictability of it all, the black and white nature of numbers and trends. But it could also be dry. This world of vibrant colors, rich scents, and the personal connections of the market was a refreshing break from that.

The sights and sounds of the market enveloped me as I wandered—the laughter of children chasing each other, the chatter of townsfolk. I let myself be carried by the current of people, taking in the stalls and their offerings.

A beautiful green pendant caught my eye, and I stepped toward the booth for a closer look. As I approached, the owner glanced up from arranging a tray of earrings. It was Marianne Delacroix, one of mom's best friends. Clad in rich, jewel-toned fabrics that hugged her frame in artfully structured layers, she exuded a refined kind of artistic elegance. Silver threads wove through her wavy brown hair, catching the sunlight just like the jewelry on display. Her hazel eyes sparkled as they met mine.

"Marianne! It's been a while." As we embraced, the scent of sandalwood clung softly to her shawl. I stepped back. "I haven't seen you since the funeral."

"I still can't believe she's gone," Marianne said. "A heart attack, of all things. Your mom was the picture of health."

A lump formed in my throat. "It was a shock. For all of us."

"And right as she was preparing to take over Charm & Petal." Marianne sighed, her fingers absently toying with a delicate silver necklace. "I was so sorry to hear about Margaret, too. Losing her daughter like that ... I suppose it was just too much."

My hand moved to straighten a small display of earrings, more to steady myself than out of any need for tidiness. "Thank you," I said softly. "It means a lot."

"Your mother and grandmother meant a lot to this town," Marianne said. "Their shop, what you're doing now, it mattered. More than you probably knew."

I raised an eyebrow. "Really? I always thought people just saw us as ... well, odd."

"Oh, some did," she said with a chuckle. "But there were plenty who came to Charm & Petal like clockwork. Your grandmother had a gift, and your mom inherited more of it than she ever admitted. Customers never stopped coming. Not until she stepped away."

I blinked, letting the words settle. So much of what I'd believed about my family's place in Serenity Falls was tangled up in half-heard whispers and childhood impressions. But here was someone who remembered them as something else. Something more.

"Thanks," I said, my voice steadier. "I guess I'm still figuring it all out. Trying to find my place."

She smiled, her expression kind and knowing. "Forget finding their footsteps, sweetheart. You've got your own. The town needs that. And remember, every great journey starts with a single step."

As I walked away from the stall, the green pendant still gleaming in the corner of my eye, Marianne's words lingered like the hint of a scent in the breeze.

I was going to make this work.

I returned to my booth, the lively energy of the market propelling me forward. Emilia was chatting with a customer while rearranging the display, and I felt a swell of gratitude that she'd agreed to leave the house and help today.

Nearby, a woman was examining a bottle of Evoko, her expression one of intrigue and appreciation. Hope sparked within me.

"That one's special," I said, my voice tinged with pride. "It's based on my grandmother's formula."

The woman looked up. "Does it do anything?" Her tone was curious rather than skeptical.

I sighed with relief. Here was someone who understood, or at least was open to, the concept of aromatherapy. I caught Emilia's knowing glance as I answered. "Yes, it does. The blend is designed as a memory aid. It's meant to evoke and strengthen recollections."

The woman considered the bottle for a moment, then reached for the sample. "May I?"

"Of course," Emilia chimed in, handing her a tester strip with a warm smile.

We both watched as the woman sprayed a small amount onto her wrist. The scent blossomed in the air, a delicate fusion of floral and citrus notes, grounded by the warmth of vanilla.

As the fragrance settled, the woman's eyes widened. "I just re-membered," she exclaimed. "I was supposed to call my sister today about our trip next month. I completely forgot until now."

Emilia grinned, and internally I raised an eyebrow. I was a firm believer in the power of aromatherapy, but crediting a perfume with immediately jogging someone's memory about a phone call seemed like a bit of a stretch.

"That's exactly what it's meant to do," I said with a smile. "Help you hold onto those important moments."

And apparently, it doubled as a personal assistant. Who knew?

The woman nodded, clearly convinced. She picked up a bottle of Evoko and handed it to me. "I'll take two. Will you be at the market next week? I want to tell all my friends to stop by this booth. They need to try this."

My heart swelled. "Yes, I'll be here. Thank you so much."

As the woman left, a sense of accomplishment washed over me. Emilia gave me a nudge, her grin uncontainable. "See? Told you this was going to be a hit."

This feeling stayed with me throughout the day as more people stopped by the booth. Each interaction, each sale, added to my growing sense of hope and validation.

Soon a pattern emerged. People who sampled Evoko often had a moment of sudden recollection, their faces lighting up as forgotten memories resurfaced. A middle-aged man remembered his mother's jasmine garden. A young couple, laughing as they tested different perfumes, recalled their first date. Each instance was a small victory, a tangible proof of my grandmother's belief in the power of scent.

Emilia and I were people-watching, sharing a quiet laugh at a man wrestling with an absurdly oversized basket of produce, when a familiar figure approached the booth. Tabitha Root, her long blonde braid swaying behind her, moved with a grace that made her flowing, earth-toned garments seem like part of the breeze. She looked exactly as I remembered—grounded and serene, like she belonged in a forest clearing surrounded by herbs and secrets.

"Ladies," she greeted us warmly, hazel eyes crinkling with delight. "There you are. I was hoping to catch you both today."

Emilia beamed, stepping around the booth to give her a quick hug. "I told you she'd be back, eventually."

I smiled. "It's good to see you again, Tabitha."

"Marianne told me you were setting up shop." Her voice was like warm tea. Comforting, familiar. "I just had to come see the next generation of Attar magic in action."

"Trying, at least," I said, gesturing around our still-sparse table of perfume vials and handcrafted labels.

Tabitha gave a soft laugh and turned to Emilia with mock severity. "And here I thought our weekly deliveries of tea and cookies might've been enough to lure her back sooner."

Emilia glanced sideways at me, amused. "Tabitha and Marianne have been showing up like clockwork for the last year. The house, my sanity ... they've been keeping both in check."

The words hit me like a sudden draft of cold air. A flush of guilt crept into my chest. While I'd been buried in client meetings and deadlines, mom's best friends had been here, checking in, showing up. Being present.

"I didn't realize," I said, the edges of my smile faltering.

Tabitha reached over and gave my hand a light squeeze. "Don't carry that, dear. We all do what we can, when we can. You're here now, and that's what matters."

I nodded, though the lump in my throat didn't budge.

Tabitha's eyes drifted to Gran's book, sitting just behind the display. Her gaze lingered, softening with recognition. "Is that what I think it is?"

"It is," I said. "Gran's scent grimoire. I've been reviving some of her recipes."

Her eyebrows lifted in surprise, a slow grin spreading across her face. "Oh, your grandmother guarded that book like it held the crown jewels. Never let me so much as peek. Said it was just for family."

Emilia nodded, her voice touched with nostalgia. "She was serious about that. She taught me a little, but Anna's the one who really had the talent."

Tabitha's attention returned to the perfume display, and she reached for a pale green bottle. "May I?"

"Of course."

She sprayed a small amount on her wrist, then inhaled deeply. Her eyes closed, and a peaceful expression settled over her face. "It's like stepping into Evelyn's kitchen again. You've got your mom's touch, Anna. Maybe even her gift."

Emotion surged behind my ribcage, but I managed to keep it contained. "Thank you. That means a lot."

"I'll take a bottle," Tabitha said, already setting it aside. "And I'll spread the word at my booth. The market's been missing this kind of magic."

She glanced again at the book. "If anything in there gives you trouble, come see me. I might not know perfumery the way Evelyn and Margaret did, but I know my flowers. Maybe I can help you make sense of some of it."

"That's really generous," I said, as I wrapped her purchase.

Emilia gave me a gentle nudge. "And if she doesn't take you up on it, I'll make sure she does."

We all laughed. The scent of bergamot and something older, earthier, lingered in the air as Tabitha gave us each a quick hug before slipping into the crowd, her braid swaying behind her as she made her way back to her flower stall.

As Tabitha walked away, her warm words lingering, a twinge of envy pricked at my heart. Mom had such good friends here. These were the kind of deep, lasting connections I would kill for. Both Marianne and Tabitha's warmth and genuine interest in our family's legacy made my heart ache.

Emilia hummed happily beside me, arranging the bottles with care, and I felt a flicker of hope that maybe, just maybe, we could build something like that for ourselves. I had fled this place years ago, convinced that as long as I lived in Serenity Falls, I would never feel welcome, never experience any deep sense of belonging. Over a decade out in the world, and I'd never really found it out there either. I'd always blamed this town, its people, for that emptiness inside me. But now, Marianne and Tabitha's easy acceptance after all these years stirred an uncomfortable thought. What if the problem wasn't the town, but me?

CHAPTER SIX

MURDER BOARD

The rain on Sunday was relentless, a steady pour that seemed to cleanse the world outside. I stepped through the back door, my arms laden with groceries. The air was thick with that earthy, green freshness that only rain could summon, as though Serenity Forest itself had released a sigh, filling every corner of the house with the scent of damp leaves and cool soil.

I placed the grocery bags down in the mudroom and shook off the droplets clinging to my jacket. My rain boots made a wet, squelching sound as I removed them.

I stepped into the kitchen, brushing my damp palms against my jeans. Then I froze.

Something was off.

A ripple of unease ran down my spine as my gaze flicked toward the corner where Emilia had set up her murder board. My pulse ticked faster. The usual photos and index cards should have greeted me.

But no. The board had transformed. Gone were the generic clues and playful speculations about unsolved true crime mysteries. In their place was something much closer to home. Photos of our mom, some dating back to her childhood, were pinned amidst images of some of her classmates and other familiar faces from around town. Amongst these were newspaper articles, a few notes scribbled in Emilia's hand, and, most jarringly, our mom's death certificate.

My heart skipped a beat. What was this? Emilia had taken Mom's death hard—we both had—but this felt different. Sharper. Like something old and tender had been peeled back.

Emilia entered the kitchen and unloaded the groceries, as though nothing was amiss. Nothing at all. I kept glancing between her and the board, processing the connections Emilia had drawn, the faces staring back at me from another life. "Emilia, what's all this about?"

Emilia stilled, her hands resting on the countertop as she turned to face me. "You saw how Evoko helped people at the market. That perfume really does restore memories. I've been testing it on myself, and I'm sure."

I raised an eyebrow. "What, now your memory is spotless?"

"Anna, this is serious! Don't you get it? This means that Gran's outburst, when she talked about Mom being murdered, wasn't her dementia. She was lucid."

I stared at her, my stomach tightening. "Em, come on. Aromatherapy isn't magic; it doesn't work that way."

Emilia finished putting the potatoes away and turned to face me. "I know it sounds far-fetched, but you've seen it work."

I sank into the kitchen chair. It was all just a bit too much to bear. A year had passed since Mom's death, and life had started to take on shape again. I'd finally started to tuck my grief away. But now, all that carefully-constructed peace threatened to unravel.

Emilia's eyes searched mine, her voice gentler now. "I know it's hard to think about. But we can't just pretend she was never here, or that we're not still hurting."

I nodded, swallowing hard. "I just ... we've been through so much. And hearing her say something like that—*murder*—it's like tearing the bandage off all over again."

Emilia's voice softened. "I know. But what if she was right? What if Mom didn't just die? Don't we owe it to her to find out the truth?"

I met her gaze, searching for the sister I knew beneath this fierce determination. Emilia looked certain, unshakable. And I wondered, maybe it wasn't just about solving a mystery for her; maybe it was a way to bring back a part of our mother that we'd lost.

Monday morning, as the last of the rain clouds drifted away, I moved through the house, opening the windows to welcome the fresh, damp scent of a world cleansed by rain. Last night's sleep had been fitful, but now, each window I opened felt like an invitation to let go of the heaviness that loomed, a way to air out more than just the rooms.

I ventured into the living room, pushing open another window to disturb the stagnant air. Here, too, I found an unsettling quiet. The couch, often molded to Emilia's form as she unwound with her favorite shows, was eerily pristine. The remote, perfectly aligned on the coffee table, seemed to be patiently awaiting its master's return.

I entered Emilia's office, drawing back the curtains to let the morning light flood the room. The sunbeams illuminated the space, revealing a scene quite different from the usual bustling workspace. Emilia's chair, typically a throne from which she commanded her empire of international trade, was occupied not by Emilia, but by Watson. The plush gray cat was curled up, resembling a serene gray puffball in the soft light. The computer sat cold and silent, even though today was supposed to be Emilia's first day back.

Finally, my search brought me to the kitchen, where a familiar, frustrated sigh met my ears. I found Emilia in the exact spot I'd feared she'd be—standing before the board wearing the same clothes as yesterday. Her shoulders were slumped, her hair a mess, and shadows bloomed under her eyes.

"This is impossible!" Emilia tossed her marker onto the table.

Since yesterday, the murder board had become an even more complex map of clues and conjecture. Photos, newspaper clippings, and handwritten notes formed a chaotic narrative. It was clear that Emilia had poured every ounce of her analytic skills into this personal investigation, trading the structured connections of her professional life for the murky depths of a mystery that was deeply personal.

My heart clenched at the sight of my sister. "Emilia."

Emilia jerked, as though pulled abruptly from her thoughts. She turned to face me. Dark circles stood out under her eyes. "Anna, I didn't hear you come in."

"I can see you've been busy." I said softly, stepping into the room. "Have you slept at all? You need to take care of yourself, too."

Emilia waved off the concern with a tired hand. "I can't rest, not when I need to find out what really happened to Mom."

I gave her a half-smile, trying to keep my tone light, careful. "Emilia, you're starting to resemble one of those conspiracy theorists with yarn and pins. I'm half expecting to see a UFO sighting linked to Mom's case on that board."

Emilia didn't laugh, but the corners of her mouth twitched.

I moved closer. "Seriously, Em. I know this matters. But you matter too. Maybe just sit down for a minute?"

There was no way I would let this cause Emilia to sink deeper into her isolation. "Let's go out, see the sun, remind ourselves what the outside world looks like. Maybe even interact with real, living people."

Emilia shook her head, her eyes fixed on the board. "I can't just walk away. There's a pattern here. I know I can figure it out."

"The only pattern I see is you turning into a zombie. And not the fun, dance-around-to-Thriller kind." I put a hand out to my sister. "Who knows, a bit of fresh air and food that doesn't magically show up at your door might just spark a new insight."

Emilia hesitated, visibly torn between her obsession and my undeniable logic.

I, seizing the moment, added, "Plus, I'm buying. You can order the fanciest, most overpriced avocado toast they have. And we can visit Gran afterward. What do you say? Hmm?"

That elicited a smile. "You're relentless, you know that?"

"It's one of my many charming qualities," I replied. "Now, come on. Let's go be normal people for a couple of hours."

Finally, Emilia stepped away from the board. She gave a faint, tired smile. "Alright, but only if we go to the Cozy Cup. They have a Monday sandwich special I usually DoorDash. And just for a little while. Then it's back to work."

"Deal. But let's try to enjoy this break from your amateur detective gig." I watched as Emilia, still looking somewhat reluctant, trudged upstairs to shower and get ready.

I settled at the kitchen table, my gaze inadvertently drawn to the murder board. Among the array of photos and notes, one particular image captured my attention—a photograph of our mom, immersed in her beloved garden. She had been a master of her botanical domain, nurturing every plant with a tender, knowledgeable touch. "From soil to scent," mom would often say, her hands tending to the blooms that were her pride and joy.

Mom had been caught mid-laugh, a moment of unguarded joy, her hands deep in the earth, her face turned towards the sun. My fingers reached out, tracing the edges of the photo. I could almost hear my mother's laughter, feel the warmth of her presence. For a brief moment, I allowed myself to get lost in the memory, a smile tugging at the corners of my lips.

I examined the board, my eyes landing on an old, faded photograph tucked in the corner. Three girls in swimsuits stood side by side, their bellies jutting out playfully, grins spread wide across their faces. The girl in the middle, with her curly red hair pulled into pigtails, was unmistakably my mother. She was covered in mud, looking utterly carefree and joyful. On either side of her stood two other girls—one with blonde braids that I guessed might be a young Tabitha, and another with long, wavy brown hair who could be Marianne. In the background, a young boy on a swing, being pushed by another girl.

The image tugged at my heart. These three girls, arms slung around each other's shoulders, seemed to embody the kind of friendship I'd always yearned for but never quite achieved. Their comfortable closeness, the shared laughter evident even in this frozen moment, reminded me again of the deep connections that had been so elusive in my own life.

I found myself lingering on the photo, drinking in the details. What adventures had led to them being covered in mud? What secrets had they shared? What inside jokes had made them laugh so freely? The questions swirled in my mind, along with a familiar ache of longing for that kind of carefree companionship.

As I was lost in my reflections, the sound of footsteps signaled Emilia's return. She descended the stairs, and I blinked in surprise.

Gone was the disheveled, obsessive investigator from earlier. In her place stood my sister, refreshed and stylishly put together. She'd swapped her oversized sweatshirt for a fitted black turtleneck, tucked neatly into high-waisted jeans. A sleek trench coat completed the look, giving her the air of a noir film detective who had just cracked the case. The effect was only slightly undercut by the mismatched socks peeking out from her ankle boots.

My lips curved into a teasing smile. "Well, look at you. All dolled up for our breakfast date. Or should I say lunch date, given the time?"

Emilia shot back with a playful grin. "I'd say it's fashionably late for breakfast but perfectly on time for lunch. Besides, I had to look my best in case we bump into any fellow *Serenity Falls Mysteries* enthusiasts. Got to represent the fanbase, you know."

"Right, because the first rule of being a true crime fan is to always look like you haven't just spent all night at a murder board."

CHAPTER SEVEN

COZY CUP

The Cozy Cup, nestled in the heart of downtown, seemed a haven for those seeking refuge from the hustle and bustle of everyday life. Its warm lighting and the soft murmur of conversation created an ambiance of comfort and familiarity.

As Emilia and I entered, we were enveloped by the rich aroma of brewing coffee and the sweet scent of baked goods. The line was long, snaking its way to the counter.

"Should we go somewhere else?" I eyed the line.

"Most of the other places are closed on Mondays. And even if they weren't, you must try this sandwich." Emilia's eyes went glassy with longing. "Slow-roasted brisket, caramelized onions, cheddar, fresh arugula, and aioli, all nestled between two slices of toasted artisan sourdough bread—"

"Okay, okay, I get it. We eat here." I laughed at the sheer passion in Emilia's voice. "You had me at 'slow-roasted brisket.'"

We got in line. As we waited, I checked out the café. Vintage posters adorned the walls, hanging above plush armchairs and small tables, perfect for intimate conversations or solitary reflection. In one corner, a small bookshelf overflowed with well-thumbed novels and local newspapers, inviting customers to linger over their drinks with a good read.

"You know," I said, "they really nailed the cozy part of 'Cozy Cup.' I half expect to see a knitting club in the corner."

"Just don't start crocheting doilies, or I'll have to stage an intervention."

I pretended to ponder the idea, my gaze following the length of the line. "Well, now that you mention it, I could see myself with a crochet hook. Imagine the possibilities. Hipster doilies, avant-garde beanies..."

"Please, no," Emilia interjected with a smile. "Let's not forget the scarf debacle of junior year."

That year, I had ambitiously decided to knit a scarf over winter break. The endeavor had started with enthusiasm and a YouTube tutorial. I had envisioned a chic, striped pattern, something that would make me the envy of my classmates. Instead, the scarf had morphed into a lopsided creation, full of unintentional holes and uneven edges. It looked less like a scarf and more like a woolen abstract art piece.

I had worn it to school once, more out of stubborn pride than anything else. The reactions had ranged from bewildered glances to outright laughter. The scarf had eventually found its place as a quirky, if not particularly effective, draft stopper for my bedroom window.

My eyes drifted to the community billboard near the counter, adorned with various flyers. I pointed. "I don't know. Maybe it's time to give it another go. Look there, Stitch and Sip on Thursday nights. It's like fate is calling me back to the world of knitting."

Emilia sighed in pretend defeat. "Okay, but I need to be there to see that."

I grinned, stepping forward as the line moved. "It's settled then. I'll start my knitting career here. Who knows? It might lead to a whole new line of scented yarns."

Reaching the front, Emilia placed her order—a caramel latte and a Rustic Brisketeer sandwich—then offered to snag us the nice corner booth that had just opened up. I stayed behind and scanned the menu. "I'll try the honey lavender latte, please," I said to the gal behind the counter. "And one of those Rustic Brisketeers too."

As I stepped aside to wait, the scent of something rich and nostalgic curled through the air. Something that spoke of home kitchens and handwritten recipes. I glanced at the handwritten chalkboard behind the counter, where one item caught my eye: *Ms. Hattie's Sweet Potato Hand Pies.*

I smiled. That name could only mean one thing.

A woman appeared through a doorway behind the serving station, her vibrant energy immediately noticeable. Under her apron, she wore a flowing floral blouse paired with simple, chic jeans. Her rich brown skin glowed in the soft café lighting, and her hair, a cascade of braids, was pulled back with a bright yellow scarf tied at the crown of her head. But it was her brilliant, welcoming smile that truly set her apart, lighting up her face and making her instantly recognizable to me.

"Vee! I can't believe it! How long has it been?" Time seemed to melt away. The years had only added a touch of grace to Vivian Thompson's features, and her eyes still sparkled with the same kindness and curiosity I remembered so fondly from our high school days.

"It feels like forever, but look at us now." Vivian laughed, stepping out from behind the counter for a heartfelt hug.

"It's nice to see you, Vee. I wish I had stayed in touch more." I gave her one more squeeze, suddenly aware of how, in my haste to put Serenity Falls in my rearview mirror, I had left behind the bad and the good. "So, you work here now, eh?"

"Work? Girl, I *own* this place," she said, grinning.

"You own the Cozy Cup? That's amazing! Congratulations."

Vivian beamed. "Thank you. It's been a journey, but I love it. Granny gave me the startup money as a graduation gift. Said she was investing in the family legacy." She winked. "No pressure or anything."

I laughed. "Ms. Hattie does have excellent instincts."

I followed her to the end of the counter, watching as Vivian skillfully crafted the drink. The hiss of the steam wand and the aromatic blend of coffee and lavender filled the air.

I have a confession to make." Vivian glanced over her shoulder as she worked. "I saw your booth at the farmer's market. Sorry I didn't stop by. I had planned to reach out soon. Things get hectic here on weekends. Especially when Ms. Hattie's hand pies hit the specials board."

She chuckled, the sound warm and familiar, before turning back to me. "Following in your mom's footsteps?"

"Just a side project for now." I leaned against the counter. "Until I find a new research job."

"I knew you'd go into something intellectual. You always were the book-smart one." She shook her head with a smile. "I swear, every time you got called on in class, I'd be sitting there thinking, *Lord, let me borrow that brain for just one quiz.*"

"*I* was always the booksmart one?" I scoffed. "Says the gal who got into *Cornell.*"

Vivian shrugged off the compliment like it was no big thing. With a practiced hand, she poured the steamed milk into the cup, the latte art forming a delicate swirl on the surface. She handed me the mug. "Here you go. Hope you like it."

I took a sip. The flavors mingled perfectly. "This is really good. The lavender isn't overpowering, and the honey adds just the right touch of sweetness."

Vivian's face lit up. "Thanks! I love playing around with flavors. Grannie says I inherited her kitchen instincts, but I like to think I put a little spin on things."

"Same for me with scents." I took another sip of my coffee. "You know, I have this wild idea. What if I created a signature perfume for the Cozy Cup? Something that captures the essence of this place."

"I *love* that!" Vivian stepped aside to let one of her workers handle a new order, but kept her attention on me. "It's a fantastic idea. You know, consider your next latte on the house. A bit of market research, right?"

"That's exactly what my sister called our coffees on Saturday!" My gaze flitted over to Emilia, who sat in the corner booth, immersed in her own thoughts.

Vivian followed my gaze. "You know, your sister is a regular, but I've never actually seen her inside the café."

"Yeah, Emilia's more of a homebody. But I'm trying to get her to branch out more."

Vivian's expression softened. "It's hard to blame her, after everything she's gone through. That you've both gone through. I know how it is. Grief can pull you in like a tide. And that stress with the Charm & Petal storefront couldn't have helped."

I paused, my coffee halfway to my lips. "Stress? What do you mean?"

Vivian looked surprised. "Oh, you know, the whole issue with the owner doubling the rent on the store without warning. It was all anyone could talk about. Your mom even fought it with the town council, but they sided with the landlord. Everyone knew they were just trying to push Charm & Petal out. That's why your grandmother retired, isn't it? Your mom was determined to keep fighting, but then..."

The cook placed two sandwiches on the counter in front of me. They really did look, and smell, delicious. "I didn't know about any rent issues. I thought Gran retired because she was getting older."

Vivian nodded. "That was part of it. But your mom was carrying a lot. She believed in Charm & Petal. Said it was her family's legacy. And she didn't want to let that go."

My mind raced. This was the first I'd heard of any controversy surrounding the family business. Why hadn't Emilia told me? Why hadn't Mom?

"Do you think this stress contributed to her heart attack?"

"It's hard to say," Vivian replied carefully. "But your mom was under a lot of pressure. Anyone who saw her could tell she was fighting with everything she had to keep that place alive."

I managed a nod, though my fingers tightened around the coffee cup. My mother was battling to keep Charm & Petal afloat, struggling against faceless landlords and rising rents, and she hadn't said a word to me. Instead, I'd pictured her happily arranging perfumes and potpourri, her biggest concern whether the rose was just the right shade. But Vivian's words painted a different picture, one I hadn't seen because, apparently, I hadn't been looking.

"Thanks, Vee." I grabbed the sandwiches, balancing them with the lattes. "I appreciate you telling me this."

Mind teeming, I returned to the booth where Emilia was waiting. I set down the sandwiches and coffees, then slipped off my rain jacket. The café's warm atmosphere felt distant now, as my mind grappled with the revelations about Charm & Petal.

Emilia grinned as she picked up her sandwich and took a big bite. Then her smile faltered as she noticed the troubled look on my face. "What's wrong?" The words were garbled, spoken around her mouthful.

I slid into the seat across from her, my movements slow, weighted. "Why didn't anyone tell me about the trouble with the store? The rent issues, the pressure Mom was under?"

Emilia swallowed, a flicker of guilt passing over her features. "We ... we didn't want to bother you with all that, Anna. You seemed so busy with your own life."

I closed my eyes, Emilia's words landing harder than she probably meant them to. My fingers tightened on the cup, as if the warmth might somehow tether me. The hum of the café faded, replaced by the echo of missed moments and words left unspoken. The weight of that guilt settled over me, pressing down with all the quiet losses I'd ignored.

And now, like a cruel reel of old footage, snippets of hurried phone calls with Mom played through my mind. How many times had I been too busy to really listen? There she was, calling to chat, her voice warm at first, but then the inevitable, "Well, it sounds like you're busy, Anna. I should let you get back to work." The hint of sadness in her voice was so easy to overlook, especially when I was halfway through a deadline or staring down another late night.

I could still see myself sitting at my desk, phone tucked between my ear and shoulder as I typed away, managing emails and sending the occasional "Mmhmm" or "Really?" in her direction. I'd always promised myself I'd listen more next time, but next time was always the same. She'd sigh, that gentle, disappointed sound that stuck with me longer than I'd let myself admit.

Mom's struggles, her unspoken worries, all the ways I'd been too distant ... regrets were their own kind of ghost, and right now, they were haunting me good and proper.

"I wish you had told me," I finally said. "No matter how busy I was, it was important. I should have been here." My eyes met Emilia's, conveying a depth of emotion words couldn't fully capture.

"Yes, you should have." Emilia's response was soft, yet within it, I detected a tone that suggested a lingering hurt that couldn't be easily brushed aside. It was a tone that spoke volumes, revealing the gap that had formed between us over the years, a chasm widened by absence and silence.

I really did leave behind the good with the bad, didn't I? In my eagerness to escape the confines of Serenity Falls, to distance myself from the whispers and shadows that clung to our family name, I had inadvertently distanced myself from the people who mattered most. From Emilia, who had remained, bearing the brunt of our mother's struggles and the town's scrutiny in my absence.

A pang of regret pierced through me, sharper and more profound than the myriad of emotions I had felt since returning. I realized, perhaps too late, the cost of my departure, the price paid not in miles but in missed moments and unshared burdens. I had some making up to do. It was too late for Mom, but at least I could be here for Emilia now.

"I'm sorry, Emilia," I whispered, my voice thick with unshed tears. "For leaving, for not being here when you and Mom needed me most. I can't change the past, but I'm here now. And I'm not going anywhere. Maybe I could even find a new research job here locally."

Emilia met my gaze, the hurt in her eyes mingling with a cautious glimmer of hope. I picked up my sandwich, letting the silence settle, giving Emilia—or let's be honest, me—a moment to pull it together.

The rain pattered softly against the café windows as I sat across from Emilia, the warmth of my coffee at odds with the chill settling in my chest. We ate in silence, the air between us heavy but not unkind, until a voice broke through, warm and bright. The woman approached our table, her eyes alight with excitement. "Anna, right? I bought that Evoko perfume from you on Saturday. You won't believe what happened!"

My hands paused mid-air, sandwich inches from my mouth, angled perfectly for a bite. A flicker of annoyance passed through me before I composed myself. Reluctantly, I put down the sandwich and turned towards the source of the voice.

"Yes, that's me," I said, my voice carrying a professional tone. "What did the perfume bring back for you?"

The woman's eyes sparkled. "It was incredible. I remembered this moment with my sister, who passed away years ago. We were dancing in the rain as kids, something I had completely forgotten. The memory was so clear. It was like she was right there with me again."

My interest was piqued despite myself. "That must have been quite a moment for you."

"It felt like magic, like a gift. I just had to come and tell you."

I nodded, my own troubles momentarily receding. Maybe there really was more to Evoko than I had initially thought.

As we chatted, a man from a nearby table leaned over, his presence impossible to ignore. He looked to be in his late fifties, with neatly combed salt-and-pepper hair and piercing eyes that scanned the room like a ledger he was keeping balanced. His skin was a warm olive tone, and the fine lines around his mouth hinted at years of habitual disdain.

He wore a dark blazer—expensive but understated—over a crisp white shirt, collar stiff, top button undone just enough to signal confidence. There was a faint trace of cologne, something woody and bittersweet, like amaretto over smoke. A scent meant to linger. To remind you he'd been here.

"Magic, huh?" His gaze slid toward the woman again, smile sharp enough to cut. "That's how they lure you in—pretty words, sweet promises. But it's always the perfume before the potion, isn't it?"

Something cold curled in my stomach. The words landed too close, too familiar.

Flash—a pencil flicked to the back of the neck, a voice hissing *witch* in the hall.

Flash—a crumpled note on my desk, a stick figure drawn with flames around it.

Flash—Emilia standing in front of me on the playground, face red, fists clenched.

I tossed my napkin onto the table like a gauntlet and stood. "Well, if I start riding a broomstick or chanting over cauldrons, I'll let you know."

Heads turned in our direction, conversations faltering as curious eyes flicked towards our table. A couple near the window whispered behind their menus, while a group of teenagers at the counter had stopped mid-order to watch the unfolding drama.

I may have been shouting.

As I scanned the room, my eyes landed on a familiar figure in line. Tabitha Root stood there, a paper cup clutched in her hands, a look of consternation etched across her face. Her brow was furrowed, lips pressed into a thin line as she watched the man's outburst. For a moment, our eyes met, and I saw a flicker of something—concern? Worry?—cross her features. Without hesitation, Tabitha stepped out of line and began making her way towards our table, her gaze fixed on the unfolding scene.

Tabitha rolled her eyes at the man's comment as she approached. "Don't mind him. That's just Lawrence Riviera, local royalty in his own mind."

He gave her a tight smile that didn't reach his eyes. Then he turned to me, lifted his espresso with fingers that barely trembled—but I noticed. With a single, practiced motion, he downed it in one gulp. The cup hit the table a little too precisely, like a period at the end of a threat.

Then, with a scrape of his chair against the floor, he stood. The sharp sound cut through the café's low hum, drawing glances from nearby tables. He grabbed his coat and stormed towards the exit. Just before leaving, he turned back, his eyes locking with mine. "You Attars think you're so special. But mark my words, *strega*. Some secrets are better left buried."

The bell above the door jingled as Lawrence left, leaving behind a thick silence.

Tabitha sighed, her shoulders sagging. "I'm sorry you had to witness that, Anna. Lawrence ... well, he's got his reasons for being upset, but that's no excuse for his behavior."

She glanced around the café, noticing the curious stares from other patrons. "Listen, I should go." Tabitha placed a comforting hand on my shoulder. "Don't let Lawrence get to you. Your family has always been good for this town."

With a final reassuring smile, Tabitha made her way to the exit, leaving Emilia and me alone at the table.

The café slowly returned to its normal hum of conversation, but I could still feel eyes occasionally darting in our direction. Emilia and I sat in silence for a moment, processing what had just happened.

Finally, Emilia cleared her throat. "Well, that was intense. You okay?"

I nodded, not entirely sure if I was being truthful. "Yeah, I think so. Just a lot to take in."

We turned our attention back to our sandwiches, which had been all but forgotten during the commotion. Emilia took a bite of hers, but I just stared at mine, my appetite having vanished along with Lawrence's parting words. *Secrets better left buried?* What could he have meant by that?

Chapter Eight

EVOKO

The drive home from Golden Pines was quiet. After the Cozy Cup, we had brought Gran ginger scones and a thermos of chamomile tea, and she'd been having a good day—sharp, if a little drowsy around the edges. Our visit had stayed light, neither of us having the energy for anything deeper after the conversation with Lawrence.

Instead, we talked about everything from the weather (unseasonably wet, even for spring), to Emilia's latest Netflix binge (a true crime documentary, of course), to the superiority of sourdough bread (a topic Gran and Emilia both had alarmingly strong opinions on). It was all surface-level chatter, cheerful and brittle, like porcelain already cracked beneath the glaze.

Now, all that remained was the steady swish of windshield wipers and the soft patter of rain. The bustling downtown faded as we turned toward Riverside Park, the cobblestones giving way to slick pavement. I let my thoughts drift to the troubling mysteries piling up: Gran's perfume and its apparent power, the cryptic warnings from Lawrence, and the nagging questions about our mom's death.

The evidence of Gran's perfume's effects was mounting. The market anecdotes, and now that woman's vivid recollection of a

long-buried memory pointed to something extraordinary. The sci-
entist in me wrestled with the implications. What if Gran's brief
clarity amid her dementia wasn't a fluke but something far more
significant? And what if Mom's death held darker truths?

Yet, how could I reconcile these thoughts with logic? The notion
of magic seemed as far-fetched as the idea that someone could induce
a heart attack from afar.

As the car wove closer to home, my gaze lingered on the
rain-blurred outlines of budding trees. Arriving home as the rain
tapered off might have felt comforting on another day, but today,
it brought only unease. The answers we sought hovered just out of
reach, like a storm refusing to clear.

I let out a heavy sigh. In this small town, where Gran had always
been a figure of mystique and whispered rumors, the line between
reality and superstition seemed to blur. Gran had always laughed
at the rumors that she was a witch. She even dressed as one for
Halloween. But magic wasn't real, or so I had always believed.

We stepped out into a world transformed. The overcast sky cast
a muted glow over the wet earth, and the garden shimmered under
its fresh rinse. But something beneath the surface prickled. The
house stood quietly against the backdrop of Serenity's dense forest,
unchanged and yet distinctly off. Even the old oak by the driveway
seemed to whisper warnings with every drip and sway of its branches.

As we walked toward the front door, the air buzzed, raising the
hairs on my arms. My heart picked up, though I couldn't say why.
From the outside, everything seemed normal: the two-story yellow
house, the windows with gently swaying curtains, the rain-washed
garden blooming wildly in Mom's absence.

Emilia, oblivious to the tension humming in my chest, led the way
to the front door, her keys jingling in the softened quiet.

A sudden movement drew my attention. Watson darted out from beneath a forsythia bush, its yellow blossoms vivid against the rain-slick leaves. The gray fluffball's movements were frantic, his little paws skidding on the wet ground as he rubbed desperately against Emilia's legs.

"Watson! How did you get out here?" Emilia bent to scoop him up.

Watson meowed in response, his wide green eyes brimming with urgency. He squirmed in her arms, his tail flicking against her wris t.Hher fingers smoothed his damp fur. "What's gotten into you?"

The rain-softened world felt impossibly still as we stepped into the dimly lit foyer. Inside, the sense of unease that had shadowed me solidified into certainty. The faint but unmistakable scent of bergamot lingered in the air.

I froze, my pulse quickening. Neither of us wore it, and I hadn't been working with it.

Someone's been here.

Without even stopping to take off my raincoat, driven by a sudden urgency, I peered into the living room. Emilia's books, usually meticulously organized on their shelves, were scattered across the floor, their pages flung open and askew, as if someone had been searching through them in a hurry.

No. The windows. I'd left them open.

Emilia dashed into the living room and frantically gathered her books. The burglars had gone through her personal items. She carefully salvaged what she could, her hands trembling as she tried to restore order to the disarray. Then, abruptly, her back stiffened. "My office," she whispered, dread in her voice. That's where she kept her laptop, her client files. Everything tied to her work. Without a moment's hesitation, she sprinted to the adjoining room.

Meanwhile, I followed Watson, who seemed intent on leading me toward the dining room. The sight that greeted me hit like a silent scream. The drawers of the curio cabinet stood ajar, their contents spilled and strewn across the floor as if a storm had torn through. My gaze landed on the dining room table. My perfume supplies were oddly untouched amid the wreckage.

A whisper of bergamot—bright, citrusy, out of place—wafted through the air, between the broken remnants of normalcy.

But it was the empty space on the hutch that stopped me cold.

Gran's scent grimoire was gone. Our family heirloom filled with recipes, with secrets passed down through generations, was no longer ours.

Someone had come here with purpose. They knew exactly what they were looking for.

Behind me, Emilia sucked in a sharp breath. "Where's the grimoire?"

I didn't answer. I was already moving, crouching down to check the bottom door of the hutch. Another emptiness gaped back at me. The box of Evoko. Gone. I sat back on my heels, the room tilting sickeningly around me.

"My guess?" My voice sounded hollow in my own ears. "It's wherever all my Evoko is."

I pressed a hand to my forehead, trying to steady myself, trying to think. That book held my only copy of the Evoko recipe. The only thing that kept Gran tethered to her memories. Without it, there would be no more flickers of clarity. No more questions answered. No more moments of her coming back to us.

Whoever had done this stole time we couldn't afford to lose. I couldn't get another glimpse of the woman she used to be before the fog took over.

I couldn't get her back. Not without Evoko.

A prickling sensation crawled up my spine. Had that been the point of the break-in? Not just the perfume bottles, not some opportunistic grab for shiny glass and delicate labels, but the recipe itself? The one thing that could bring Gran back to herself, even if only for a few fleeting moments?

Was this all about keeping Gran quiet? Keeping us from finding out what Gran knew?

Could the theft be connected to Mom's death?

I motioned for Emilia to follow me into the kitchen.

There, chaos greeted us.

The murder board lay in ruins. Photographs torn down, some slashed through the middle. Sticky notes curled and crumpled like dead leaves. Red thread dangled like veins cut mid-course. A push-pin rolled across the tile with an eerie little clatter, the sound far too loud in the silence.

Emilia stopped cold. For a second, she just stared. Then her hand flew to her mouth, and a strangled sound escaped her throat—half sob, half gasp.

"No," she whispered. She dropped to her knees so hard I winced. Her hands moved frantically, trying to gather torn notes, reattach thread, rescue the mess. "No, no, no. This was everything."

"They knew what you were doing," I said. "They knew exactly what we had."

I knelt beside her, my stomach twisting. "This was a message. Someone wanted to shut us down."

She picked up a photo with shaking fingers. It was of the Charm & Petal closing event, now ripped in two. Her handwriting was still visible beneath the jagged edge: *What was Lawrence doing at the party?*

"I worked so hard on this." She clutched the photo to her chest. "I finally felt like I was close. Like maybe we were finally going to prove it." She looked around the room as if she could undo it all by sheer force of will. "They came in here and *ripped it apart.*"

The fury in her voice startled me. But beneath it was something even sharper: grief.

"Em," I said, reaching out. She flinched back for a second, then leaned into my arm.

For a moment, neither of us moved. The only sound was the soft rustle of paper as the wind from the open window stirred a scrap across the floor.

"They think this will stop us?" Her voice was ragged. "They think I'll give up now?"

I looked down at the scraps in my hand, the broken trail of a story someone wanted buried. And I realized she had been right all along.

I reached across the mess and pulled her into a hug, paper crinkling beneath our knees.

"I'm sorry I didn't believe you before," I murmured into her hair.

She pulled back just enough to meet my gaze, eyes fierce and wet.

"Mom was murdered," she said. "And I'm going to prove it."

Chapter Nine

POLICE VISIT

An hour later, I was still reeling from the break-in. Emilia and I sat on the front porch, the evening air cool against our skin. She was curled up in one of the wicker chairs, bundled in a knitted blanket, scrolling rapidly through her phone as we waited for the police.

I couldn't sit still. I paced the length of the porch, boots thudding against the worn floorboards, the familiar creak of a loose plank punctuating each turn.

Watson perched at the top of the steps like a furry sentinel, his tail flicking with restless energy, fur puffed ever so slightly. The porch light buzzed quietly overhead, throwing a soft circle of gold against the growing twilight. Somewhere out in the distance, a dog barked, the sound sharp against the quiet.

Suddenly, Watson let out a sharp *mrrrp* and his posture stiff with attention. A pair of headlights turned into the driveway, tires crunching over the gravel.

"That's probably them," I paused mid-pace.

A police cruiser rolled to a stop, and the driver's door swung open. David Miller stepped out. I immediately recognized my old lab partner from junior year chemistry. Back then, he'd been all awkward angles and quiet apologies, forever pushing his glasses up the bridge of his nose while the other kids snickered at me. He'd never joined in. Just gave me small, hesitant smiles and focused on balancing chemical equations.

Now, David looked every bit the officer. Taller, broader, his stride steady and sure. The glasses were gone, replaced by a clear, steady gaze. I felt a strange pang seeing him like this. Official and imposing, a world away from the boy I'd known.

As he walked up the path, I caught myself smoothing my hair.

"Anna Attar?" David's voice was deeper than I remembered, tinged with surprise. His eyes flickered with recognition as he took me in. "It's been a long time."

"David Miller," I said, a little breathless. "I almost didn't recognize you." What with all the muscles and whatnot. "You're ... wow. A cop."

He chuckled. "That's the general idea." His expression shifted to professional. "I'm here about the break-in."

"Right, come in."

As we stepped inside, David gave the foyer a long, sweeping glance. The sleek gray walls and abstract art earned a slow nod, but his gaze snagged on the empty space where the photo gallery used to be.

Emilia quickly took the lead. "I'm sorry about the ... clean ... in here. I instinctively started picking things up." She gestured to the slightly tidier living room.

"But we haven't touched anything else," she added.

"No problem." David nodded. "I'd like to take a look around, if that's okay."

"Of course," Emilia said. She was already pulling out her phone and tapping notes into it with the efficiency of someone who had read too many procedural thrillers.

"She's starting a case file," I murmured to David as we followed him deeper into the house.

David cracked a smile. "Still the same sisters, huh?"

Emilia, without missing a beat, stepped in front of him and gestured deeper into the house. "Officer, I think we should begin in the dining room. That's where the perfumes were kept, and also where we last saw Gran's grimoire."

David blinked. "Grimoire?"

"A family heirloom," I explained quickly. "A book."

As we stepped into the dining room, David eyed our dining room curtains, flapping like surrender flags. "Were the windows open like this while you were out?"

I winced. "I didn't think ... we were just stepping out for lunch."

"Open windows can be an invitation for opportunistic thieves." He looked up, likely realizing how that sounded. "Not that I'm blaming you. I just mean it's good to be cautious."

His ears turned pink. I bit back a smile. There's the David I remembered.

Emilia shot me a look. Less nostalgia, more *you had one job.*

David moved with quiet focus as he tested locks and nudged window latches with the same precision he'd once used to balance chemical equations. He paused near the dining table and crouched to inspect the floor beside the carved legs of the antique hutch.

How many afternoons had we spent at that table? Our elbows brushing as we worked through equations, sunlight sliding across our notebooks, his pencil tapping nervously whenever he hit a snag. David had always blushed when confused, his gaze darting between me and the paper. Unlike other boys, he never blustered his way through. He listened. And sometimes, he smiled at me like he meant i
t.

Once, he spilled orange juice all over his shirt, and we'd rushed upstairs to find—

Upstairs! That's right. All was not lost. Emilia and I each had personal bottles of Evoko in our bedrooms. Surely the thief hadn't thought to check there. "We should check upstairs," I said.

We followed David upstairs. When we reached my bedroom, I immediately went to my old dresser.

No! My bottle of Evoko should have been sitting next to the Whisperwind Whimsy that Emilia and I had crafted together.

Whisperwind Whimsy was still there.

I pulled open the drawer, hoping perhaps I'd moved it there for safekeeping. My heart sank as I found nothing nothing. "My personal bottle of Evoko is also missing."

Emilia emerged from her room. "Mine too."

I shuddered. The thief had been upstairs. Standing over where I slept.

Emilia crossed her arms. "If the thief took the time to find even the bottles we kept for ourselves, they were searching deliberately."

David's brow furrowed as he wrote. "That suggests this wasn't a random burglary."

"We'll need to piece together a timeline, maybe get a description of any suspicious individuals seen in the area," offered Emilia.

David opened his notebook again, writing while talking. "I'll file a report on the break-in and theft. Now, you also mentioned a ... what did you call it? Grimoire? Was it worth a lot?"

"Sentimentally, yes. But monetarily? Hard to say." I hugged my arms close, like that might somehow fill the space Gran's book had left behind. "I care more about it than the perfumes. That book was Gran's. It's a family heirloom."

David paused his writing, his hazel eyes meeting mine. "I understand. We'll do everything we can to find your book. Can you describe it?"

As I described the perfume book, David's expression shifted from professional to intrigued. "Ms. Attar's spell book?" David brought his pen to his mouth. "Do you mean that was real? I remember the stories. All us kids thought she was some kind of witch, selling her magic potions at Charm & Petal."

I smiled at the memory. "She loved those rumors."

"But why now?" he asked. "Why steal her book after all this time?"

Emilia straightened, her eyes sharpening with sudden focus. "Maybe someone wanted the recipes for themselves!"

"I just reopened a perfume booth at the farmer's market under the company name. I even had Gran's book out on the table as part of the display. Maybe someone saw it and wanted Gran's perfume recipes."

David shook his head. "Then why not take the ingredients? There's a whole apothecary's worth downstairs."

I gave a dry laugh. "Well, Evoko is a memory perfume. What if someone out there *does* believe the rumors about our family? I can only think of two reasons to steal just the Evoko and the book containing its recipe. Either they wanted to stir up some long-lost memory ... or make sure we never do."

David chuckled. "You know, it might just be a prank. We've seen similar things happen before in town. A few years back, someone swiped Harold Jenkins' prized garden gnome. It ended up on top of the water tower, of all places. Caused quite a stir."

"This is not a prank," Emilia said flatly. "The thief also destroyed my murder board."

David blinked. "Murder board?"

"She means family history project," I interjected.

"No," Emilia insisted. "We're investigating our mother's death. Gran had a lucid moment. Said mom's death wasn't an accident."

David went still. "That's a serious allegation."

"It is," Emilia agreed. "But we made her a memory perfume that day. She was clearer than she'd been in months."

I quickly added, "Probably a psychological response. A familiar scent. But she said our mom was murdered."

Emilia cast me a look that broadcasted in sister language, *I know we're not supposed to talk about magic to the nice cop, but you and I both know there's more to it than just psychology.*

He paused for a moment. "I could have sworn I'd heard your mom died of a heart attack."

"That's what her death certificate states," said Emilia. "But they didn't do an autopsy to confirm, either."

David nodded. "I'd like to interview your grandmother. Anna, would you be willing to come along? It might make things easier, given her condition."

"Yes, of course."

David's eyes sparkled. He jotted down a note, a faint blush spreading across his cheeks. Standing up, he conveyed a sense of quiet anticipation. "I'll arrange the interview and get in touch with the details. In the meantime, I'll file a report about the break-in and keep an eye out for anything related to your mother's case."

"Thank you," said Emilia. She gave me a knowing look I could not quite interpret.

David nodded. "I'll keep you both updated on any developments. In the meantime, try to stay safe." He pulled out a business card, wrote a number on the back, then handed it to me. "This is my personal cell. Don't hesitate to call if you remember anything else."

On Tuesday morning, the dining room transformed into my personal sanctuary, filled with an array of vials and bottles, each containing an essence of nature's own brew. I found myself engrossed in the art of perfumery, my senses enveloped by scents.

The atmosphere in the Attar household had noticeably shifted in the wake of David's departure. The investigation into the break-in, and the theft of Evoko and of our grandmother's grimoire, had left a lingering tension, like a dense fog that refused to lift.

I sought solace in creating a blend that spoke of peace and tranquility. Lavender, with its soothing qualities, paired beautifully with chamomile's gentle embrace and a hint of sandalwood's grounding effect. Each droplet became a calm counterpoint to the storm raging in my life.

While working, I revisited the spreadsheet I had begun for my new formula. Why hadn't I started a digital formula book sooner? Though I had sufficient notes to get close to recreating Evoko, it just wasn't the same. So, I resolved to take this time to begin crafting my own blend.

As I blended and tested, I felt a deep connection to Gran, a silent conversation carried through the language of scents and memories. The act of creation was therapeutic. In the midst of uncertainty and fear, the world of perfumes became my haven, a place where I could exert control and find a semblance of peace, one drop at a time.

Emilia, on the other hand, threw herself into her work with a fervor that bordered on obsessiveness. She only left her office to use the restroom and grab her DoorDash orders from the front porch. Then, after logging off from her job at precisely five o'clock, she migrated to the kitchen, where she pieced her murder board back together. The board had become her world, a puzzle she was determined to solve.

By Wednesday, our home had become a silent hub, with me lost in my world of perfumes and Emilia consumed with reconstructing the murder board. I ventured into the kitchen occasionally, offering to help or simply to share a quiet moment with my sister. Deep down, I harbored the belief that we should leave the investigation to the police. Yet, I knew suggesting as much to Emilia would be futile.

My sister was living in her own real-life murder mystery, and there was no way she would step back now.

A wave of guilt washed over me. I shouldn't have been so flippant. This was about our mother. Of course Emilia was invested. Throwing herself into the investigation was just her way to cope.

As the clock struck five on Thursday, I heard my sister shut down her computer with a sigh before immediately drifting back to the murder board in the kitchen.

It was time for a change.

"Hey, Emilia," I called out, leaning against the kitchen doorway. "How about we do something different tonight? There's a concert at the park. Live music, food ... It could be fun."

Emilia looked up. "A concert? On a Thursday?"

"Yeah, I saw an ad for it online. It's part of the town's spring series honoring the fiftieth anniversary of the opening of Riverside Park. You know, local bands, restaurant booths. A change of scenery might do us some good." I tried to inject a bit of enthusiasm into my voice.

Emilia hesitated, her gaze lingering on the murder board. Then, to my surprise, she nodded. "You know what? That actually sounds nice. I could use a break from all this."

As we prepared to leave, I felt a sense of relief wash over me. "I think this will be good for us. A little fresh air, some Ivy Nook sandwiches. It's exactly what we need right now."

Emilia gave a slow smile. "I do love sandwiches."

We got ready in silence, but just before we left, I walked the perimeter again, locking every window and checking every latch. As we made sure all the windows were closed and locked, then shut the front door and locked it securely, Emilia glanced back.

"Let's hope this ends better than the last time we left the house," she muttered.

I nodded. "Agreed."

Chapter Ten

RIVERSIDE PARK

The lively atmosphere of Riverside Park enveloped Emilia and me as we stepped into the throng of the Thursday night concert. Soulful strains of music mingled with the laughter and chatter of the community. The air was rich with the aroma of various cuisines. Each local restaurant seemed to compete in an unspoken culinary contest as scents of grilling meats, fresh bread, and spices wafted through the air.

Above us, banners fluttered from the light poles, proudly announcing the park's fiftieth anniversary. Gold and green lettering proclaimed, *"Celebrating 50 Years of Riverside Park!"* alongside charming illustrations of the park's iconic bridge.

Even some artists had set up booths, all in a row on the other side of the stage from where the food was. Lights had been strung along the path between the booths, illuminating the way for potential shoppers. I gazed longingly in that direction. I wanted to explore those before leaving. And maybe, someday, set up a table of my own at something like this. I'd have to use my own blends now, not Gran's. The thought filled me with both excitement and dread. Without the grimoire, it would all have to come from me. Was I ready for that?

I needed food.

The Ivy Nook truck was a hub of activity. Behind the counter, a younger woman with a bright smile and an animated black ponytail greeted me and Emilia. "Hey there! What can I get for you ladies tonight?" she chirped. Her energy was infectious.

"Two of your best sandwiches, please." I returned the woman's smile.

As the worker bustled about preparing our order, Emilia leaned in. "You know, I order from Ivy Nook all the time, but I've never actually been in."

The woman, placing the sandwiches on the counter, looked up. "Really? You should come by sometime. I'm Sophia, by the way. I waitress there part-time, but it's just something to pay the bills. I'm in the creative writing program at Serenity Falls College."

Emilia's interest visibly perked up. "Creative writing? That sounds amazing. I'm a huge fan of true crime novels myself."

I watched as Emilia's shoulders relaxed, her gaze softening under the strands of twinkling lights overhead. I could almost pretend she was the sister I remembered from years ago, back when she had friends—a ragtag group of them, but friends, nonetheless. She used to be part of the world.

I had been so jealous of my sister in high school, seeing Emilia with her small crowd of "misfits," as my mother had called them. I was a loner. Other than Vee, the kids all gave me a wide berth. But Emilia had managed to find a way to connect. She'd be at the bonfires, laughing with that scruffy-haired guy who always wore the same band T-shirt, and with Juniper, the quiet gal who filled the margins of her notebooks with doodles. They were their own little band of outcasts, united against the world.

Emilia had seemed so carefree back then, so unburdened by what we all quietly called "the Attar curse." But she had an edge, too. Her laughter could flip to fury in a heartbeat, and anyone who dared to whisper behind her back often got a front-row seat to her temper. She'd sent more than one rumor-monger scurrying with a single, withering glare. Or worse, the sharp edge of her fist. Wild, mysterious, and just a little dangerous, she'd been unstoppable in my eyes.

Then Danny happened.

He was a reckless dreamer with the kind of charm that parents side-eyed and daughters adored. Emilia was so *alive* with him. I could still remember watching them speed off down the road together, his motorcycle roaring, my heart thudding with some mix of envy and admiration. And then, just like that, he was gone. Skidded out on a rain-slick road leaving our house one night, and the town's whispers turned vicious.

Did you hear? And only sixteen. They say he hit the brakes too late. I say he never had a chance once an Attar set her eyes on him.

Emilia withdrew after that. Disappeared from the bonfires, the school events, even from Juniper and that scraggly boy. It was like she'd retreated into the shadows, closing the door on the world. And, sometimes, I wondered, on me. But I'd never really asked. Never wanted to touch the wound in case it still hurt.

I had been a senior in high school, already busy daydreaming about life outside Serenity Falls, where I could be logical and rational and not from a family of freaks. But I made a perfume For Emilia—a bottle of Joy I'd crafted with every shred of love and desperation I had left, hoping it would bring her back from her grief.

When it didn't work, I quit perfume for good. I told myself if magic couldn't help the person I loved most, then it wasn't worth anything. That magic was a child's fantasy.

Sophia's voice broke me out of my thoughts. She was still chattering away, oblivious to the ache of memories hovering in the air. "...book club! You should join us sometime. It's a lot of fun, and we love having new people."

She practically bounced as she handed over the sandwiches.

I glanced at Emilia, catching the polite half-smile she'd perfected. It was that same smile she used every time someone tried to tug her back out into the world. A smile that said *not in a million years,* wrapped in a blanket of niceness.

"That sounds great," Emilia said in her fake nice voice, and the familiar pang of sadness twisted in my chest.

At home, it was easy to forget. When she was curled on the couch arguing plot holes or laughing at old movies, I could almost believe nothing had changed. But out here, in the midst of other people, I could see the edges of the mask she wore. The girl she used to be still lingered, like the faint scent of something beautiful, and just out of r each.

Sophia nodded, turning to help the next customer, and I shot Emilia a small smile, trying to cut through her polite distance. "Come on," I said, nudging her shoulder with mine, "let's find a spot to eat."

Sandwiches in hand, we meandered away from the heart of the festivities. We strolled along a path that led us closer to the river. The strumming of guitars, the beat of drums, and the distant laughter of children became a pleasant backdrop to our walk.

As Emilia and I approached Whisperwind Bridge, the boisterous sounds from the concert and crowd gradually faded, overtaken by the tranquil rustling of leaves and the melodious murmur of the river. We sat on a park bench nestled under a canopy of trees.

I unwrapped my sandwich, revealing a gourmet take on a classic peanut butter and jelly. The bread was a rustic, artisanal sourdough, its crust golden and crisp. Between the slices, a generous spread of crunchy peanut butter melded perfectly with slices of strawberry and a layer of homemade strawberry jam, its vibrant hues promising a burst of sweetness.

"Sophia seems nice," I said, taking a bite. Fresh strawberries burst in my mouth. "You should take her up on her offer."

Emilia picked at her turkey club. "I don't know. Do you think they meet over zoom?"

I laughed. "No, this sounds like an in-person thing. You would actually have to—gasp—get dressed and go."

Emilia did a theatrical shudder. "And leave my couch?"

I laughed. "Come to think of it, I can't believe I got you out of the house twice this week!" Of course, we had triple-checked all the doors and windows before leaving this time. Emilia insisted.

"Well, it helps that Riverside Park is practically in our front yard," Emilia remarked, holding up her club sandwich with a smile.

As we sat together on the park bench, savoring our food and the cool night air, an elderly couple walked past. The woman leaned towards her husband and whispered in a voice she probably thought was soft but carried clearly, "Look, isn't that the Attar girls?"

Hearing this, Emilia visibly sank deeper into her seat, her focus shifting to her sandwich as if it held the secrets of the universe. I, on the other hand, faced the couple squarely. "Yes, I'm Anna."

"Oh, you're the spitting image of Evelyn back when she was a girl," the elder woman commented. "Shame what happened to her."

"Thank you," I said.

As the couple walked off, the woman's voice, still not as hushed as she likely intended, floated back. "It was probably the curse, poor woman. Fate is finally enacting revenge for the flood."

Without missing a beat, Emilia called out after them, "Don't worry, you'll be safe on the bridge. We left our weather-controlling machine in our other pants!"

The couple looked back, then furtively veered away from the bridge. Good riddance.

This stretch of the river, peaceful and inviting, had once been lined with houses. Not just the one that belonged to our family.

Just over fifty years ago, a devastating flood swept through the area, leaving ruin in its wake, and taking the life of thirteen-year-old Carolyne Morgan.

No one knew exactly how she ended up in the river with the floodwaters raging. Some said she had been swimming when the storm came in. Others say she fell in trying to save someone else. Whatever the reason, Carolyne never made it back. Her death became a scar on the town's collective memory, but it also became a weapon. The Morgans, devastated and looking for someone to blame, pointed fingers squarely at the Attar "witches." It didn't take much for the rest of the town to follow their lead. Whispers of strange herbs and midnight lights in the windows fed the fire.

The accusation stuck, long after the Morgans moved away, and our family went from peculiar to problem.

The fact that the whole Morgan family was alive and well two towns over should have been proof enough we weren't witches. If I ever ran into a Morgan, I'd have a few choice words about the suspicion they lit and left behind.

Then, as if to cement our reputation, when the town decided to buy out the riverfront properties to make way for a flood wall and Riverside Park, all but one homeowner agreed. Our great-grandmother refused to sell. Her defiance was the final straw for many. To me, she was a fierce symbol of independence, a woman who stood her ground in the face of unimaginable pressure. To the town, she was evidence of the worst rumors. Proof that the Attar witches cared more about their own desires than the safety and harmony of the town.

I scoffed at the absurdity of the town's logic. "I mean, notwithstanding the fact that no one can cause a flood, think about how ridiculous it sounds. Would Great-Gran really flood her own home just in the hopes the town would build a wall and buy up all the surrounding property? For what? So she could have no neighbors?"

Emilia shrugged, a look of admiration on her face. "If she did, she was a genius."

I shook my head, my eyes rolling in exasperation. "If anything, it shows how quick the town is to create villains out of our family with no logical reason. See, nonsense like this is why I left. How do you deal with it?"

"Easy. I don't go out much." Emilia then proceeded to dig into her sandwich.

CHAPTER ELEVEN

WHISPERWIND BRIDGE

Finishing our dinner, Emilia and I meandered to the spiral ramp leading up to Whisperwind Bridge. I marveled once again at the ingenuity of it. What once carried the weight of trains now had a second life as a scenic walkway for pedestrians.

Upon reaching the bridge's flat expanse, we strolled across, exchanging brief nods with people coming from the opposite direction. Classical music drifted from speakers. Lights strung along the bridge's length, bathing the structure in a display of slowly changing colors, turning a simple crossing into something almost magical.

"It's like walking through a rainbow." My eyes followed the transition of hues.

"Personally, I'm more entranced by the *Bach beats burglars* strategy," said Emilia. "I remember when the town council decided on classical music, hoping to sway more 'unsavory' folk from using the bridge as a hangout spot. Because nothing scares off potential criminals like a dose of Beethoven."

I perked my ears to listen. "Or maybe they're hoping to cultivate a generation of cultured pickpockets."

Emilia, with a mischievous glint in her eye, changed the subject. "So, about David Miller. He's got quite the crush on you, doesn't he?"

I laughed, brushing off the suggestion. "No, that's silly. We just went to high school together, that's all."

"But did you not notice how he kept looking at you when he was over? And he specifically asked you, not me, to come with him to interview Gran tomorrow." Emilia playfully bumped her shoulder against mine.

I waved my hand dismissively. "It's because he knows me from school. We were lab partners, remember? It's just familiarity."

Up ahead, I caught sight of a familiar figure leaning casually against the bridge railing. Parker. The shifting lights of the bridge bathed him in a soft, ethereal glow, transitioning from green to blue. The hues played across his features, accentuating his easy confidence as he gazed out over the river. My cheeks warmed.

Emilia noticed immediately. "Well, well," she said, her voice teasing. "Isn't that Mr. Farmers Market?"

I tried for nonchalance, though I could already feel the heat creeping up my neck. "Yeah, I remember him. He sells bowls. Nice ones. Very practical."

Emilia's lips quirked into a knowing smirk. "Uh-huh. And here I thought you were brushing off David because you weren't interested. But now I'm starting to think it's because of this guy. You like him."

"That's ridiculous," I protested, the words coming out faster than I intended. "We've barely spoken."

But Emilia chose this most embarassing moment for her old social self to break through. Before I could stop her, she strode confidently toward Parker, her determination clear.

"Well, I guess it's time for a proper introduction," she said to me over her shoulder.

"Emilia!" I hissed. I considered bolting, but my feet were glued to the bridge by my own curiosity.

"Hi!" Emilia said brightly as she reached Parker. "I don't think we've been properly introduced. I'm Emilia, Anna's sister."

As I rushed to catch up, Parker turned towards us, a look of surprise crossing his face, quickly replaced by a welcoming smile. "Nice to meet you."

I found myself compulsively fiddling with my hair, a nervous habit I thought I'd left behind years ago. My gaze kept darting away from Parker's striking green eyes, only to be drawn back again. My mind raced for something to say but came up empty. Instead, I stood there, shuffling my feet, acutely aware of how my hands seemed to have no natural resting place.

Emilia, on the other hand, somehow managed to carry the conversation as if she were a seasoned socialite. "So, Parker, how long have you been in Serenity Falls?"

"About a year." Parker's voice drifted somewhere above my head as I scrambled to keep my expression calm and casual. Anything but the flustered mess I felt underneath. I could practically feel my inner teenager groaning, rolling her eyes at my pathetic attempt to keep it together.

Emilia's voice chimed in next, asking about his work. Parker started describing his carpentry, something about shaping wood into custom furniture, the way he could see a table or chair in the grain before he even started. His words painted images of elegant lines and rich, polished finishes, but they only half-registered as I focused all my energy on not gawking like some moony-eyed schoolgirl.

I nodded along, hoping I looked interested rather than flustered, but the way my cheeks burned told me I was failing miserably.

Emilia, with the eagerness of a detective from her beloved murder shows, continued her interrogation. Her eyebrows danced with intrigue. "Do you know about the legend of this bridge?"

Parker shook his head, his gaze shifting towards me. Was there a hint of curiosity, or something more, in that brief glance?

"The legend goes that the bridge listens to your deepest, darkest secrets and grants wishes," Emilia continued. For a fleeting moment, I caught Parker's eyes lingering on me again, a thoughtful, almost wistful look in them.

"Some say it's the lights and music. They attract mystical beings who love to eavesdrop on all the juicy gossip. And," Emilia added with a waggle of her eyebrows, "if they love your secret enough, they'll reward you with a granted wish."

I took a deep breath and jumped into the conversation. "Yeah, local folklore at its finest. You'll have folks around here swearing they've seen fairies or heard mermaids in the river. I guess even mystical beings can't resist a good light show and some Mozart."

Parker glanced around at the vibrant lights. "Sounds intriguing. Maybe I should start whispering to the bridge, see if any wishes come true."

I laughed, the sound more genuine this time, thankfully. "Just be careful what you wish for. With our town's track record, you might end up with a garden gnome appearing mysteriously on your rooftop."

Parker smiled at that, and I felt a warmth spread through me. There was something about his smile that made my heart flutter.

"So, how do we make a wish here?" asked Parker. "Any special protocol?"

"Well, traditionally, you're supposed to close your eyes, stand on one leg and turn around three times. Then facing due East, offer your deepest, darkest secret to the river as a form of payment." I shrugged. "But, you know, results may vary."

"It needs to be a good secret," added Emilia. "Something juicy. Otherwise they won't grant your wish."

"Challenge accepted." Parker stepped back, a twinkle in his eye. "Why don't we all give it a try?"

Emilia grinned. "I'm in. After all, what's a night on a magical bridge without a little ritual?"

Emilia and Parker squeezed their eyes shut, faces bright with laughter as they wobbled on one leg, arms stretched wide like kids playing a game of balance. Their giggles drifted through the cool evening air, and I grinned, feeling warmth rise in my chest. Maybe these outings were working. Maybe Emilia was slowly leaving her hermit status behind.

And there was something so disarming about seeing Parker like this, eyes closed, a soft smile tugging at his lips as he twirled in place. He looked ... happy. Unfiltered, even. And he didn't seem to mind one bit how silly he might look, spinning around under the flickering lights of the bridge.

Then, feeling a surge of joyous spontaneity, I closed my own eyes, breathing in the crisp night air, letting the sounds and sensations swirl around me. Balancing on one leg, I tilted into my own slow turn, feeling the weight I carried lift ever so slightly. Just me and the night and the laughter of my sister beside me. My heart felt lighter, almost as if it could float up with the lights swaying gently on the breeze. The worries I'd been holding on to felt distant, like I could leave them behind with each spin.

I completed my rotations and faced east—at least, I thought it was east—my heart still racing from the giddy joy of it all. I closed my eyes tighter, focusing on the wish that had lodged itself so deeply in my heart.

Mom. Her laughter, her arms wrapping around me in the quiet of the evening, her voice always soft but sure. The floral scent that always lingered in her hair. How many years had it been since I'd felt her warmth? Too many. I hadn't meant to stay away so long. But one missed visit became two, and suddenly the chance to sit beside her, to ask the things I'd never thought to ask, was gone.

I'd give anything to find out what really happened to her. But the Whisperwind Bridge didn't grant wishes without a price. What secret could I offer it in return? Something meaningful enough, something deep enough to earn its favor.

A sharp voice cut through the night, smooth but laced with an edge. "Practicing your *craft*, are we? Out here for everyone to see?"

The warmth of the moment slipped away, leaving a chill that curled up my spine. My eyes snapped open, and the whimsical bubble we had created around ourselves popped, replaced by the harsher reality of Lawrence Riviera.

He stood on the far side of the bridge, his tailored coat buttoned neatly, his posture stiff with disapproval. Even as the full moon began to slip behind an encroaching veil of clouds, the glint of disdain in his piercing eyes was unmistakable.

"Is this what the Attar legacy has come to?" he continued, his tone dripping with disdain. As he walked toward us, his movements were measured, almost overly deliberate. "Playing witch under the stars? Just being near you is enough to make my head pound." He pinched the bridge of his nose for emphasis.

Emilia didn't miss a beat. "Oh, don't worry, Lawrence," she shot back with a saccharine smile. "We keep the cauldron brewing out of sight. Wouldn't want to violate any zoning laws."

His lips curved into a thin smile, as if humoring a child who didn't know better. "Charming. It seems sarcasm runs in the family."

His gaze flicked to Parker, who had been standing quietly nearby. "I'd be careful if I were you. Men who get close to the Attars tend to disappear or die. Ask them where their grandfather is. Or their dad. Ask them about *Danny Vance*."

The name landed like a stone in my gut. But it was Emilia who flinched, sharp and silent, like she'd been punched in the ribs. Her breath caught, her jaw tightened, and the color drained from her face before rushing back in a hot flush.

I stepped in before she could speak. "What's that supposed to mean?"

The wind picked up, brushing past us with an insistent tug, carrying with it the faint metallic scent of rain.

Lawrence's expression didn't waver, his calm unshaken by the tension crackling in the air.

"Just an observation," he said, almost lazily. "And come to think of it, maybe we should add your mother to that list of mysterious deaths. Margaret was always mixing up her little concoctions. Strange, isn't it, how her mind started to slip around the same time Evelyn passed away? Makes one wonder if a mistake in her recipes had something to do with it."

That was it. Emilia stepped forward, her eyes lit with fire. "You think we don't know what you're doing?" she hissed. "You show up everywhere we go, always with some veiled threat or nasty little comment. You hated our mom and you hate magic. And now Anna's memory perfume's gone, and so is Gran's grimoire. Doesn't take a detective to connect the dots."

Lawrence arched a brow. "Are you accusing me of something?"

"I'm saying it's awfully convenient," she snapped. "You had motive, opportunity, and the access to cover it up. You knew exactly what Gran was working on. You've always been watching this family, waiting for a moment to strike. Maybe you couldn't stand that people actually believed in her work."

The clouds overhead swallowed the last of the moonlight, casting the scene in eerie darkness. The wind surged again, sending leaves skittering across the path.

"Careful," Lawrence said, his voice suddenly colder. "Wild accusations have consequences."

"So do guilty consciences," Emilia growled.

I felt a sinking sense of dread coil in my stomach as I watched her unravel. I'd thought she'd left these explosions behind, that she'd finally wrestled her anger into submission after all these years. But it had always lurked beneath the surface, ready to flare up when she felt wronged.

Lawrence didn't flinch. If anything, he looked mildly amused, as though he were watching a particularly tiresome performance. "That temper might be just as dangerous as your grandmother's 'perfumes.'" I could hear the air quotes around that last word.

And we were beginning to draw an audience.

"Emilia, let's just go." I reached out, grabbing her arm, trying to ground her before the rage took full control.

She shook me off, her attention fixed on Lawrence with a burning intensity. Her hands balled into fists, her words turning into sharp, stinging expletives as she advanced on him, pointing a finger right in his face.

"Emilia!" I called, chasing after her as her voice rose, fury practically radiating off her. A low rumble of thunder rolled in the distance, and the air felt charged. The first fat raindrop landed on my cheek, startling me, and then another splashed on the pavement.

Around us, the crowd grew. One woman clutched her purse closer, while a group of teenagers exchanged gleeful glances, clearly thrilled to witness a public spectacle.

Before I could reach her, Emilia shoved Lawrence hard, forcing him to stumble back a step. Gasps rippled through the small gathering that had formed.

The rain fell in earnest now. Though some people hurried off to find shelter, others sprang open their umbrellas, their murmurs blending with the rising wind.

Lawrence's eyes narrowed, his polished demeanor cracking just enough to reveal a flicker of indignation. He straightened his coat with deliberate precision, but his hands lingered on the fabric for a moment too long, a subtle tremor betraying the effort. His voice, low and cutting, carried just enough volume to reach the onlookers. "Temper, temper, Miss Attar. Is this how your family handles criticism? With violence in plain view of the public?"

A man near the back muttered, "What's going on here?" while a pair of children craned their necks for a better look.

Emilia jabbed a finger at Lawrence, her voice trembling with rage. "You don't get to talk about my family like that! Not here, not anywhere!"

I felt my stomach sink as the weight of the onlookers' stares pressed in on us. This was a spectacle, and Lawrence knew it. His smirk returned, faint but maddening, as if he were savoring every moment of the drama unfolding around him. But behind his veneer of composure, I saw him take a step back, his hand touching his temple as though steadying himself.

My sister was making him nervous, and that could not possibly be good.

Parker stepped in beside her, his hand a steady anchor on her back, his voice low and soothing. "Hey, hey. Come on," he murmured, his calm presence like a soft tide trying to pull her back from the edge. "This isn't worth it."

But Emilia wasn't ready to be pulled back. Her breaths were short and hard, her chest rising and falling like she'd just run a mile, and each expletive she hurled seemed to land with enough force to make Lawrence flinch. It took everything Parker and I had to steer her away, even as she kept throwing words over her shoulder, each one sharper than the last. The onlookers shuffled aside as we passed, some whispering, others outright gawking.

By the time we reached the end of the bridge, the rain was soaking into my jacket and plastering my hair to my face. The onlookers had dispersed, leaving only the sound of raindrops against the pavement and the rumble of thunder. Emilia's steps hit the sidewalk like punctuation marks, her anger a warning flare that hadn't fully burned out. I caught Parker's eye and gave him a grateful look, one that hopefully conveyed my thanks for his help.

The evening's fun had dissolved entirely, replaced by the cold, heavy reminder of Lawrence's ugly words. I drew in a deep breath, but even the air felt different now, damp and laced with the tang of rain. Whatever secrets and whispers had drawn us to Whisperwind Bridge, they weren't the comforting kind tonight.

CHAPTER TWELVE

GOLDEN PINES

The crisp morning air nipped at my cheeks as I stepped out of David's police car, filling my lungs with the fresh scent of early spring. I shivered, pulling my jacket tighter as I followed him into the lobby of Golden Pines Assisted Living Facility. Inside, soft classical music played from overhead speakers, filling the space with an easy, almost sleepy calm.

"Peaceful, isn't it?" David murmured, giving me a sidelong look as we paused by the front desk.

"Almost makes me wish for a recliner and a knitting project," I joked, but my thoughts had already drifted. The music brought me back to last night on the Whisperwind Bridge, before everything went awry. When Parker had been twirling around, eyes closed, hopping on one leg with a grin that lit up his face. The memory tugged a smile from me. Why didn't I ask him more about himself? I'd barely managed to stammer a few polite questions, too tangled up in my own awkwardness to ask him about his life before Serenity Falls or what had brought him here.

David glanced at me as we waited for the receptionist, raising an eyebrow. "Something funny?"

"Sorry," I said, shaking my head. "I was, uh ... distracted."

He chuckled. "Well, that's a first."

I rolled my eyes, fighting a smile. Maybe he was right. Maybe I was slipping. But I couldn't help it. The image of Parker under the shifting lights, carefree and open, stayed with me, like a soft spot I felt compelled to press.

My reverie was broken by Helen approaching. The nurse stood before us, eyeing David and me. "The doctor felt it was important for me to be present during your visit with Margaret."

She scanned me with those sharp eyes again, and inwardly I cringed. I thought I had won Helen over last time with my kindness, but it seemed like I was still receiving judgement for my lack of visits this past year.

"If you'll follow me, please." Helen led us toward the set of double doors marked 'Silverleaf Crossing,' her silver tree pendant catching the light as she moved.

Helen's gaze, sharp as a hawk's, landed on me, carrying a tinge of suspicion. "You didn't bring anything to upset her this time, did you?"

Ah, so that was the look. Not *why haven't you visited more often*, but *please don't start a geriatric riot again*.

"No, nothing." Unfortunately. Ever since the break-in, I'd been trying to recreate Evoko from memory, but something was always off—a missing note here, an imbalance there. If only I had Gran's original formula. Without it, I felt helpless. I hated not having any Evoko to properly test if the perfume really could pierce through Gran's fog. It was like having the key to a locked door, only to have it stolen away.

Helen reached for her badge to swipe us into Silverleaf Crossing. The doors clicked open, revealing the carefully crafted 1950s streetscape beyond. As we crossed the threshold, a hushed conversation drifted from the nearby nurse's station, designed to look like a bus depot.

"...need to adjust her medication again," Susan's voice carried. "We can't risk another episode like last week."

The other voice murmured something inaudible, and Susan responded sharply, "Just do as I say. I know what's best for Margaret."

I felt a surge of indignation, my mind racing back to the last time I was here. Susan had insisted Gran's outburst was normal, yet here she was, pushing for more medication. Whereas a week ago, hearing this would have made me feel vindicated—and newly concerned about Gran—now I knew better. Gran hadn't been confused or agitated. She'd been lucid. The realization that they might be increasing her medication unnecessarily made my stomach churn.

Then a worse thought struck me. What if Susan was behind the entire thing? The theft, the grimoire, the perfume, the destruction of Emilia's board ... maybe even the murders. A chill skated down my spine. She looked so harmless, with her rosy cheeks and plump, grandmotherly frame. But serial killers didn't look like monsters. They looked like overly friendly nonnas in their sixties with perms and cookie-sweet voices who worked at retirement homes. Because, really, who would question a death in a place like this? No one suspects the woman who smells like roses and wears cat pins.

Macabre, Anna. Get a grip.

David's elbow bumped mine, just lightly, and when I glanced up, he gave me a look. One brow arched, half skeptical, half amused. As if he could sense the wheels turning in my head and was bracing for whatever half-baked theory I was cooking up. The corner of his mouth twitched in that way it always had when I was about to say something ridiculous in class and he was trying not to laugh. It was annoyingly effective.

I exhaled and shook my head, offering him a sheepish smile. "Don't ask," I muttered.

As we rounded the candy shop, I steeled myself for another visit with a grandmother who didn't remember me. Helen continued leading us through the recreated downtown until we reached the diner. Inside, we found Gran sitting at the red vinyl booth beneath the drive-in theater mural, her eyes distant as she watched other residents chatting over milkshakes. The morning sunlight streaming through the large windows cast a gentle glow on her face, highlighting the lines of time.

I approached with a cautious smile.

Gran turned, a shadow of recognition flickering in her eyes. "Evelyn?"

David, Helen, and I slid into the booth with my grandmother. As Gran continued to gaze at me with that distant look of recognition, I recalled Susan and Emilia's advice not to correct Gran when she gets things mixed up. It only confuses and upsets her more.

So, swallowing the lump in my throat, I said. "Yes, it's me." A bittersweet ache filled my chest as I embraced the role of my mother.

Gran's eyes brightened slightly, a touch of relief passing over her features. "Evelyn, my dear." Her hand squeezed mine. The moment was tender, yet tinged with the sadness of untruth.

"It's good to see you ... mom." I took my grandmother's delicate, papery hands. Immediately, a wave of familiar scents enveloped me. Clary sage. Mugwort. A hint of wormwood. The aromas were subtle but distinct, not the faded ghosts of an old wardrobe, but the living language of perfumery.

I glanced at Helen, my brow furrowing. "I thought you said no fragrances were allowed in the facility?"

Helen leaned toward Gran, sniffing. "Oh, that's just how she smells," she said, straightening. "Rest assured, we don't use any fragrances here at Golden Pines. It's all hypoallergenic and fragrance-free. What you're smelling must be a residual scent from her old belongings."

I nodded, keeping my expression neutral, but the explanation didn't sit right. These weren't vague traces clinging to old scarves or pillows. These were active notes, balanced and intentional. It smelled like Gran had been working with herbs that morning.

But I didn't press. Not here. Not with Helen watching.

Gran coughed, and Helen placed a hand on her shoulder in support.

It was sweet that Helen was so attentive, but good grief! We were here on official police business. Weren't we entitled to a moment of privacy? I studied Helen, trying not to scowl at her sharp, almost birdlike features. Maybe she's descended from hawks. Helen Hawk-Eye, Guardian of the Geriatric Order.

"How is the store doing, dear?" Gran asked.

And then I had an idea. Maybe pretending to be Evelyn could be more than just a compassionate deception; it might also be a way to glean some insights. Understanding more about Mom's life could be key to discovering who murdered her.

I glanced at David sitting next to me, trying to telepathically communicate my plan. Then I leaned in closer to Gran, adopting a tone I imagined my mother might have used. "Oh, the store is doing well. But there have been some challenges. The landlord has been giving us a hard time about the rent, and the town council is no help at all."

Helen's expression was unreadable, but David's showed a flicker of interest at the turn the conversation was taking.

Gran's brow furrowed, her gaze drifting. "Those council folk, always causing trouble."

My heart raced; this was a path worth pursuing. I just needed to deftly navigate between the roles of concerned daughter and sly investigator, all under the watchful eyes of Helen Hawk-Eye.

David leaned forward. "Margaret, was there anyone in particular giving you trouble? Anyone who made things difficult for the store?"

Gran looked up, her eyes widening with a mixture of surprise and delight. "Oh, the police are here to help with my store?" A spark of her old self flickered in her voice. "Well, isn't that something? Evelyn, dear, we have such important people looking out for us!"

I gave David a quick, appreciative glance.

"Well, yes," I played along, "we're trying to sort everything out. Do you know of anyone causing problems? Any names?"

Gran's gaze drifted, her mind reaching back through the haze. "There's one man, always so pushy. Always talking about rules and money and the reputation of the town..." Her voice trailed off, lost in a tangle of half-formed thoughts.

David leaned forward slightly, his voice gentle. "Do you remember his name, Margaret?"

She shook her head slowly, a shadow of frustration crossing her face. "Names escape me these days ... but he's a stern man. Always in a suit. Always frowning."

My pulse quickened. A man on the town council, obsessed with money and rules, who had a personal grudge against our family? That narrowed it down. Unfortunately.

"Let me guess," I said dryly. "Slick hair, sharp suit, talks like he thinks he's the godfather of Serenity Falls?"

Gran let out a faint chuckle. "Yes, that's him."

"I'd bet my last bottle of vetiver she means Lawrence Riviera," I said to David. "He's on the town council. I've run into him twice since coming back, and let's just say the welcome wasn't warm."

Gran's eyes flickered. Recognition, then doubt, then recognition again. "Of course, Evelyn. You know who he is. Always sniffing around, trying to grow his little empire. Lawerence wanted that shop for years." Her voice softened, fading a bit. "The building owners were willing to sell to him, but the offer was useless. He couldn't force me out. No one could. The lease had a clause. That was your grandmother's doing, Evelyn. It guaranteed I could stay as long as I wanted, and any new owner had to honor it."

I exchanged a look with David, unease knotting in my stomach.

David picked up the thread, his voice calm but firm. "Was he trying to get around that clause?"

Gran nodded slowly. "He tried everything. Building inspections, code violations, town ordinances. Always something. Then somehow, he convinced the landlord to double my rent, and the town council to turn a blind eye. I know Lawrence was behind it, but I was tired. I had to let go."

Gran's gaze turned to David, her expression softening. "But my Evelyn here," she said, resting a hand on mine. "She's a fighter. Not one to back down easily."

I listened, playing my part while internally piecing together the timeline.

Gran continued, "Lawrence has his ways, connections that aren't always … proper. He has a certain sway over the other council members."

David nodded, his expression grave as he took notes.

Eventually, somehow, after the heavy talk about landlords and shady council dealings, Gran, David, and I tumbled into a spirited debate about whether squirrels were plotting something sinister in the courtyard. Gran swore they were organizing. "They're too coordinated," she insisted, eyeing a plump one nibbling on a cracker just beyond the diner's broad window.

David looked baffled but played along, and I found myself laughing for the first time in days. For a moment, beneath the drive-in mural's soft glow, Gran looked like her old self again.

Soon, we made our way out into the recreated downtown. By the time I slid into the passenger seat of David's car, my thoughts were a tangled web of enlightenment and unease. Today had opened a window into a past fraught with tension and hidden agendas.

Lawrence Riviera, with his real estate front and unnervingly pointed accusations, loomed larger now as someone tangled in the mystery of my family's history, and perhaps, my mother's untimely death.

David paused, turning to me, car keys in hand. "You okay?" he asked quietly.

I hesitated, then nodded. "Getting there."

As we drove off, the reflection of the building's glass atrium shimmered in the side mirror, like a memory just out of reach. But I wasn't done. Not even close.

CHAPTER THIRTEEN

THE LIST OF SUSPECTS

David dropped me off back home, my mind abuzz. I shoved open the back door, Gran's words about Lawrence still rattling in my head. The smell of french fries hit me first, followed by the low hum of Emilia's voice. I entered the kitchen to find her in a steady stream of theories aimed at Watson, who looked appropriately indifferent.

I checked my phone. It *was* still the middle of the afternoon on a Friday, right?

The kitchen table was cluttered with takeout boxes from yet another DoorDash order. I considered chiding my sister for relying so much on food delivery. Or for taking another day off work. However, the seriousness of our situation held my tongue. This *was* more important.

But Emilia, with that uncanny sister telepathy, seemed to tune into my wavelength without a word being exchanged. "It's fine, Anna," she said, her voice laced with the calm of someone who had rehearsed this defense. "I've worked at that company for seven years, and I've racked up about three weeks of vacation time. It's practically begging to be used. Besides," she waved a hand toward the murder board, her eyes alight with the flame of her mission, "this is a tad more critical, wouldn't you say?"

I raised my hands in mock surrender. "I didn't say anything."

"You said it." Emilia pointed at her eyes, mimicking the international sign for I'm watching you. "With your eyes."

I sunk into a chair opposite Emilia, snagging a fry from the take-out box. "Well, you won't believe what I found out from Gran." I told her about Lawrence Riviera's influence over Gran's landlord and how he wanted the Charm & Petal property.

Emilia wore a look of smug satisfaction, continuing to pet an equally smug-looking Watson. She listened to me with a knowing air.

I hesitated. My eyes narrowed. I had expected surprise, maybe even shock from Emilia. "What's with the face?"

Without a word, Emilia pointed to a section of the murder board. I leaned closer. Lawrence Riviera's name was circled in red, and beneath it, a printout of town council minutes was pinned up, with an arrow point to the agenda item "discuss prospective buyer with vested interest in the 208 Pearl Street unit." Next to it, Emilia had scrawled a sticky note in her tidy handwriting: *If Lawrence bought it, why is it still sitting empty?*

There were already photos of him, of course, along with detailed profiles and string-drawn connections to the other five members of the town council.

My eyebrows shot up. "You figured that out on your own?"

"I did," Emilia said, sounding thoroughly pleased. "Google is my sidekick, and town council meeting minutes are public record."

"So much for dramatic reveals," I muttered.

"After his outburst last night, I had a hunch he was more involved than he let on." Emilia's eyes sparkled with an almost infectious enthusiasm. "So I did some research."

I leaned back, giving Emilia room to shine. She was clearly in her element, discussing potential murder suspects and unraveling mysteries. "Looks like we're on the same page then. What else have you found?"

"Well, obviously, there's Lawrence. He's at the top of my suspect list. But we need to be thorough. He may have had an accomplice, and of course, the top suspect is rarely the right one." Emilia paused. "At least, that's how it goes in the crime shows."

"Ah, so we're basing our investigation on TV logic. Should I expect a dramatic courtroom revelation next? Maybe I should start practicing my 'shocked and betrayed' face for the jury."

Emilia rolled her eyes. "Please, if we were truly going by TV logic, we'd have solved the case in an hour, including commercial breaks. And you'd need to work on your dramatic pause. But sure, go ahead and practice your courtroom faces. It might come in handy when we finally confront our villain."

I reached out and put a hand on my sister's. "Emilia, I have no doubt that you will figure out who killed mom. Probably even before David."

"Thanks, sis. Shall we review the councilors?"

Emilia's gaze returned to the murder board. She pointed to a photo of a man wearing a brown suede jacket and jeans. "First, there's Tom Kline. He owns the Enchanted Oven bakery next door to where Charm & Petal used to be. There's talk he wanted to expand his store, and Gran's shop was in the way."

I followed Emilia's pointer, considering this. "Wait, Tom Kline? Wasn't he in your grade?"

"Yeah." Emilia nodded. "He seems like a good guy. All the girls swooned over him. Everyone thought Megan was so lucky. Until. Well."

"That's right. I heard about that. She died in a car accident not even a year after they got married. Such a shame. Can you imagine being a widower at twenty-five?"

"It would be horrible."

I peered at Tom's photo. I could see why the women swooned over him—those dimples alone. "A baker, really? What's next? Does the butcher have a secret underground fight club?"

"Don't knock it," Emilia said. "TV crime shows have taught me that bakers are surprisingly dangerous. Remember *Pastry Pusher: Crimes of Confection*?"

"That was a *parody*."

"Details."

I nodded, feeling like a student in a murder class. "Who's next on our list?"

"Check out who else is on the council." Emilia said, tapping a photo with her pen.

I leaned in, my eyes landing on a familiar face framed by sleek dark hair, its luster as commanding as the confident smirk that played on her lips. "Ah, my old high school nemesis, Lisa Marconi. Queen bee of high school and forever a thorn in my side."

The photo of Lisa depicted her in a light that was all too familiar to me—poised, polished, and exuding an air of unshakable confidence. Her eyes, sharp and calculating, seemed to pierce through the photograph, mirroring the same intensity she carried through the hallways of our high school years ago. The smirk on her face, half-amused and wholly self-assured, brought back memories of the social dynamics that had once ruled our teenage lives.

"And now she's working her way towards Queen Bee of the town," said Emilia. "I hear she's planning to run for mayor."

I leaned back. "Clearly, the killer is Lisa. We had her last Saturday, red-handed, picking out strawberries at the market. It's the perfect alibi ... or so she thought."

Emilia laughed, shaking her head. "Yes, because picking strawberries is the hallmark of a criminal mastermind. What's next? Discovering she's been leading a double life as a strawberry thief?"

"Exactly. It's all coming together. By day, a council member and by night, the strawberry bandit of Serenity Falls. It's the perfect cover. Does she have any connection to Lawrence?"

Emilia shook her head. "Not that I'm aware of. But we'll keep her on the suspect list, just for you."

"She once tried to sabotage my science fair project with glitter and lies. Murder's not a huge leap."

Emilia smirked. "Honestly, that sounds like most of your exes."

I scanned the board again, then stopped short. "Seriously? Marianne?"

Emilia arched a brow, pen tapping against her chin.

I let out half a laugh. "The woman who has been bringing you tea and muffins every Thursday for the past year? Who used to braid my hair at the solstice festivals? Mom's best friend?"

Emilia didn't smile. "Which means she was close enough to know things we didn't."

"She's also the kind of person who wears scarves like armor and gives relationship advice like it's gospel," I countered. "I saw her at the market on Saturday. She said Mom and Gran meant a lot to this town. She seemed ... I don't know. Gentle."

Emilia gave a short shrug. "Sometimes the gentle ones are the best at keeping secrets."

"That's a stretch," I said. But the words felt thin, fragile. Because while I didn't believe Marianne could've hurt Mom, I couldn't say for sure that she couldn't have.

My eyes locked onto another photo—Susan, cheerful in a floral blouse. But the image made my stomach lurch. It was too fresh, too close. I'd *just* overheard her earlier today pushing for a change in Gran's medication.

"Susan, on the other hand," I pointed to her face and her saccharine smile, "is definitely worth looking into more deeply."

Emilia tilted her head, the ghost of a grin playing at the corner of her mouth. "Interesting. You jump to defend Marianne like she's a living hug in human form, but Susan? You're ready to slap the cuffs on her before I've even made tea."

I scowled at her, but it lacked heat. "During my visit today, I overheard Susan talking about upping Gran's medication. I thought I was just being paranoid. Gran had an outburst, Susan's a nurse—it made sense. But now?"

Emilia blinked, her skepticism giving way to a flicker of unease.

"What if she killed mom?" I said, the words tasting bitter even as I said them. "And now she's trying to keep Gran quiet, too?"

The room went still, the only sound Watson's soft snore as he lay curled on the table between us.

Emilia didn't speak for a moment. When she did, her voice was low. "If that were true..."

I nodded. "We need to keep a better eye on Gran. No more assumptions. I'm going to start visiting her every day."

"She'd like that, I'm sure."

We sat and stared at the board, like it was some sort of zen garden for conspiracy theorists.

"But who would go as far as to..." I shuddered.

"We can't rule out anyone yet. But this," she gestured to the board, "is our starting point. We need to dig deeper into each of these connections."

I nodded, swiping another fry from the takeout. "Tomorrow is the farmer's market. I can visit Tom's booth. And maybe pick up a Danish or two. And I'll invite Marianne out to lunch. I don't think she's our killer, but she may have some sort of information that might point more clearly to Lawrence, or someone else on the council. Or both."

"And I'm going to take what I have to David at the police station," said Emilia. "Maybe some of it will be useful to their investigation."

I placed my hand over my heart in mock shock. Even Watson gazed up at Emilia with a look of surprise. "You're going to leave the house? On your own? In public? To ... talk to people?"

Emilia raised an eyebrow, a playful smirk on her lips. "Yes, believe it or not, I do occasionally interact with the outside world," she said. "Besides, someone has to do the legwork while you're off peddling your wares at the farmer's market."

"Well, if you see sunlight, don't panic. It's just that big round thing in the sky. I hear it's quite popular among the humans."

"And here I was, thinking it was an elaborate government conspiracy. I'll make sure to wear my tinfoil hat, just in case."

"Tomorrow," I said, tossing the last fry into my mouth, "we stop theorizing and start digging. If there's a killer out there, they've made a mistake somewhere. And we're going to find it."

Emilia nodded. "We'll crack this case yet. For Mom."

"For mom."

Chapter Fourteen

Market Investigations

The next morning dawned bright and cool. Serenity Falls Farmers' Market was already humming with life, the usual patchwork of stalls spilling over with handmade goods, fresh produce, and eager locals. I sat at my booth, alone this time. My perfumes were lined up in neat, glinting rows. For the first time, they completely mine. No inherited formulas. Just me, my intuition, and a few sleepless nights of trial and error.

Across the square, a young woman stumbled toward my booth, frazzled and clearly on the verge of tears. She rocked a wailing infant against her chest, her movements sharp with exhaustion. The baby, red-faced and inconsolable, screamed with the determination of someone small and entirely fed up.

I acted on instinct and reached beneath my table for my newest creation. I caught the woman's eye with a compassionate smile. "This could help. May I?"

The woman looked up, eyebrows drawn together. "I can't put perfume on my baby."

My smile widened, reassuring. "No, it's not for him. It's for you. Babies are incredibly in tune with our emotions. If you're calm, it helps them settle down too. This," I held up the bottle, "is designed to soothe and calm the wearer. Would you like to try?"

Hesitant but clearly desperate, the woman nodded. I pulled back the woman's hair and spritzed a small amount onto the nape of her neck, encouraging her to inhale deeply. The fragrance was a blend of calming chamomile and uplifting herbal fragrances, grounded in a resinous base.

Within moments, the woman's shoulders relaxed, her breaths deepened, and the baby, as if by magic, began to mirror her new-found calm, his cries softening to whimpers before dissolving into a contented silence.

"Oh, my," the woman breathed out. "That's ... incredible." She looked at me, a newfound respect in her eyes.

A familiar voice chimed in. "Wow, that's impressive. I'll have what she's having."

Parker's presence made the air around me feel charged with electricity. As he strolled over, his eyes, bright with humor, locked onto mine, stirring a warmth in me that went beyond the springtime air.

My gaze flitted between the now calm baby and Parker, my heart thumping a little louder than before.

The woman, now holding her peaceful baby with a look of astonishment and gratitude, said, "I'll take a bottle." She shifted the baby to her hip and dug out her wallet. "What's it called?"

"Solamen." I wrapped the bottle in tissue paper before bagging it and handing it over. "Just dab a bit on your pulse points—wrists, neck, even behind your ears—whenever you feel a bit overwhelmed or anxious."

The woman nodded, cradling the perfume like a talisman against the chaos of parenthood. "Thank you. You have no idea how much this means." With a final grateful glance, she made her way through the crowd, the baby still nestled contentedly in her arms.

I watched her go, a warm bloom of satisfaction in my chest. Then I turned to find Parker watching me with that lopsided smile of his, the one that seemed to know more than he said.

"You here for emotional support," I asked, "or just sniffing around for free samples?"

He stepped a little closer, the corners of his mouth twitching. "Can't a man multitask? Emotional support, keen sense of smell, and an appreciation for artistry..."

I raised an eyebrow. "You forgot humble."

Lisa Marconi sliced through our warm bubble. "Anna, darling. I had heard you were back in town. You sure work fast, don't you? Already acquainting yourself with our Parker." Her voice dripping with a sweetness that I knew all too well was laced with venom.

She turned her attention to Parker, her smile widening. "And Parker, how lovely to see you. We've missed you at the town meetings."

Parker offered a polite smile. "I do enjoy the market's atmosphere; it's a bit more my speed than the council events, I guess."

Lisa laughed, a sound that seemed too rehearsed to be genuine. She stepped closer to Parker, her movements graceful and deliberate. She leaned in, her hand finding a brief rest on Parker's chest. "I've been trying to convince our Mr. Ekstrom here to run in the next election for months now. We could really use a fresh perspective, especially from someone so ... *unencumbered* by Serenity Falls' past. A newcomer's insight could be invaluable. I'm sure you understand, Anna."

Lisa's maneuvering was seamless, as though she were merely including me in the conversation rather than shifting her target.

Her eyes flicked back to Parker, a conspiratorial glint in them. "Anna here used to be quite the antenna back in high school. Always picking up on things others missed." A flicker of something crossed Lisa's eye when she looked at me. "Isn't that right, Antenna Anna?"

Evil. That's what the flicker was.

And who was she to hang all over Parker like that? Were they dating? He didn't act like they were dating. *Our* Parker. Like she could lay claim to a human. *My* human! I tried to formulate a response, but all of a sudden it was like I was back in those high school hallways, bumbling and awkward.

Parker's brow furrowed. "Antenna, huh? Sounds like a superhero name. I guess every town needs one. Someone to tune into the things that the rest of us might miss."

I managed a smile. "Well, every superhero needs a sidekick. What do you say, Parker Ekstrom? Ready to join forces at the market today?"

Parker chuckled. "I'd like that. But only if I get a cool nickname too."

"Well, I'll leave you two to your ... partnership," said Lisa. "Don't forget, Parker, the council could use your insights." Her tone dripped with something that sounded a lot like defeat masked as magnanimity.

As Lisa sauntered away, the tension she brought dissipated like morning fog under the sun. I turned back to Parker. "Thanks for that."

"Anytime, Antenna," Parker replied. The nickname now felt like a badge of honor rather than a weapon of shame. "Now, about that sample of Cozy Cup? Or better yet," he leaned in closer, his gaze locking onto mine with an intensity that made my pulse race, "what do you say we grab the real thing, after the market shuts down?"

A date! Was he asking me out on a date? Yet, as I opened my mouth to respond, reality rudely interjected. "I'd like that. But I can't today. I've already made plans for lunch."

The words hung between us, heavier than I'd intended, and I cursed myself silently for not being able to get through this simple social interaction without feeling like I was navigating a minefield.

Quickly, to patch the gap my refusal might have created, I added, "But how about dinner instead?" The moment the suggestion left my lips, I wanted to reel it back in. Dinner? My mind screamed at my boldness. Everyone knew a coffee date was just dipping your toes in the water, but dinner? That was diving headfirst into the deep end.

Parker's expression was unreadable for a fraction of a second that felt like an eternity. Had I just torpedoed what could have been a simple, sweet beginning with an overzealous leap?

Then, breaking through my whirlwind of self-doubt, Parker's face split into a wide grin. "Dinner sounds great." His voice carried a warmth that enveloped me. I found myself returning his smile with one that felt both shy and exhilarated.

As Parker strolled back to his booth, I watched him go, my heart doing somersaults. I pulled out my phone, my fingers dancing over the screen with a newfound excitement tinged with a hint of nerves. I texted Emilia, the words pouring out in a rush of adrenaline: *Change of plans. Dinner date with Parker!*

The morning bustle of the farmers' market had settled into a rhythmic hum. My booth had been steady, with customers stopping to sniff bottles and chat, but as the crowd thinned for the moment, I allowed myself a breather. Across the way, Tom Kline stood behind his booth for The Enchanted Oven, chatting with a woman who practically glowed as he handed her a bag of pastries.

Tom hadn't changed much since high school—still tousled blond hair that looked like he'd just rolled out of bed in the most charming way possible, a dimple that flashed whenever he smiled, and that easygoing warmth that made you feel like you'd known him forever. He wore a faded apron over a navy henley, sleeves pushed up to reveal forearms dusted with flour.

Tom's booth was as charming as his reputation suggested. The display of breads, cookies, and pastries was impeccably arranged, and a small chalkboard with delicate flourishes announced the specials of the day. The scent of cinnamon and butter wafted toward me.

I glanced at my own table to ensure everything was in order and caught sight of the jam vendor a few stalls over, keeping an eye on her two young grandkids as they giggled over a jar of strawberry preserves. My booth would be fine for a minute.

Straightening my jacket, I made my way to Tom's booth, rehearsing the casual tone I'd use. "Hey, I'll take a pastry," I murmured under my breath, as though practicing would help my voice stay even. My questions about the town council loomed in my mind, but I couldn't come off as too eager. Or suspicious.

Tom noticed me approaching and flashed a smile that could power the entire market. "Anna! What a surprise. Finally escaping your own booth, huh?"

Of course the town heartthrob remembered my name. I smiled back, careful not to let my nerves show. "Just for a minute. I figured I deserved a treat, and your booth smells amazing."

His dimples deepened as he gestured toward his display. "You've come to the right place. What's your poison? Apple strudel, cherry almond plunder, or my famous purple swirl schnecken?"

"Purple swirl schnecken," I said, pulling a few bills from my pocket. "I need the energy boost."

As Tom wrapped the pastry, I took the opportunity to look around his booth, searching for a way to steer the conversation. A small sign at the corner of his table caught my eye: *Vote Kline for a Better Serenity Falls!*

"So, running for office again?" I asked, taking the Danish from him.

"Yep," he said with a nod. "It's just for reelection to the town council. Nothing too glamorous."

I pretended to examine the schnecken, as though the elderberry swirls required my full attention. "Council elections are every two, or is it three years?"

"Three years," Tom replied, leaning an elbow on his table. "But I've only been on the council for a few months. I took over after Jim Weaver moved out of town. It's been interesting, to say the least."

I nodded, the gears in my head turning. Tom had only joined the council after the trouble with Charm & Petal had started. If he had any interest in expanding The Enchanted Oven back then, it hadn't been through political maneuvering.

"Interesting, huh? What made you want to go into politics?"

"Honestly? Megan used to always say I needed to get more involved in the community. I guess I finally took her advice." Tom chuckled, shaking his head. "Besides, the council has a lot of say in things that affect small businesses. I figured I might as well have a seat at the table."

"Well, it sounds like you're doing good work," I said, hoping I sounded sincere. "Thanks for the pastry."

I headed back toward my table and settled behind my display. I took a bite of the purple swirl schnecken, the rich elderberry flavor doing little to sweeten my mood. The mystery was no clearer than before, but at least I could cross one name off my list. Tom Kline wasn't part of whatever had happened to my mother—or Charm & Petal. Now, I just had to figure out who was.

Chapter Fifteen

BRUNCH

As the farmer's market shut down for the day, I packed up the last of my perfumes. The ritual filled me with memories of my childhood at Gran's shop. After securing the last bottle, I snuck a glance across the way, where Parker was also breaking down his booth. The ease with which he interacted with his customers, even in these closing moments, was endearing. Did I really have a date tonight with this man? Parker flashed me a knowing smile. Shaking off the butterflies, I focused on the task at hand.

After packing up, I checked my phone. Emilia had not texted back yet. But she was probably still at the police station. I could just see my sister standing in front of David, passionately pointing out connections she had made on her elaborate murder board. Heck, I wouldn't be surprised if Emilia had boxed up the entire board and was doing a presentation for everyone in the station. With an accompanying PowerPoint. Emilia could be forgiven for not being glued to her phone.

Just as I was transferring the boxes to my car, Marianne appeared, her artful jewelry shimmering in the soft sunlight. "Hey, you ready for lunch?"

"Absolutely. I'm starving." Together, we began our short walk to the Ivy Nook.

The weather was perfect. A gentle breeze carried the scent of blooming flowers mixed with the earthy aroma of the recent rain, cooling the sun's warmth just enough to make the day pleasantly crisp. The streets were as inviting as ever, lined with quaint shops whose windows boasted colorful displays, from hand-crafted jewelry to freshly baked goods. Folks going about their Saturday afternoon dotted the sidewalks.

The Ivy Nook sat nestled among a row of welcoming storefronts, its façade lushly overgrown with climbing ivy that framed the doorway and windows. Hence the name. The sign swung gently in the breeze, beckoning passersby with the promise of a delicious meal.

"Wow, it's just like I remember." I turned to Marianne. "My family used to come here every Sunday. It feels like a lifetime ago."

Gran, Mom, Emilia, and I would gather around our favorite table, the one by the window with the best view of the street, and spend hours talking, laughing, and enjoying each other's company. Those were simpler times.

Marianne smiled. "This place has always had a special kind of magic, hasn't it?"

I nodded. The familiar jingle of the bell above the door and the comforting aroma of coffee and baked goods greeted me as I stepped into the restaurant.

We had just settled into our seats when Sophia approached with menus in hand. Her face instantly brightened with recognition upon seeing me. "Hey! I remember you from the concert last Thursday. You and your sister were really enjoying the music. And oh, I invited her to our book club, didn't I?"

"Yes, that was us. I'm trying to encourage her to go, but don't take offense if she doesn't. My sister is something of a homebody."

Sophia's hand flew to her mouth in a comical wave of horror. "Oh no, I just realized I didn't invite you, too! How rude of me!"

With a chuckle, I waved off the apology. "It's totally fine. Honestly, I'm more of a 'judge a book by its movie' kind of person."

Sophia's earlier mortification gave way to laughter. "Oh, you're one of those. Well, if we ever start a film club, you'll be the first to know." She promised to return with our drinks, then bounced off, her ponytail swaying cheerfully.

I smiled at Marianne across the table, bathed in a golden light that seemed to lift the weight of the world. The murmur of other diners added a layer of normalcy to the murder investigation that brought us together.

How should I navigate the conversation toward Lawrence Riviera? The idea of being straightforward was tempting. After all, wasn't there some merit in laying all cards on the table? But small towns have an intricate web of relationships, and I did not know what Marianne and Lawrence's might be.

What if Marianne, with her easy smile and shared memories of my mother, was more than just a bystander in the tragedy that unfolded?

I toyed with the edge of my napkin. The idea of suspecting Marianne, of suspecting anyone who had been a part of my mother's life, felt like a betrayal in itself. Yet, wasn't it my duty to explore every avenue, no matter how painful? After all, she is a suspect on the murder board, even if it's only because she is on the town council.

With a deep breath, I centered myself. I was turning into Emilia, seeing a potential murderer in every face. But the journey to uncover the truth about my mother's death was bound to lead me down paths riddled with doubt and discomfort.

Marianne's voice drew me back into the moment. "You know, this is the same table that Evelyn, Tabitha, and I used to share when we would lunch here. It's special, being here with you now. Thank you for reaching out."

"It's strange, being back in this place full of memories I've barely touched. After high school, I was so eager to leave, to escape the small-town gossip and the shadow my family seemed to cast. But in doing so, I missed so much time with my mom, with Gran." My voice wavered.

Marianne reached across the table. "Evelyn understood more than you know, Anna. Sure, she missed you dearly, but she was also proud of your accomplishments, and recognized your need to find your own path."

A pang struck my heart. I glanced out the window, where the streets of my hometown stretched out. I had strolled those sidewalks with dreams that extended far beyond their edges, leaving them behind in search of the life I thought I wanted.

Now, those same streets were calling me back, whispering secrets from a past that refused to stay buried.

Sophia brought our drinks and took our food order. I asked for the meatloaf—my mom's favorite.

As I looked at Marianne, something shifted. She was a connection to my mother's life. And a part of my own. A link to the girl I used to be, and maybe a guide to help me find the woman I was still becoming. A lingering connection to my mom.

"Marianne, I need to know about Lawrence Riviera and his feud with my mom. I was so caught up in my own world back then, I missed the signs. Could that conflict have led to something as drastic as ... murder?"

Marianne's pause was thoughtful, her gaze drifting to a spot just over my shoulder as if gathering her thoughts. "Why do you think it was murder? Your mother's death was a shock to all of us, but it was ruled a heart attack."

I leaned forward, my voice low. "But don't you think it was a bit odd for Mom to die of a heart attack when she was so healthy?"

"These things do happen," she said gently.

"Maybe. But it still doesn't sit right with me. If there were any signs, any warning, then we never saw them."

Pausing, I gathered the courage to share a piece of our investigation that sounded almost too fantastical to be true. "There's more, though. I brought Gran a bottle of her memory perfume, Evoko, not really thinking it would do anything. But it did. She had a brief window of lucidity, and during it ... she asked if we'd found Mom's killer."

I let the words hang there, as unreal as they still felt.

"But then, someone broke into our house," I continued. "They took all my Evoko. And they took Gran's scent grimoire and destroyed the murder board Emilia had been putting together. It was a targeted act. Someone's trying to silence our questions, erase any trail we might be on."

Marianne's eyes widened. "Margaret's grimoire was stolen?"

Sophia returned with our lunches. I took the opportunity to watch Marianne closely, searching for any sign of disbelief or skepticism. Or guilt. All I saw, though, was a woman deep in thought.

"I admit, it was hard to accept Evelyn's sudden passing as merely a heart attack." She glanced down at her plate but didn't move to take a bite. "When I first heard the news, my thoughts turned to the Morgans. You wouldn't know them. They moved away before you were born. But their hatred for the Attars runs deep."

I paused mid-cut, my fork halfway through a bite of meatloaf. Of course I knew about the Morgans. Carolyne's death was practically town lore.

She looked up, meeting my eyes. "It happened on Attar land, did you know that? Awful, awful thing. Of course it was just a tragic accident, but grief has a way of planting doubts."

I nodded slowly, though my appetite was fading fast. *Attar land*—as if the dirt itself were guilty. The Morgans may have left town decades ago, but the stain they left on our name still clung like mildew. Could they have come back? Enacted some fifty-year old revenge?

I shook off the thought. That was ancient past. If they wanted revenge, why wait so long?

She paused, then asked, "Have you found anything? Anything that directly points to someone being responsible?"

"Emilia's been putting together some theories. She's actually at the police station today, presenting what we've found so far to David." I quickly checked my phone. Still no text. "In the meantime, that's why I'm here, digging into the past, trying to piece together what really happened. We have reason to suspect Lawrence."

"I can see why he'd be your top suspect. You know, I was on the town council at the time everything happened with Charm & Petal. Terrible stuff, what that landlord was doing to Evelyn and Margaret. And Lawrence tried to buy the building. Luckily, he didn't succeed. But to think it could all lead to such a tragic end..."

Marianne placed her fork on the table and leaned back in her seat. "Faking a heart attack requires special knowledge. Lawrence may have built a real estate empire, but outside of building codes and tax loopholes, his knowledge is limited. I can't imagine Lawrence even knowing how to fake a heart attack."

I nodded, absorbing her insight. The thought had crossed my mind too; it seemed almost beyond Lawrence's reach. And yet the suspicion gnawed at me. "If Lawrence didn't have the knowledge himself, could he have found someone who did? Someone with the means and motive to help him?"

Marianne tilted her head, considering. Her fork idly traced a pattern across her plate.

"Lawrence Riviera doesn't have many friends," she said. Then, after a pause, she added, almost offhandedly, "Outside of family, that is."

I froze. "Family?"

Marianne's eyes sharpened as they met mine. "A sister, Susan Eldridge. She has always been close to him, ever since they were kids. Protective to a fault, if you ask me."

I stared at her, stunned. "Susan—the head nurse at Golden Pines—is Lawrence's sister?"

Marianne nodded. "You didn't know?"

"No," I said, the pieces starting to shift and slide into place. "If anyone in Lawrence's immediate circle had the medical knowledge to make a heart attack look natural, it would be her."

Marianne's mouth tightened. "Susan's smart. And fiercely loyal. Especially when it comes to Lawrence. She's spent her whole life covering for him, smoothing things over, making sure he stayed out of real trouble. I wouldn't put it past her to step in if she thought it would protect him—or the family name."

A chill threaded down my spine. "I need to look into this further. If Susan had a hand in this, there has to be something that ties it back to Lawrence. And maybe even to my mother's death."

"You need to tread carefully," Marianne warned, leaning in. "This investigation of yours is creeping into dangerous territory, especially with your grandmother still at Golden Pines."

My heart clenched at the thought of the easy access Susan had to Gran. "I need to do something."

"Why don't you talk to Tabitha? She could help you understand what signs to look for."

"Tabitha?" I echoed.

"She may have traded her lab coat for linen and lavender, but don't be fooled," Marianne said with a smile. "Before she opened her flower shop, she spent years as a pharmacist. She's got a sharp mind for science, and a keen instinct for when something's not right."

I thought back to Tabitha's recent visits—the way she'd shown up at the market, the firm grace with which she'd stood up to Lawrence, the watchfulness in her eyes. She'd always seemed to appear right when we needed her.

I hesitated, voice catching on the question that had been needling at me since the idea first took root. "What if she thinks I'm reaching? That I've let grief and paranoia get the better of me?"

Marianne's expression softened. "She won't. Tabitha's not one to dismiss someone she cares about. But she might pause. Not because she doubts *you*, Anna, but because she's afraid you're onto something real. Something dangerous."

CHAPTER SIXTEEN

THE BIG NIGHT

"Well, Watson, what do you think?" I flung open my wardrobe doors and surveyed the meager options awaiting inside.

Watson buried his face in his paw.

"I know, right?" My fingers itched to find something that would make me look … well, just right. This was a date, and I felt a tickle of panic in the back of my mind that I'd never be ready in time. I tried to ignore it, but my heart sped up a little each time I imagined Parker's face waiting at the door. I'd never planned for dates while here, though, and the proof stared back at me in the form of exactly zero dresses.

One hour until the date, and every second seemed to slip away from me. I pulled out my interview suit and held up to Watson, who was watching the whole performance from his spot in the doorway, head tilted as if to say, *Is that really the look you want to go with?*

"You're right, Watson. This is not going to work," I sighed, feeling a reluctant grin tug at the corner of my mouth.

With a quick decision, I padded down the hall to Emilia's room. She and I were roughly the same size, and I could already hear her voice in my head: *Just take what you need. Make it work.*

Still, I pulled out my phone, sent off a hasty text and dropped it back in my pocket, a small pang of worry creeping in at the sight of our thread, where too many of my messages sat waiting for replies. She was just busy, I told myself, pushing back the niggling feeling. Emilia knew how to take care of herself. Right? And if anything, it's good that she's been out this long. Maybe she made some friends. Perhaps she went to that book club after all.

I crossed the room to her closet. My fingers skimmed a row of dresses until they paused on a soft yellow one with clean lines, effortless drape. It was so very Emilia—easygoing on the surface, razor-sharp underneath.

I held it up in front of the mirror, tilting my head one way, then the other, imagining myself wearing it. Imagining Mom here to help me prepare for my date, brushing my hair and telling me how beautiful I looked.

Then my gaze shifted to a deep blue wrap dress. It was elegant and confident. Just the kind of thing I needed tonight. With Parker, and in general. I was going to need more than resolve for what lay ahead.

As I mulled over my choices, the silence of my phone became increasingly pronounced. Surely Emilia could have at least texted back. Should I call, just to check in? Or would that be venturing into 'controlling older sister' territory? Besides, Emilia never answered the phone, anyway.

Watson poked his head up and meowed. "Where's your mommy, Watson?" He curled up on the yellow dress and licked his paw. No help at all.

Deciding on the wrap dress, I brought it back into my bedroom and laid it out on my bed. Then, I gathered up my toiletries and slipped into the bathroom, flipping the shower dial to as hot as I could stand. The hot water served as a sanctuary, the steam enveloping me in a comforting embrace as I tried to wash away the complexities of my investigation. I allowed the cascade to soothe my tense muscles, my thoughts adrift from the mystery that had consumed me.

Like, could it be a coincidence that someone stole my perfumes and Gran's scent grimoire? Maybe it's not connected to mom's murder at all. Maybe there's a perfume competitor in town that wanted to shut me down. A shadowy villain wearing a trenchcoat, the interior lined with an array of colourful perfumes, each with a different power, shifting from town to town, taking out the competition.

The *perfumurdurer*.

But no, it seemed far more likely that someone had caught wind of Evoko's memory powers and wanted to stop me from creating magical perfumes entirely. Then again, Lawrence could easily have stolen everything out of pure spite just to watch me flounder. I scrubbed my legs furiously until red patches appeared, frustration bubbling under my skin.

No. I let out a deep sigh. Tonight was meant to be a reprieve, to live in the present and enjoy my budding connection with Parker.

Stepping out of the shower, I wrapped my bathrobe snugly around me, then grabbed a microfiber wrap and twisted it over my damp hair, securing it neatly at the nape of my neck. Time to let the curls of my youth return. Who decided straight hair was more professional, anyway? I was ready to embrace the natural look and let go of outdated notions.

As I padded back into my room, the cool air kissed my freshly steamed skin. I moved to my bed, where my chosen outfit lay waiting.

Just as I was about to change, my phone rang. My heart sank and my hands trembled as I answered. "Emilia?"

"Anna, I need you to come to the police station right away." Emilia's voice was tense.

"What happened? Are you okay?"

"It's ... no," Emilia's voice cracked, a tumultuous blend of crying and righteous anger seeping through. "I've been arrested."

My sister's words struck me like a physical blow. I sank onto the edge of my bed. "Arrested? For what?"

A sob broke through Emilia's attempts at explanation. The sound of Emilia's distress was a knife to my heart.

"Just ... just wait there. I'll be right over."

The call ended, and I barely remembered dropping my phone onto the bed. My legs moved before I could think. The dress I'd laid out was suddenly ridiculous. I scrambled for the pants and shirt I'd worn earlier. My fingers fumbled with the buttons, my mind spinning.

Emilia. Arrested. The words looped in my head. What on earth happened?

Every second felt like it was slipping away too fast. I flew down the stairs, yanking the door closed behind me, the slam echoing. But as I skidded to the end of the driveway, I stumbled to a stop, my mind coming up blank at the sight of ... nothing.

Because I didn't have a car.

I swore under my breath, racing back to the house, my hands already reaching for the shed key hanging by the door. My old bike. It would have to do. I'd pedal like my life depended on it.

But as I swung open the shed doors, defeat hit me like a punch to the gut. The bike tires sagged uselessly against the ground. For a split second, I could only stand there, clenching my fists so hard my nails bit into my palms. My pulse drummed louder in my ears, every moment slipping away while Emilia was stuck at the police station, waiting for me. I forced down the rising panic and forced myself to think, reaching for something that could help.

Then it hit me—Roger, the town's one-man Uber service.

I called him. "Roger, I need a ride to the police station, as fast as you can."

"Lucky for you, I'm just around the corner. Be there in a flash," Roger responded.

True to his word, Roger arrived in record time, and I barely had the door closed behind me before we were speeding toward the police station. The streets of Serenity Falls blurred past my window, the familiar storefronts and tidy flowerbeds rushing by in streaks of spring color.

I pressed my hand against the cool glass, heart hammering. Emilia was my anchor, my impossible opposite who somehow always fit. My sister. And now she was in a holding cell while I'd spent the day having long lunches with old family friends and planning a date.

I closed my eyes and inhaled, catching the faintest trace of my perfume on my wrist—a blend I hadn't named yet, something warm and sharp and strange. Something unfinished.

Hang on, Em, I thought, as Roger turned the corner. *I'm coming.*

CHAPTER SEVENTEEN

THE POLICE STATION

I didn't wait for the car to fully stop before I was out the door and rushing inside the police station . The sterile, buzzing lights did nothing to calm my nerves as I approached the front desk.

"I need to see Emilia Attar. Now." Every second felt like an eternity, and I was prepared to fight tooth and nail to be by Emilia's side, to confront whatever nightmare had led to her arrest and to stand unwaveringly in the face of the unfolding chaos.

As I turned, my eyes caught sight of David. The sight of my old lab partner felt like a beacon. His presence brought a wash of relief.

David handed me a cup of coffee and gestured for me to follow him into the interrogation room. As he took a seat opposite me, I could see him mentally preparing to bridge the gap between his role as a police officer and his history with me. I could hardly contain myself. I paced the small confines of the room, coffee gripped in my hand. "What's going on? What happened?"

David motioned for me to sit. I reluctantly settled into the chair. The cold metal felt alien against my back.

David sat opposite me, shuffling a stack of papers before him. He cleared his throat. "Let's start with the ... ahem ... murder investigation. I understand Emilia's settled on Lawrence Riviera as a main suspect?"

"Well, we've been researching interactions between Mom and various town council members leading up to her death, any potential motives we could think of. And yes, Lawrence Riviera's name does appear prominently."

David's pen hovered above his notepad as he listened, his gaze never leaving my face. "And these connections, the ones you've drawn between Lawrence and your mother ... How did you come to highlight him as a suspect?"

I felt a surge of defensiveness. "It's not just wild speculation," I said. "Lawrence had motive. There was animosity between him and Mom over the Charm & Petal. Plus, his behavior towards me and Emilia raised red flags for us."

David made a note, then looked up, his expression unreadable. "You're referring to the altercation on Thursday night? What led to that?"

I shifted in my seat. I was so stupid! David hadn't brought me here for privacy. He's not talking to me as a friend. He brought me to the interrogation room to *interrogate* me.

"What's going on? Why has Emilia been arrested? She came here to tell you all this, to share what we've found. Why are you asking me these questions again now?" My gaze was steady, demanding answers from a man I once knew as a safe space, now seated across from me in a role that seemed to place us worlds apart.

The air in the room shifted as surprise registered on David's face. "Anna..." He rubbed the back of his neck, a hint of discomfort passing over his face before he met my eyes again. "Your sister never came to the police station."

My stomach tightened.

David cleared his throat, looking almost like he wished he were anywhere but here. "I got a call about someone snooping around Lawrence Riviera's property this morning." He paused, glancing at me as if to gauge my reaction, as if wondering how much more I could handle. "When I went to check it out ... I found Emilia." Another pause, his words hanging in the air. "She was breaking and entering."

The scenario David described was so far removed from what I had imagined that it took me a moment to process the implications. "Breaking and entering? But why? She was supposed to be here, talking to you, not ... not doing something like that."

David leaned forward. His eyes, which had always held a hint of warmth for me, searched my face, as though seeking evidence of something. "When we processed her, we found a notebook in her car. It was full of research into your mother's murder. Lawrence Riviera was highlighted as her prime suspect, over and over again. It seems she is convinced he was behind it."

"Well, that's what she was supposed to come talk to you about," I said, the words coming out too quickly, as if I could make sense of them just by saying them aloud. The idea of Emilia actually breaking into Lawrence's house was unsettling. And yet, as I pictured her, hunched over her computer, the faint blue glow lighting up her face as she embarked upon yet another late-night dive into crime articles and notes, it wasn't exactly a shock. She had this intensity, a determination that could easily look like obsession from the outside.

I swallowed, feeling a strange mix of horror and reluctant under-standing. "David, she ... she's really into those true crime shows," I said, the words tumbling out as the realization took hold. "I think she might have thought she was being helpful, playing detective or something. I know it sounds crazy, but she just wants answers, to find justice for Mom."

David's expression shifted, his mouth pressing into a hard line. "If only that were all it was." His tone was low, edged with something that felt like warning. "Lawrence Riviera is in the hospital. He wasn't home because of that."

He paused, his face turning grave. "We suspect foul play. And with your sister breaking in at such an opportune time ... it doesn't look good. Your sister is convinced Lawerence killed your mom. It's not a stretch to think she wanted revenge."

His words hung in the air, heavy and impossible, the weight of them pressing down until I could barely breathe. Emilia could never have taken such drastic actions. "David, come on. She's not out for blood. We're not. We just want to find out the truth."

David's phone rang, the sharp sound slicing through the tense quiet. I watched as he answered, his face shifting from controlled calm to something more raw, the color draining from his cheeks as if he were being pulled into some dark place he didn't want to go. He listened in silence, jaw tightening, and when he finally nodded curtly and ended the call, the heaviness in his gaze made my stomach clench.

"Lawrence Riviera is suffering from cyanide poisoning," he said, his voice low, each word dropping like a stone. "And just now, officers at your house found bitter almond oil among your things."

My mind reeled. "But that's from Gran's perfume supplies!" My voice caught as the shock crashed over me. "The kind she used wouldn't even contain amygdalin. It's completely harmless. And how could they search our house without me there?"

David looked at me, his eyes clouded with something that looked uncomfortably like sympathy. "They had a warrant, Anna. Given the circumstances, they're taking every precaution. They're confiscating all of your perfume materials, and a specialist is examining them for potential poisons."

I felt as if the ground were shifting beneath me, the weight of it threatening to bring me to my knees. "But I use those materials for the perfumes I sell at the farmer's market." My voice rose, a tremor of desperation threading through it. "This is a mistake."

David shook his head slowly, his expression resolute. "Until this is cleared up, you're not allowed to sell at the farmer's market. I'm sorry, but until they can rule out any risk, they have to treat everything in your perfume business as potential evidence."

A cold heaviness settled in my chest as I processed what he was saying. This wasn't just about Emilia now. It was my work, my Gran's legacy. All of it now under suspicion, tangled up in the chaos our search for the truth had created.

David's face softened, the hard lines of duty blurring as he looked at me, a flicker of regret passing through his eyes. "I know this is hard to hear. And I want to help you through this." Each word was measured, as though he were weighing them carefully before releasing them. "But you need to be careful. Speaking to me any further without a lawyer, given everything, might not be in your best interest."

The interrogation room door swung open with a low, reluctant groan, and there was Emilia, standing in the doorway like a kid who just realized the haunted house *wasn't* a ride. She looked like she was trying for a smirk, but it was more of a grimace stretched thin across her face, half bravado, half barely-contained panic.

David stood, gave her a curt nod, then turned to me. "I'll give you two some privacy." Then he was gone, the door clicking shut behind him.

Silence fell, heavy and awful. I took in her messy bun, the circles under her eyes, that twitch in her jaw she got when she was trying *very* hard not to cry or scream or both. The spark she usually carried—that ridiculous thrill she got from connecting red-string-and-pushpin dots—was gone. What was left looked hollowed out.

I crossed the room in a heartbeat and wrapped her in a hug. Tight. Hard. Probably too much. Her whole body was tense, like she hadn't unclenched in days.

Then I stepped back and punched her in the arm. "You finally leave your house on your own and this is what you do? Breaking and entering? Seriously?"

She winced, rubbing the spot. "Ow."

"You broke into Lawrence's house. In broad daylight."

"I *know*," she said, eyes wide, defensive.

"Do you?"

She opened her mouth, then closed it. "Guess I'm not winning any detective awards this year, huh?"

The smile she gave me was so flimsy it may as well have been made of tissue paper. She glanced at the chair David had vacated and dropped into it with a sigh. "I didn't think they'd actually arrest me."

I blinked at her. "That's your defense? *You didn't think?*"

"I was trying to *help*," she snapped, eyes flashing. "No one else was going to look into this, not really. And if Lawrence killed Mom—"

"But you didn't *know* that," I said. "You guessed. And now you're in a police interrogation room, one bad headline away from an orange jumpsuit."

She rubbed her temples. "I found something. Okay?"

I folded my arms. I was fully prepared to lecture her for the next ten minutes, but apparently my curiosity had other plans. "What kind of something?"

"Letters between Lawrence and GreenMart. He was negotiating a lease for the Charm & Petal property, promising them a competitive deal."

"GreenMart? In Serenity Falls?" The thought of a big-box retailer taking root in our quaint, tightly knit community felt like a betrayal of everything the town stood for.

"Yeah, exactly." Emilia leaned in. The fatigue seemed to lift from her shoulders, replaced by the familiar thrill of the chase. "But here's where it gets even weirder. He had to back out."

"Back out? Why?"

"Because someone else swooped in and bought the property right out from under Lawrence and his meticulously laid plans. Paid in cash, just like that." Emilia snapped her fingers. "And you know what's even more bizarre? It's still sitting empty. Not a single Green-Mart shelf in sight."

I tried to piece together the implications. "Why go through all the trouble to secure the property so urgently, then let it sit there, unused?"

"I don't know." A shadow of frustration crossed Emilia's features. "But it means Lawrence had no motive. This deal falling through would've been a blow to him, but it also meant that he would not benefit from … you know … hurting mom."

The news sent my mind spinning. The pieces of the puzzle we had been trying to solve were shifting, forming a picture far different from what we had initially imagined. "But if Lawrence lost out on the deal, he would have been livid. Could he have done something out of spite?"

"To mom?" Emilia shook her head. "It wouldn't make sense. She and Gran lost out just as much as Lawrence did."

I sat back, the weight of Emilia's findings pressing down on me. I tried to reconcile the image of Lawrence as a suspect with the new information Emilia presented. "Are you sure about this?"

Emilia sighed. "Yeah, I'm sure. Turns out, Lawrence was just a red herring."

"A red what now?" I blinked.

"A red herring, you know?" Emilia leaned back, the spark of her investigative zeal flickering despite the circumstances. "Means something that misleads or distracts you from the actual issue. And boy, did I get distracted."

I let out a half-hearted chuckle. "So, you're saying we've been chasing our tails? Because of a fish metaphor? Should I say we've been chasing our fins?"

"Yes. And now I smell like one." She tried to grin. It didn't quite stick.

"God." I raked a hand through my hair. "Okay. So we're starting over. No more fish. No more breaking into homes. We cast a wider net."

Emilia raised an eyebrow. "Really? *Another* fish pun?"

I held up my hands. "I'm stressed. It's coming out in dad jokes."

My chuckle died in my throat as the door opened again and David stepped back in. His expression was serious. No trace of his usual warmth. Just cop-mode activated.

"The judge has set bail," he said. "You can leave, but you have to stay in town until your arraignment on Wednesday. And no more playing detective. I mean it. This is serious."

I opened my mouth, objections already forming, but David's expression stopped me cold.

"If Lawrence dies," he said, "Emilia could be facing murder charges."

I felt a chill settle into my bones, a reminder that this was real. Far too real.

As we prepared to leave, I turned to Emilia, a question lingering in my mind. "Why red, though? Why call it a red herring?"

Emilia offered a small smile. "It comes from an old technique of training dogs. Smoked herrings are red and have a strong smell. They were used to lay false trails for hounds to follow, to test their ability to stay on the scent of the actual quarry."

"Do you mean to say that a scent-based metaphor tripped up the granddaughters of the town perfumer?"

Emilia stopped in her tracks. "Huh. I guess so."

We stepped into the cold hallway of the station, the hum of fluorescent lights buzzing above us. A storm of unanswered questions brewed in my head. We had to clear Emilia's name. We had to find out who bought that property. We had to figure out who actually killed our mother. And why.

Oh, and I still needed to find my missing bottles of Evoko.

And Gran's stolen grimoire.

And we had four days until the arraignment, because apparently the local court system only runs like clockwork when your entire life's on the line.

CHAPTER EIGHTEEN

SUSPECT EVERYONE

The streets of downtown Serenity Falls felt oddly peaceful after the suffocating weight of the police station. The hum of life carried on as though the world hadn't tilted on its axis. Shopkeepers flipped signs to 'closed,' pulled shutters down with weary hands, and locked up for the night, their routines untouched by the chaos Emilia and I had just lived through.

I clutched my arms around myself as if bracing against the cool breeze, though the real chill came from David's words, still ringing in my ears: *If Lawrence dies, Emilia could be facing murder charges.* Even now, the thought made my stomach twist.

Beside me, Emilia's footsteps matched mine, steady and deliberate. But the slump in her shoulders betrayed the weight she carried. Her usual quips were absent, and the silence stretched between us.

"I still can't believe they searched the house," I said finally, breaking the quiet. "Our materials. Our work. Gran's legacy. All just treated like potential evidence." My voice cracked at the end, and I quickly looked away, blinking back the frustration welling in my eyes.

"They'll find nothing," Emilia said, her voice quieter than I'd expected. "We clearly haven't poisoned anyone. But until they figure that out..." She let out a humorless laugh.

I nodded, not trusting myself to respond. Every step we took brought a new wave of doubt. Our once-simple mission to uncover the truth about Mom's death had grown into a labyrinth of poisoned suspects and tangled motives. And now, Emilia's arrest had thrown us headfirst into the center of it.

The cobblestones glistened under the glow of the streetlamps as we walked past familiar storefronts. Serenity Falls was quiet now, but its gentle rhythms did nothing to calm the storm raging inside me. It was all I could do to put one foot in front of the other.

"We can't keep stumbling around like this," I said. "We need a plan. One that doesn't involve breaking into houses."

Emilia shot me a sidelong glance, her mouth quirking into a wry half-smile. "What, you don't trust me to stage another flawless B&E?"

"Not even slightly. And after what just happened, you shouldn't trust yourself either."

She let out a huff that might've been a laugh. "Fair point."

"So, what now?"

"Well, first, we clear my name. And yours, considering your perfume business is now part of the investigation." She gave me a sidelong glance. "Other than that, I don't know. Keep digging?"

Digging. The word stirred something in my memory, tugging me back to lunch with Marianne at the Ivy Nook. Was that really only hours ago? It felt like a lifetime had passed since then.

"Actually," I said, slowing my pace, "there might be a lead we can follow. Before your life of crime blew up, Marianne said we should talk to Tabitha Root. Apparently, before she got into flowers, she was a pharmacist. Marianne thinks she might be able to help us understand if something could've been engineered."

Emilia frowned, her brow furrowing. "Tabitha? As in herbal teas and moonstone necklaces? The woman who's basically the farmers market's fairy godmother?"

I nodded. "That one. If anyone understands how something could be masked as a heart attack, it's her."

I hesitated, then added, "But we should also put her on the board."

Emilia stopped mid-step, turning to look at me with one perfectly arched brow. "You want to suspect *Tabitha*? The same Tabitha who used to sneak us honey sticks and tell us bedtime stories about enchanted forests?"

I winced. "I know how it sounds. But you were the one who insisted we keep Marianne on the board, even though she was one of Mom's best friends, too. We can't give Tabitha a pass just because she bakes cookies and floats instead of walks."

Emilia considered that, her expression sharpening. "You're right. She's got the knowledge, and the access. And if we're serious about this, we can't leave any stone—or crystal—unturned."

I folded my arms. "No exceptions. Not Tabitha, not the sweet old ladies in the knitting club."

"Not even your new crush, Parker," Emilia said sweetly, the sass curling like steam off hot tea.

I stopped mid-step. "Wait. Didn't he say he moved here about a year ago? Was that before or after Mom died?"

Her teasing expression dropped into one of exaggerated disbelief. "I was joking, Anna. Please don't tell me you're actually considering Parker as a suspect now."

"Well," I said, drawing out the word as the thought latched on, "come to think of it..."

"Oh, for the love of lavender!" Emilia groaned, throwing her hands in the air.

But the idea was already worming its way into my mind, unwelcome but persistent. Parker had shown up in town right around the time everything fell apart. It was nothing, of course. A coincidence. But were there ever really true coincidences?

My brain, restless and primed by all the clue chasing, refused to let the matter drop. Since losing my job as a researcher, I'd been grasping for something to latch onto, some puzzle to solve. And this mystery—this mess of suspects, secrets, and misdirection—had filled that void with an intensity I hadn't expected.

I tried to tell myself it was healthy. Productive, even. But there was no denying the darker side of it. The hypervigilance that kept me awake at night. The nagging suspicion that turned everyone I knew into a potential culprit. Even Parker, with his warm smile and quiet kindness, wasn't safe from my scrutinizing gaze.

I rubbed my temples, as if that could massage the racing thoughts out of my brain. "Ever since we started looking into this, I can't turn my brain off. It just won't quit."

"Welcome to my world," Emilia said with a dry laugh. Her tone softened as she glanced at me, the teasing giving way to something gentler. "Maybe this mystery is just your brain's way of keeping busy."

"Maybe," I admitted, a reluctant smile tugging at my lips at hearing my sister voice the exact same thoughts I just had. "But I'd still prefer to solve this and get back to a life where I'm not suspecting everyone."

"Like your new boyfriend, Parker," Emilia cooed, nudging her elbow into me.

I let out a laugh and pushed her off. "You're impossible."

"Anna? Emilia?"

Parker's voice rang out behind us, and I spun around so fast I nearly dropped my purse. There he stood, framed by the golden lamplight like something out of a particularly rugged rom-com. Hair neatly combed and dressed in a button-up shirt and creased slacks, he was fancier than I was used to seeing him.

And just like that, my heart dropped into my shoes.

Oh no. The date. *Tonight.*

I slapped a hand to my forehead. "Parker! I completely forgot. Our dinner. I was supposed to meet you at Ivy Nook at seven and—oh my gosh—I'm so sorry."

His eyebrows lifted. "You forgot?"

"I didn't mean to. I was getting ready. I had a dress picked out and everything. But then I got a call that Emilia had been arrested and I just ran. I didn't even think to text. Or call. Or anything." I could feel my face blazing. "You must think I'm the worst."

Parker blinked again and turned to Emilia. "You got *arrested*?"

Emilia crossed her arms. "It was a misunderstanding. Apparently, the police don't appreciate it when you crawl through a real estate magnate's dog door."

A laugh escaped him before he could stop it. "Okay, that's not even the weirdest thing I've heard this week."

My breath whooshed out in a relieved little huff. "Still. I hate that I left you hanging."

He tilted his head, a flicker of warmth softening his features. "Honestly, I figured something big must've come up. So, I used the time to get some work in."

That's when I noticed the toolbox in his hand and the dusting of sawdust on his sleeves. His shirt clung in all the right places, and the slacks looked like they'd been made for him. *Lumberjack meets dreamboat* was apparently my type now.

"Oh. Right. Work," I said, awkwardly gesturing to the toolbox like it was a prop I didn't quite know what to do with. "What kind of job were you working on this late?"

"Just finishing up a shelving install nearby."

I nodded, grateful that he wasn't holding a grudge. "Still, I feel terrible."

"It's okay," he said, and it actually sounded like he meant it. "You had a family emergency. I get it."

He paused, then smiled, slow and easy, with that little crinkle at the corners of his eyes. "How about a rain check? Coffee at the Cozy Cup on Monday?"

I felt my heart trip over itself. "Yes. Absolutely. Coffee sounds perfect."

His grin widened. "Great. And don't worry, your secret's safe with me. Although, if I disappear under mysterious circumstances, I'm absolutely haunting you both."

With a wink, he turned and headed off down the sidewalk, toolbox swinging, sawdust trailing in his wake like fairy dust for the hardware-inclined.

I watched him go, still mildly sizzling.

Emilia nudged me with a wicked smile. "So. Flannel. Muscles. Twinkly eyes. Coffee date. Should I start planning a wedding theme?"

I rolled my eyes, but the smile tugging at the corners of my mouth was impossible to suppress. "Come on. We've got a mystery or three to solve, remember? I want to take a look at Gran's old shop while we're close. Maybe we can peek in the windows and get a clue about who bought the place."

We continued our stroll, the evening breeze bringing in the rich, earthy aroma of the nearby river. The cobblestone streets glistened with a post-rain sheen, casting a soft glow under the lamplights. I admired the shop windows, lined with geraniums and trailing ivy. As much as I hated to admit it, I missed this. Maybe I even enjoyed it slightly more than the hustle and bustle of the city.

As Emilia and I neared Gran's old Charm & Petal shop, a sensation settled over me, a prickling at the back of my neck. I glanced at the ginkgo tree outside, its fan-shaped leaves just beginning to unfurl. The tree, with its ancient limbs stretching protectively over the sidewalk, had always been a silent sentinel, watching over this corner of the world.

Walking down this very street as a kid, my hand clasped in Gran's, I would eagerly tug her towards her aromatic wonderland. The shop had been a treasure trove of scents and curiosities, where jars of dried herbs and glass bottles of essential oils lined the wooden shelves, each holding a promise of enchantment. Sometimes Gran would slip me a tiny vial of perfume to take home, her eyes twinkling as she put her finger to her lips, like we were lifting something from the store.

Now, standing in front of the shop, I felt a pang. The once lively storefront was now muted and mysterious, its large display windows covered from the inside with butcher block paper. The glass, smudged with fingerprints and dust, reflected the nearby streetlamp's glow, giving it an eerie, almost spectral appearance. I pressed my face against the cool glass, peering through a gap in the paper into the murky interior.

Inside, a shaft of light sliced through the darkness, just enough to catch on the haze of dust drifting in the air. Furniture loomed under white sheets, hulking shapes like sleeping ghosts. The air leaking through the window crack carried the scent of dry wood and old books.

Then something moved.

A figure passed through the beam of light. It was too tall for a cat, too slow for a shadow trick. Just a flicker. Enough.

I stumbled back. "There's someone in there."

Emilia squinted at the papered-over windows. "What? Are you sure?"

"I saw them. Just for a second, but yeah. Definitely."

She tilted her head, frowning. "Maybe it's the new owner? Cleaning up or something?"

"Sure," I said, the words sour in my mouth. "Cleaning in the dark. In a building that's been empty for a year."

She shrugged. "Could be a night owl."

I gave her a look. "A night owl who prefers lurking to lighting a single bulb?"

A long pause.

"Let's knock," she said.

"What? No."

"Why not?"

"Because it's *weird*, Emilia! Late at night, papered windows, mysterious figure lurking in the shadows? This is literally how people get murdered in movies."

She crossed her arms. "Or maybe they're up to something they don't want anyone to see."

"Exactly my point," I hissed. "Which is why we *don't* knock."

We stood there, both staring at the door like it was going to explain itself.

Emilia leaned closer, ear near the crack in the door.

"Don't," I said.

"I'm just listening."

"I *know* that tone."

She straightened, eyes locked on the entrance, jaw tight. "We could say we're interested in renting the space. Play it casual. Curious. Confused."

I stared at her. "No. We do *not* play real estate roulette with whomever the heck that was. We go home. We make something warm, pretend we're not amateur detectives on the verge of a felony, and tomorrow, we search property records like normal people."

Emilia sighed but followed as I turned back toward the street. The quiet was heavy now, like the air didn't want us leaving. My skin buzzed with the kind of nervous energy that didn't usually kick in unless something was about to go very wrong.

"Whoever owns this place now," she muttered, "they're in it. I can feel it. If Mom was fighting the sale, then maybe someone had a reason to shut her up."

I stopped walking. She wasn't wrong. And I hated how much that *made sense*. "We start first thing tomorrow. We're finding out who bought this place."

Emilia nodded, already plotting. "But tomorrow's Sunday. Municipal office is closed."

I groaned. "Right. Because the world is inconvenient."

"So we go see Tabitha."

I hesitated, then gave a resigned nod. "Fine. Tabitha first thing tomorrow. Then Monday, we dig into property records and start shaking some trees."

Emilia smirked. "Sure, just don't forget your other plans for Monday. You know, your hot coffee date with Parker?"

I groaned, covering my face with both hands. "I still can't believe I forgot about that. Our first date. And I was excited too!"

"You were bailing me out of jail," she said with a shrug. "It happens."

"You owe me, you know."

She grinned and looped her arm through mine. "Of course. Sisters first. Coffee with Dreamboat Carpenter second."

Despite everything, a laugh bubbled up. The road ahead might be tangled with secrets and suspects, but at least I wouldn't be walking it alone.

CHAPTER NINETEEN

TABITHA'S GREENHOUSE

The Sunday morning air was crisp as Emilia and I stepped out of the car and stood in front of Tabitha Root's cottage. A chill breeze tousled my hair and nipped my cheeks, like winter wasn't quite ready to give up its grip. It was a new day, but yesterday's shadows still clung to me.

I glanced at my sister, grateful to see her upright, free, and fully caffeinated. Today, Emilia had traded her typical comfy chaos for a pair of nearly-new jeans and a determined expression. Her auburn hair was swept into an artful bun. Seeing her like this made something tighten in my chest. My sister's arraignment was in three days.

She couldn't go to prison. I wouldn't let it happen.

Yet, the police seemed convinced Emilia poisoned Lawrence. It was up to us to prove otherwise. And figure out how Lawrence's poisoning and our mom's murder were connected.

Tabitha's cottage was charming in its own right, but the attached greenhouse was a wonder, like someone had captured a bit of spring and told it to bloom forever. Emilia and I used to play inside as kids, and I was looking forward to seeing it again.

We spotted a familiar silhouette moving through the foliage, hazy behind the greenhouse's misted glass.

"There she is," Emilia said, a smile tugging at the corner of her mouth.

We veered toward the greenhouse, bypassing the front door entirely. I knocked on the glass, and the woman inside turned with a bright, knowing grin.

"About time," Tabitha called, her voice muffled but unmistakably affectionate. "Come in, girls!"

The warmth of the greenhouse embraced us the moment we stepped through the door. The humid air was alive with scent—loamy soil, sweet jasmine, sharp geranium leaves, a teasing flicker of bergamot and rose. My whole body eased.

Tabitha Root looked like the embodiment of botanical wisdom. Her clothes flowed like petals, her blonde hair pinned up in organized disarray. Even though I was the one who lobbied to add her to the murder board, I felt guilty and foolish about it now, standing in front of the woman who was a fixture in our lives growing up. Tabitha was part fairy godmother, part science teacher, part partner-in-crime.

She pulled off her gardening gloves and enveloped us both in a warm hug. "I was starting to worry you'd show up after the second apocalypse. Come in, come in."

"We brought chaos," Emilia said cheerfully.

Tabitha snorted. "Good. I was running low."

She gave us a once-over with the eyes of someone who already knew something was wrong and was just waiting for us to spill it. "So. How bad is it?"

I exhaled. "We think someone murdered our mom."

Tabitha blinked. She stepped back and braced herself against the edge of the potting bench, her fingers curling around the worn wood. Her gaze dropped for a moment, fixed on nothing.

"Oh, darlings." Her voice, so often light and ironic, trembled at the edges. "You know, I still talk to her sometimes. Out loud, like a fool."

Silence swelled between us, filled only by the soft drip of condensation and the rustle of a breeze through palm fronds.

When she looked up again, her expression had changed. Calmer. Sharper. She wiped a smudge of soil from her thumb with the edge of her apron and said, "Do you know how?"

"Not yet," I said, voice low. "But Emilia thinks it was poison."

Tabitha nodded slowly.

"That would track," she said, eyes narrowing. "If someone wanted it to look natural. And if they knew what they were doing. Have you gone to the police?"

"Well, yes. But they're focused on a different culprit right now," I said.

Emilia raised her hand like a reluctant volunteer. "That'd be me."

"We want to know how someone might have done it."

Tabitha's mouth tightened. "Well, then. We'd better get to work." She waved us deeper into the greenhouse.

"The line between healing and harm is finer than most realize." Tabitha's eyes softened as she regarded a plant, her fingers brushing one of its delicate purple flowers. "Nature provides us with powerful tools. Things that can mend, soothe, save. But those same gifts, in the wrong hands, can be twisted to serve dark ends."

Her gaze shifted, and a faint, knowing smile played at her lips as she looked back at us. "But in the right hands, they can do wonders."

We stopped beside a table laden with various herbs and dried flowers. Tabitha picked up a small, nondescript leaf, holding it between her fingers. "Knowledge of these substances requires a deep understanding of their properties and effects, but someone with this knowledge and malicious intent could indeed have orchestrated Evelyn's death."

Emilia leaned in, her brow furrowed. "Could they do this remotely?"

"With enough planning, yes." Tabitha set down the leaf and picked up a dried flower, brittle and delicate in her hands. "Consider foxglove, for example. In the right dosage, it's used medicinally for heart conditions, but in excess, it causes symptoms indistinguishable from a heart attack. A murderer could easily mask it in a seemingly benign herbal tea, presented as a gift."

She moved to another part of the table, where a small, unassuming plant sat in a pot. "Or take aconite, also known as wolfsbane. Just a few milligrams can disrupt the heart's electrical conduction. Imagine it being ground into a fine powder and slipped into a spice jar, the label suggesting it's something innocuous like powdered ginger or turmeric, used in daily cooking."

"Could there have been a way to use prescription medication to achieve the same effect?" I asked.

"Absolutely." Tabitha walked over to a shelf lined with old pharmacopeia and pulled down a thick, dusty tome. Flipping it open, she pointed to a list of common medications. "Beta-blockers, for instance, are prescribed for managing high blood pressure and heart conditions. Yet, an overdose can lead to heart failure. Coupled with drugs that can alter potassium or magnesium levels in the body, the heart's rhythm can be disrupted enough to cause death without raising immediate suspicion."

Tabitha's gaze met mine. "It's a more technical and precise method, but in the hands of a skilled individual, just as undetectable as using a natural toxin. Especially if they planned it to coincide with the victim's existing health issues."

"Well, Mom didn't have heart issues," Emilia said, her eyes never leaving the foxglove. "So plant-based poisons make more sense. Especially for someone with *access*."

I caught Emilia's slight emphasis and winced internally. Subtle, but not subtle enough.

"Not necessarily. It just means no one tampered with her prescriptions." Tabitha's gaze shifted thoughtfully to the dried foxglove hanging nearby before finally settling on Emilia. "Synthetic compounds could be administered much like the natural poisons we've discussed. And although they may be easier to detect in an autopsy, they're often more accessible. Especially if someone already had a prescription."

Or if your sister was a nurse, I thought, the idea sneaking into my mind unbidden. I forced it away. Lawrence had been cleared.

"Could someone have stolen something from here?" I asked.

"Absolutely not." Tabitha's response was swift, her head shaking firmly. "This place is locked tight whenever I'm not here, and I know each plant down to the last leaf. I would know if something had been disturbed."

Emilia raised a brow. "But do you sell them? Could someone have bought foxglove or wolfsbane from you?"

Tabitha brought a finger to her chin, frowning in thought. "It's possible. I do keep records, but you have to understand. Someone could have bought the plants years ago and held on to them, waiting for the right moment."

"Could we look at those records?" Emilia asked, her tone politely sharp.

Tabitha hesitated. "Customer details are private."

I stepped in. "It's our mom."

Tabitha's expression softened, the steel easing out of her voice. "I understand. I'll review my records myself. If anyone bought something dangerous in the past year, I'll let you know."

"Thank you." Emilia's eyes darted around the nursery. "Tabitha, do you sell anything here that could be used for cyanide poisoning?"

Tabitha's eyebrows raised. "Well, yes, I do sell hydrangeas, which contain cyanogenic compounds. But it's not the season for them right now." She paused. "Besides, you can't exactly feed someone a hydrangea without them raising an eyebrow. And extracting cyanide from one would require considerable skill."

I could see Emilia's shoulders drop at the lack of a lead.

Tabitha seemed to note my sister's disappointment. She continued, "elderberries, on the other hand, would be easier to work with. The unripe berries, leaves, and stems all contain cyanogenic glycosides. Someone could have purchased them under the guise of making jam or wine. You might want to check with The Purple Pantry, the local elderberry shop. They'd be more likely to have sold larger quantities without raising eyebrows."

We thanked Tabitha for her time and headed back to the car, loaded up at her insistence with fresh bouquets. With these new insights illuminating the dark path we were navigating, I felt a mix of gratitude and heaviness settle over me.

As we made our way back to Emilia's car, the quiet between us was filled with the distant call of birds. Nature carried on, oblivious to the human complexities we were unraveling.

"Okay, one thing still bothers me about mom's death," I said. "How could the murderer ensure the right person took the poison? Gran lived there, too. And you were there eating dinner that night."

"That's a good point," said Emilia. "The killer would have needed intimate knowledge of Mom's routine. They'd have to know not just what Mom consumed, but when and how to introduce the toxin without arousing suspicion."

"And they'd need to understand your and Gran's habits too, to ensure they didn't accidentally poison the wrong person."

The car came into view, a silent witness waiting to carry us back into the fray. Emilia reached for the door handle, then paused, turning to me. "Whoever did this had to have been close to Mom. It's unsettling to think the murderer might be someone who was part of our everyday life."

Chapter Twenty

The next morning, Emilia and I stepped into the grand old municipal building, a cornerstone of Serenity Falls. Its red brick façade was softened by decades of weather and ivy tendrils, while its marble accents gleamed in the spring sun. The structure loomed with an air of quiet authority. Tall arched windows caught glints of light that played on the heavy oak doors that had borne witness to generations of small-town deliberations, whispered confessions, and bureaucratic drama.

As we climbed the wide steps, the dogwood trees flanking the entrance swayed, their branches casting dappled shadows on the stone.

Inside, the atmosphere shifted from serene to bustling. The scent of lemon polish mingled with the musty aroma of paper that had soaked up decades of ink and secrets. The hum of ringing phones and clattering keyboards provided an unrelenting backdrop, underscored by the occasional low murmur of conversation or the squeak of a wheeled cart ferrying an unwieldy stack of file folders.

The clerk's office was no exception to the building's sense of history. Rows of tall oak filing cabinets stretched along the walls, their brass handles gleaming. Each drawer bore a neatly typed label, signaling the careful orderliness of decades past.

A worn but stately mahogany desk dominated the center of the room, its surface polished to a sheen. Behind it sat a woman. Her eyes flitted between her computer screen and a thin notepad, her fingers clicking away on the keyboard in a rhythmic cadence.

She glanced up as we approached.

"Good morning," I said. The sheer weight of history in the room seemed to demand a more formal tone. "We're here to inquire about the ownership of a building. The one housing the old Charm & Petal shop, specifically."

Her gaze flicked briefly back to the screen before settling on us. "And what exactly is your interest in that property?"

I hesitated and glanced at Emilia. She gave me an encouraging nod, her expression calm but watchful. Taking a breath, I mustered a smile. "We're, uh, investigating some changes in the neighborhood," I replied, aiming for a casual tone. "Just curious about the new owners."

"The information *is* public record, is it not?" Emilia asked, her voice taking on a clipped, authoritative tone. It was all I could do not to laugh. She sounded just like one of the hardened detectives from her favorite crime shows. But there was a determined spark in her eye that told me she wasn't playing around.

Before the clerk could answer, a door behind her creaked open, and a familiar voice sliced through the air like a razor wrapped in velvet.

"Anna Attar? Fancy running into you twice in one week."

Emilia and I spun around. Lisa Marconi strode out of a back office like a queen descending from her throne. She was flawless, as always—crisp white blouse buttoned to the throat, dark hair coiled into a sleek twist, glossy pumps clicking across the tile with unshakable authority.

A memory smacked me. High school debate finals, her voice smooth as honey as she dismantled my arguments with surgical precision. Her smile had been a weapon back then, and judging by the sharp curve of her lips now, it still was.

The air between us buzzed with old, unsaid things. My spine went rigid, irritation bubbling up beneath a familiar, unwelcome sense of inadequacy.

My first instinct was to run. Escape. Anything to avoid standing here, exposed to the full force of her dissection of my existence. I took an involuntary step back, but Emilia, as if sensing my flight response, clamped a hand around my arm.

"Don't even think about it," she whispered, her grip firm enough to keep me rooted in place. "We need answers."

"I'd rather chew broken glass," I muttered under my breath, watching as Lisa's smile widened just a fraction. She was enjoying this. Of course, she was.

Emilia leaned closer, her tone low and insistent. "Then smile. Pretend you're happy to see her. Just for five minutes."

I summoned a smile that felt about as natural as a taxidermied squirrel. "Lisa. What a ... surprise. I didn't realize you were working here."

"Oh, I took over the county clerk position a few months ago," she replied, her voice breezy as if this were a casual coffee catch-up instead of a calculated power play. "It's been quite the transition, but you know me. Always up for a challenge."

"Of course." My voice was a touch too sharp, but if she noticed, she didn't let on.

"Can I help you with something?" Lisa asked, tilting her head ever so slightly, the picture of polite curiosity.

"Yes," Emilia cut in, her tone brisk, stepping into the awkward void before I could flounder further. "We're looking for information about the ownership of the old Charm & Petal shop."

Lisa's smile faltered, her expression twisting with a look of disdain that I suspected she reserved for tax evaders and people who wore last season's shoes. "Ah, yes. I don't even need to look that up. The place was snatched up by some out-of-town conglomerate. COWW, they call themselves. Swooped in and bought it right out from under Lawrence Riviera. Poor man was heartbroken. Then they just left it sitting there, untouched, for over a year." She huffed. "The nerve! It's becoming an eyesore. The city should have done more to keep that building in local hands."

I exchanged a bewildered glance with Emilia. "Cow?" I repeated, fighting back a grin. "Like the animal?"

Lisa raised an eyebrow. "Yes, I know it sounds ridiculous. C-O-W-W. It stands for something, though I couldn't tell you what. Just another faceless corporation, as far as I'm concerned."

"Mysterious," I said, barely resisting the urge to moo for emphasis. "I suppose their headquarters are in a barn somewhere?"

Lisa chuckled. The sound was surprisingly genuine. Did I just make Lisa Marconi chuckle? Was that a snowball I saw whizzing past in the underworld?

"We should have let Lawrence buy the building." Lisa's expression hardened. "At least he had plans for it. Even a GreenMart would be better than nothing."

Emilia, ever the opportunist, pounced on this opening, her voice smooth as silk. "Seems like you've got some strong opinions about the property. It must be frustrating not knowing who's really behind COWW. Maybe if we knew more about them, we could address these eyesore issues."

Lisa's eyes narrowed, her gaze shifting between us with cautious interest. She straightened, smoothing her blouse with a practiced hand. "That's part of the problem," she admitted, her tone begrudgingly candid. "COWW's details are murky at best. They've kept everything under wraps. It's as if they just appeared out of nowhere."

"So, there's no way to find out who is behind COWW?" I pressed.

Lisa's expression turned thoughtful, and for a moment, she seemed to drop her polished façade. "Not from the local records, no. Their registration is out-of-state. But if you're really interested in digging, you might want to start looking into corporate registries in other jurisdictions."

"Makes sense," Emilia nodded, her eyes sparkling with faux innocence. "But maybe when you're mayor, you could push for more transparency with these out-of-town companies. After all, you'd want to ensure Serenity Falls doesn't become a haven for absentee landlords, right?"

I stood in awe of my sister's acting ability.

Lisa's gaze sharpened, a flicker of something unreadable passing across her face. "That's a thought," she replied, her tone carefully measured. "And as for those mayoral rumors, let's just say I'm considering all my options."

"Oh, I'm sure you are," Emilia said with a knowing smile. "And I bet you'd make quite the impact on this town. Starting with tackling these mysterious ownership issues."

Seriously. Why didn't Emilia ever try out for the school play as a kid?

Lisa's expression softened just a touch, a hint of pride flickering in her eyes. "I suppose it wouldn't hurt to bring a bit of change. There's a lot that could be improved around here."

"Well, good luck with that, Lisa," I added, trying to sound sincere. "We'll be watching your campaign closely."

Lisa nodded, her smooth smile returning. "Thank you. If you need any more information, feel free to stop by."

As we turned to leave, Emilia's elbow nudged me. "Looks like we've got another lead to chase down. COWW. What a name.

Sounds like either a tech start-up or a secret society from a conspiracy thriller."

I snorted. "Maybe it's both. The Coalition of World Wonders? Cult of Weird Wealth?"

Emilia's lips quirked up in a grin. "Ooh, or Cyber Operatives Working Worldwide. That'd explain all the secrecy."

Despite the knot of worry in my chest, I laughed. "Let's just hope it doesn't stand for *Collective of Wicked Whackos.*"

"I just hope this isn't leading us on a wild goose chase. Or should I say, a wild cow chase?"

We stepped out into the crisp morning air, the cool breeze carrying the sweet scent of dogwood blossoms. The white and pink petals tumbled around us like confetti, dancing against the impossibly blue sky.

As Emilia and I walked down the steps, I grappled with a mix of intrigue and dread. Was COWW merely an odd corporate entity, or could it hold the key to understanding the events surrounding Mom's death?

Reaching the bottom step, Emilia turned to me, her eyes sparkling with curiosity. "So, what's next? More digging into COWW?"

I shook my head, a reluctant smile tugging at my lips. "Not just yet. Remember my coffee date with Parker?"

Emilia's eyes widened with realization, and a teasing grin spread across her face. "Ah, yes. And more importantly, *you* remembered! Can't keep the man waiting, can we?"

"Exactly," I said, though the thought of Parker waiting for me stirred a nervous flutter in my stomach. "Besides, maybe a bit of normalcy will do me some good."

Emilia gave my shoulder an encouraging pat. "You deserve a break. Go get some caffeine and conversation. I'll keep poking around and we can regroup later."

I narrowed my eyes. "Okay, but maybe *no* solo breaking and entering this time? Let's aim for a day without handcuffs."

She smirked, completely unrepentant. "Hey, I didn't *technically* break anything."

"That's the spirit," I muttered, already imagining what kind of chaos she might stir up next. "Just don't interrogate anyone who carries pepper spray."

"No promises," she said with a wink. "Now go. Flirt shamelessly. Leave the meddling to me."

Chapter Twenty-One

COFFEE AND CONSPIRACIES

I stood outside The Cozy Cup, fidgeting with the strap of my purse and wondering if it was too late to fake a sudden onset of bubonic plague. After all, I'd already stood Parker up once. What was one more time between almost-strangers?

But before I could convince myself that the Black Death was making a comeback in Serenity Falls, the door swung open, and out stepped Parker, in all his tall, broad-shouldered glory. His green eyes lit up when he saw me, and my stomach did a little flip.

"Anna," he said, his voice as warm and rich as the coffee scents wafting from the café. "I was starting to think *you* might've gotten arrested this time."

I winced.

"Too soon?" he asked, looking a bit sheepish.

"Nah." I mustered a grin. "I save my felonies for at least the third date. Gotta keep some mystery alive, you know?"

"Fair." He stepped aside to usher me in. "I snagged the good booth."

I raised an eyebrow. "*The* booth?"

"The one with the lumpy cushions and the daisy vase." He waggled his brows. "Very high-end."

He wasn't wrong. The booth was cozy incarnate, with overstuffed cushions, a tabletop polished to a warm gleam, and yes, a cheery little vase of daisies. I set down my purse and raincoat, pretending not to be impressed.

Parker headed to the counter to order—lavender latte for me, black and unsweetened for him—and settled into our corner. I watched him as he chatted with the barista, leaning on the counter like he belonged there, like he belonged *anywhere*. It was unfair, really, how easy he made it look.

I glanced out the window, where rain still misted against the glass, and tried not to read too much into anything. It was just coffee. Just a second chance at a first date. No big deal.

He returned a few minutes later, two mugs in hand and a glint in his eye. "So, what finally convinced you to keep this date? Did the stars align? Did your parole officer insist on socialization?"

"Mostly guilt." I deadpanned. "But the booth helped."

Parker lifted his coffee to take a sip. My eyes were drawn to the large, calloused hands that dwarfed his mug. It was oddly mesmerizing. What would those hands feel like wrapped around mine instead?

"How are you finding Serenity Falls after so much time away?" he asked. "Aside from the aggressive small talk and mandatory pie tastings."

I shrugged, playing it breezy. "Comforting. Disorienting. Like finding your favorite sweater at the bottom of a moving box, only to realize it smells like attic and lost time."

He tilted his head, smiling like he was filing that one away. "That's oddly poetic."

"I dabble," I said, tapping my mug. "So what about you? You've been here what? A year?"

"That's about right. Long enough to know where the good coffee is. Not long enough to know why everyone in town thinks the librarian's cat is clairvoyant."

I smirked. "Moonbeam *is* clairvoyant. Or at least, she pretends to be."

"Really, isn't that half the job?"

I chuckled, but there was a quiet pause after. Parker was looking at me, but not with the usual first-date curiosity. It was more like … he was taking a reading. Like he was trying to decide what kind of story I was and whether it was safe to flip to the next page.

I set down my mug. "So how does a guy like you end up in a place like Serenity Falls? Wrong turn at Chicago?"

For a moment, Parker's eyes clouded over, and I could have sworn I saw a flicker of … something. Guilt? Worry? But then it was gone, replaced by his usual easy smile. "Would you believe me if I said a coven of witches summoned me?"

I nearly choked on my latte. "W-what?"

Great. Just great. As if the rumors about my family weren't bad enough already. Serenity Falls had been buzzing with Lawrence's loud accusations that my sister and I were witches. Sure, Lawrence wasn't guilty of murder, but he was still a grade-A buzzard. Now I was facing Parker's amused grin, praying he wasn't about to mention a certain family legacy.

He waved a hand dismissively. "Kidding, kidding. Just your average small-town carpentry gig. Though sometimes, the way Ms. Fletcher talks about her cat, I do wonder…"

I laughed, relief flooding through me. Of course he was joking.

"And what about you?" Parker asked, leaning forward. "What brought the intrepid Anna Attar back to our little slice of paradise?"

I considered my options. *Oh, you know, just your typical unemployment, family secrets, and murder mystery trifecta* probably wouldn't go over well on a first date.

"Would you believe me if I said a coven of witches summoned me?" I parroted back at him with a grin.

Parker's laugh was even better the second time around. "Touché. Although in your case, I might actually believe it. There's something magical about you, Anna."

I felt a blush creeping up my neck. If only he knew how close to the truth he was. But that was a can of worms—or maybe a bottle of perfume—better left unopened for now. I searched for an answer that felt true.

"My gran's not well," I said finally. "And my sister needed help. It just felt like time."

His expression shifted, gentled. "That's good of you. Not everyone would come back."

I gave a soft snort. "It's not a war zone."

"No," he said, "but sometimes family feels like one."

The honesty in his voice caught me off guard. I wanted to ask him what he'd left behind, why he didn't talk about his family, but I didn't. Instead, I reached for a safer thread.

"So ... any recent woodworking triumphs?" I asked, wrapping both hands around my mug like it could anchor me to the present.

Parker's eyes lit up, and he launched into a story about a recent project involving a massive treehouse he'd built for the mayor's kids, complete with rope bridge, skylight, and a trapdoor "for dramatic exits," he said, grinning.

As he talked, his hands moved with easy grace, sketching invisible blueprints in the air. I didn't catch every detail—something about mismeasured beams and a very vocal squirrel—but the sound of his voice was steady, grounding, like the low hum of a favorite song.

I let myself sink into it. The murmur of other customers, the clink of spoons in ceramic cups, the soft scrape of Parker's mug on the table. For a little while, I wasn't the woman with a grandmother slipping away, or a sister tangled in legal limbo. I wasn't clutching a half-empty bottle of family secrets.

Sure, my life was currently a Shakespearean tragedy with a dash of Hitchcock, but for these few hours, I could pretend to be normal. Just a girl, sitting across from a boy, drinking coffee and definitely not thinking about magic or murder.

He leaned in toward the end of the tale, eyes sparkling. "And then, just as I'm testing the trapdoor, the youngest, maybe six, pops up and says, 'You're my favorite grown-up. You build dreams.'"

I blinked. "That's ... wow."

He gave a sheepish shrug. "I think he just wanted extra cookies. But still. Kinda stuck with me."

There was something quiet in his expression then. A flicker of pride, maybe. Or loneliness. Or something deeper I couldn't quite name. I smiled and took another sip of my latte, letting the lavender sweetness fill the silence.

And if I happened to be memorizing the exact shade of green in Parker's eyes for a future perfume, well, that was just good business sense, right?

They weren't just green, though. That would have been too simple. No, his eyes were more like the way sunlight filters through leaves in early spring. Bright, fresh, full of life, with just a hint of gold near the center, like a secret he wasn't quite ready to share. I could practically hear the scent notes forming in my mind: crisp fern, a whisper of cedar, maybe a dash of blue tansy—

I blinked and gave my head a tiny shake, realizing I'd completely tuned him out. He could've been talking about treehouses or nuclear fusion for all I knew.

Get it together, Anna. You're supposed to be paying attention to the man, not composing an olfactory love letter to his irises.

"So," Parker said, leaning in a little, "how is your grandmother doing these days?"

I glanced down at my coffee, watching the pale swirls settle into stillness. "She's ... stable. Golden Pines takes good care of her. They know what to do when she forgets where she is. Or who I am."

Parker didn't offer platitudes or rush to fill the silence. Just listened.

"She taught me everything I know about perfumes. But now," my throat tightened unexpectedly, "Well, dementia's a beast."

He reached across the table, covering my hand. The gesture was simple, grounding. I let myself sit in the comfort of it as the background hum of the café faded. "I'm sorry, Anna. That's rough."

Parker didn't move his hand right away, and for a split second, I thought he might say something more. But then he leaned back, giving me space.

"What about you?" I asked, eager to shift the focus. "Any family in Serenity Falls?"

Something I couldn't quite place passed over his face.

"Ah, no. It's just me here. Bit of a lone wolf, I guess," he said, his tone light but not quite masking something heavier beneath.

"You ever miss them?"

"I try not to."

Something in his face kept me from pressing. I didn't mind. After all, I had my own secrets to keep.

"Can I ask you something?" I said, surprising myself with my boldness. I took a deep breath. "What have you heard about my mother's death?"

Parker's eyebrows shot up. "Your mother? I'm not sure I follow."

"It's just..." I hesitated, wondering how much to reveal. "We always thought she died of a heart attack, but lately, I'm not so sure."

His expression turned serious. "What makes you say that?"

"Just some things that don't add up. And something my Gran said last week in a moment of clarity made me wonder."

Parker leaned forward, his voice low. "Have you talked to the police?"

"Funny you should ask. When our house was broken into, a cop, David—an old friend—came by. Emilia even showed him her murder board."

Parker's eyebrows shot up. "Your house was broken into? Murder board?"

"Yeah, she's got a bit of a true crime obsession." I explained about the theft, the murder board, and David's visit.

"So, the police are involved?"

I sighed, running a hand through my hair. "Sort of. But now, it all feels complicated."

Parker reached across the table, squeezing my hand. "And how are you holding up?"

I let out a dry laugh. "Oh, you know, just your average week. Family drama, stolen grimoire, potential murder, and a sister on the verge of incarceration. I'm thinking of taking up juggling. Might as well make the chaos metaphor literal."

"Did you say stolen *grimoire*?" Parker set down his cup.

I sighed, running a hand through my hair. "Yeah, whoever broke into our house took my gran's book. It's sort of like a recipe book, but for fragrances. They also took all my Evoko."

"Your, um, aromatherapy perfume? The one you showed me at the market?"

I nodded, the loss pressing against my ribs like a bruise. "That's the one. Now it's gone, and the police confiscated all my other materials to test for toxins. I've got nothing for the farmer's market this weekend."

Parker sat back, shaking his head. "That's awful. And they just took everything?"

"Like a scented crime scene," I muttered.

"I can see why this is hitting you so hard," Parker said softly. "Your family, your creations. They clearly mean a lot to you."

Why was I telling him all this? Didn't I start this date intending to steer clear of talk of magic and murder? I sank even further into my seat. "I don't know what to think anymore. It feels like I'm going crazy."

"Hey." Parker's hand found mine again, and I could hear the blood pump in my ears. "Sometimes what seems crazy is just really just a truth we're not ready to face yet."

I smiled, my pulse kicking up just a bit. There was something about the way he was looking at me, like he saw through the chaos and worry, straight to the heart of who I was. And liked it.

"You're handling all of this surprisingly well," he said after a beat. "If I had police confiscating my tools and a sister with a flair for felonies, I'd probably be hiding under a table somewhere."

"Tempting," I admitted. "But I don't think they let you hide under tables indefinitely. At some point, someone offers you soup and tells you to face your problems."

"Still, you've got guts. And you care."

My stomach did a little loop-the-loop. And just like that, sitting across from Parker Ekstrom in the Cozy Cup with half-drunk coffee and full-blown complications, I realized something dangerous.

I really liked him.

Also, I'd just unloaded a full tragicomedy's worth of drama onto someone who'd probably just wanted a pleasant latte and light banter.

"Sorry," I said, heat creeping up my neck. "That was probably more than you bargained for."

"Don't apologize. That sounds like a nightmare."

"Thank you," I managed, my voice smaller than I meant it to be.

We stayed a while longer after that. Long enough for the coffee to go lukewarm and the shadows outside to stretch into afternoon shapes. We talked about nothing and everything—the best kind of wood for porch swings, the weirdest farmer's market customers, whether or not Moonbeam the cat had once predicted a hailstorm. The conversation drifted easily, like leaves on a stream.

"Well," Parker said, draining the last of his coffee, "I should probably get going. Got a, uh, project to finish up."

We stood, and he walked me to the door. Outside, the late afternoon sun cast a honeyed glow across the street, stretching shadows like whispered secrets.

"This was nice," I said, suddenly shy. "We should do it again sometime."

Parker's smile came easy. "Definitely. And if you need help with ... any of this, just say the word. I'm quite good at navigating chaos."

He lingered for a beat longer, then gave a little wave and headed down the sidewalk. And yes, I watched him go. Of course I did. The view was worth it. But more than that, I watched because something about Parker felt like an unopened door in a familiar house. One I hadn't noticed until now.

Chapter Twenty-Two

THE PURPLE PANTRY

As much as I wanted to linger in the glow of a date that had been more than I'd expected, reality had other plans. I meandered toward the town square, my thoughts a tangled mess. The spring air carried the sweet scent of blooming honeysuckle, but even that couldn't lift the heaviness settling over me. Each step felt like I was wading through molasses, stuck between too many urgent tasks and not knowing which direction to take.

The mystery of COWW nagged at me. What kind of company buys a prime downtown property with cash, only to leave it empty? And that movement Emilia and I had seen inside Charm & Petal meant someone was using that shop, but for what? The whole thing reeked of secrets, but pursuing that lead meant more digging through bureaucratic paperwork, and time wasn't exactly on our side.

I paused at the corner, watching a pair of sparrows squabble over a piece of bread. Two days. That's all we had until Emilia's arraignment. My sister's freedom hung by a thread, and I was drowning in a sea of dead ends.

Then there was Gran's grimoire and my stolen Evoko. Without the grimoire, I felt like I was trying to bake without a recipe. And without ingredients. Not that it mattered. I was barred from selling at the farmer's market for now, anyway. More importantly, those bottles of Evoko might have been our best shot at getting more information from Gran. If someone was trying to silence her memories, they were doing a darned good job of it.

Susan was already increasing her medication, and the thought of my grandmother being drugged into compliance made my blood boil. Yet barging into Golden Pines and demanding answers would likely only make things worse.

I shook my head, trying to clear it. I couldn't afford to get distracted by potential romance or paranoia. Emilia needed me focused. Mom deserved justice. And right now, I had exactly one lead that felt concrete: The Purple Pantry.

Tabitha had suggested that someone could have purchased raw elderberries under the guise of making jam or wine. If someone bought supplies to create cyanide to poison Lawrence, there might be a record of it. It might not help get mom justice, but if I could prove Emilia wasn't the one that poisoned Lawrence, at least I'd keep her out of jail.

The Purple Pantry was only a few blocks away, its cheerful purple and silver awning visible from where I stood. My steps felt lighter as I headed in that direction, finally having a clear purpose.

A bell tinkled as I pushed open the door to The Purple Pantry. Inside, the shop was lined with weathered wooden shelves and antique apothecary cabinets that created narrow aisles. A purple-tinted glow filtered through stained glass panels high in the windows, casting everything in a moody hue. Jars of deep purple jams, syrups, and elderberry wine filled the displays, their glass catching the light like little amethysts. The air smelled sweet and earthy, with an underlying tang that hinted at fermentation.

"Hello?" I called out.

"Just a minute!" A voice rang out from the back, followed by a crash and a string of muffled curses, half in English, half in Spanish. A moment later, a woman emerged from behind a beaded curtain, brushing purple dust from her apron. She was around Emilia' age, with loose curls dyed a shocking shade of violet and multiple piercings in each ear. Her name tag read *Juniper*.

She glanced up—and froze.

Her eyes widened. "Anna Attar?"

The voice triggered something in my memory. A flicker of a time when I'd stood on the outside looking in. "Juniper Martinez?"

I hadn't recognized her at first, not with the violet curls, but now I could see it. The same Juniper who used to sit cross-legged on the school lawn with Emilia and that other boy, doodling magical creatures in the margins of her notebooks.

"I can't believe it's you!" Juniper bounced slightly on her toes, a habit she apparently hadn't outgrown. "I heard you were back in town, but I figured you'd be too busy with..." She hesitated, the excitement in her face dimming slightly. "Well. Everything."

I stiffened. *What does she know? What has she heard?* Gossip moved fast in towns like this.

Juniper tilted her head, her smile softening like she'd caught the flicker of discomfort on my face. "Don't worry. I didn't hear it from anyone *too* nosy. My abuela lives over at Golden Pines, and gossip is basically her full-time job." She rolled her eyes affectionately.

I let out a breath and laughed, tension easing. "Well, I guess I can't blame her. It's good material. But look at you! Your hair is amazing. Still drawing unicorns?"

Juniper laughed, raking her fingers through her curls. "Not as much. But my old sketches are still around, just hidden under all this responsible adult stuff." She gestured to her apron. "Speaking of which, what can I help you with?"

"I'm actually here to ask about raw elderberries. Specifically, who might have bought them recently."

"Oh, we get tons of bulk orders," Juniper said. "Tom Kline's probably our biggest local customer. He makes his own elderberry reduction for those famous purple swirl schnecken of his. The Enchanted Oven goes through about thirty pounds a month." She started counting off on her fingers. "Then there's the wine-making club, a few restaurants, some health food stores in the next county over..."

She grinned, leaning forward conspiratorially. "We even get these super official-looking purchase orders from companies with ridiculous names. Want to hear something funny? There's this one outfit called COWW. I kid you not. Every time I process their order, I have to resist drawing a little moo-cow on the invoice."

My heart skipped a beat. "COWW? That's the same company that bought the old Charm & Petal shop."

"Oh yeah? Small world!" Juniper's eyes sparkled with gossip. "They've been ordering from us for years."

I tried not to look too eager, but this could be the very connection Emilia and I've been looking for. I was about to ask more when the bell above the door chimed. We both turned to see Susan Eldridge entering the shop, her arms laden with grocery bags.

My whole body tensed. Would she blame Emilia for her brother's poisoning? Would she blame *me*? I shifted my weight, ready to defend myself or my sister if needed.

"Oh, hello Anna." Susan shifted her grocery bags. "I didn't expect to see you here."

"Hi, Susan," I managed, my voice cautious but polite. Susan's demeanor was muted from her normal overbearing self, but that was to be expected, with her brother in the hospital. I debated whether to convey my sympathies on that matter. Could I do it and sound sufficiently sincere? Would mention of Lawrence launch Susan into a tidal wave of accusations?

Susan glanced around, then lowered her voice. "Actually, I've been hoping to run into you. I wanted you to know, I know Emilia did not poison Lawrence."

I blinked. "You do?"

"Of course." Her hand found my arm, cold and damp as always. "That girl has her flaws but poisoning? That's not her way."

The tension in my chest eased a fraction. Susan's brother hated my family. Emilia had been caught breaking into his house, for goodness' sake. And with Susan's access to Gran, to records, to ... everything ... if she wanted to make trouble for us, she could.

I studied her face, searching for any hint of deception, of hidden motives beneath her warmth. But her expression remained open, her concern disarmingly genuine.

She didn't believe Emilia had done it.

Susan turned to Juniper before I could respond. "I'll need my order, please."

"Of course, Ms. Eldridge." Juniper stepped briskly behind the counter. She pulled out a large brown paper bag and began scooping dark, glossy—raw—berries into it with practiced efficiency.

"Here you go," Juniper said brightly, folding the top of the bag with a crisp crease and handing it over. The elderberries had vanished as quickly as they'd appeared, and I suddenly wished I'd had more time to study them.

"Raw elderberries?" I asked, trying to sound offhand.

"That's right." Susan nodded absentmindedly, then noticed my interest. "Elderberries are wonderful for maintaining a healthy immune system. I prefer to make my own syrup. It's easy to control the ingredients that way. The sugar-free version here has artificial sweeteners, and I don't trust those."

Juniper returned with a small paper bag, and Susan tucked it away. She turned to leave, then paused. "Oh, and Anna? Be careful. Someone targeting both our families ... well, just watch your back, dear."

The bell chimed as Susan left, leaving behind the faint scent of antiseptic and something else. Something bittersweet that tickled the back of my throat. Was Susan's warning genuine? Why did it feel more like a threat?

"So, she's a regular?" I asked Juniper, trying to keep my voice casual.

Juniper nodded. "Every month, like clockwork. Always the same order."

I filed that information away, my mind already spinning with possibilities.

"Hey," Juniper hesitated, twirling the edge of her apron between her fingers. "Do you think Emilia would want to catch up sometime? I know things are probably messy right now, but," she sighed, "I just keep thinking about how we used to be. I'd love to see her."

Something in my chest twisted. The answer should've been easy. But the Emilia Juniper remembered—the outgoing girl sneaking cigarettes under the bleachers—was harder to find these days, hidden away behind closed doors and unanswered texts.

"I don't know," I admitted. "But, I could ask."

Juniper studied me for a beat, then nodded. "I'd really like that. And hey, if you're free sometime, we should catch up properly, too. I still have some of those old sketchbooks, and I bet we could both use a laugh at my teenage artistic attempts."

"I'd like that," I said, meaning it.

As I left The Purple Pantry, the soft tinkling of the bell overhead did little to quiet the buzzing in my head. New connections were forming, then tangling like threads in an unraveling scarf I couldn't quite knit back together.

CHAPTER TWENTY-THREE

SLIPPING AWAY

I hung my rainjacket by the door, still damp from the incessant drizzle, and kicked off my shoes with a sigh. On the couch, Emilia was fully burritoed in her favorite throw blanket, surrounded by pillows, chopsticks in one hand, remote in the other. Watson sat curled at her side. On screen, a Netflix narrator droned on about a serial killer who turned his victims into furniture.

"Please tell me that's not your dinner inspiration," I said, eyeing the spring roll dangling from her fingers.

Emilia didn't even blink. "Relax. I'd at least marinate you first."

"Truly, your generosity knows no bounds."

"I am indeed the Best Sister Ever." She waggled the spring roll like a tiny edible scepter. "So, where'd you go? You've been gone for ages."

"Stopped by The Purple Pantry after my date." I plucked a spring roll from the takeout box and dropped onto the couch. The cushions smelled faintly herbal—sharp, green, just slightly bitter. "Get this. COWW has been buying raw elderberries from them for *years*."

She didn't respond. She was too busy smoothing a damp paper towel over her arm. I leaned closer.

"Is that ... a glitter dolphin?"

Emilia held up her arm proudly. "Temporary tattoos. Found them in my old craft drawer. This one's name is Justice."

"You gave it a name?"

"I'm channeling the spirit of the sea to help me crack this case."

I watched her for a second longer. Her hair was twisted up with sparkly chopsticks—high school era, back when she had a minor addiction to Claire's Accessories—and her socked feet were propped on the coffee table, toes wiggling to a beat I couldn't hear. She looked like a kid playing queen of the castle, high on sugar and zero responsibilities.

And she hadn't even asked me how my date went yet.

"It's called grounding, Anna," she says, carefully peeling the wet paper from her arm, revealing a glittery dolphin mid-leap. "Dolphins represent truth and murder-solving prowess."

This morning, she was talking cybercrime over coffee. Now she was draped in a blanket fort, decorating herself like a Lisa Frank folder. Something was not right.

"You okay?" I asked, keeping it casual. Trying to, anyway. Maybe she took some drugs?

"Never better." She grinned and paused the TV. "Ooh, the date! Tell me everything. No, wait." She held up a finger. "First, rate his shoes on a scale of serial killer to marriage material."

I blinked at her. "Okay, you *are* high."

She rolled her eyes. "I'm not high."

"Drunk?"

"No."

"Did you eat gummies out of a stranger's trench coat again?"

"That was one time, and they were vegan."

I narrowed my eyes. "Because you're acting like someone who just licked a frog and saw God."

She clutched her heart dramatically. "Maybe I just had a really good spring roll."

"Em, come on." I sat up straighter. "What's going on? You're nesting like a stoned raccoon with a Netflix addiction."

She waved her chopsticks again. "Netflix documentaries are an essential part of any investigation. Also, did you know you can turn a ribcage into a coffee table?"

I sighed. "Sure. That's what this is about. Furniture tips."

She blinked innocently.

"The *Purple Pantry*," I said. "Remember? I told you I went there after the date?"

She paused. Something flickered behind her eyes. "Right. Yeah. Why were you there again?"

"I *just* said. Elderberries. Turns out COWW's a regular customer."

Her face twitched. She straightened up slightly, blanket still wrapped around her like armor. "Wait, what? You think COWW is poisoning Lawrence?"

"I think it's a possibility."

The Netflix narrator, still in the background, described the best way to upholster a femur.

Emilia sat up straighter, pulling the blanket tighter, only her hands emerging to gesture as she spoke. "What if none of this is even really about us? What if it's all about Lawrence, and Mom got caught in the crossfire?"

"What do you mean?"

Emilia's voice grew stronger, more like herself. "Sure, Charm & Petal was Gran's shop, but it was in the building Lawrence was trying to buy. Maybe COWW didn't even care about Gran's shop. Maybe they wanted to take the building from Lawrence." She frowned. "And they've been buying elderberries? Why does that feel important?"

"Because elderberries can be used to make cyanide," I said slowly, watching her carefully. "Tabitha told us that. You knew that."

She clicked her tongue. "Right. I forgot."

I stared at her. "You forgot *cyanide*?"

She shrugged, all nonchalance and blanket fluff. She dropped her spring roll, then dove into the folds of her blanket nest to retrieve it.

"Em."

She popped back up a second later, victorious. "Oh my gosh, Anna. Do you remember that time you hid Mom's grocery list in the couch because you didn't want her to buy brussel sprouts?"

I pinched the bridge of my nose. "You seriously don't remember the elderberry conversation?"

"Of course I do. I just ... forgot for a second."

I glanced at the uneaten spring roll in my hand. "I swear to God, if there's weed in these..."

I trailed off.

No. This wasn't like the time someone spiked the punch at homecoming, or that one disastrous girls' night with too much Jäger.

The shift in her was too sudden. Too sharp.

And it wasn't just the random memory. She completely mixed up which sister had done it.

My throat went dry. "That was you."

Emilia froze, spring roll retrieved, her triumphant grin flickering. "What?"

"The Brussel Sprouts Incident. That wasn't me. *You* hid the list. I cried about it for, like, an hour because Mom thought I was the one who did it and I didn't even know what was going on."

She blinked. "No. I—are you sure?"

I stared at her. "Em, I had to write an apology card. In crayon. You made me sign it *with a glitter pen*."

She laughed, weakly. "That sounds like something I'd do."

But her smile didn't reach her eyes.

And now my heart was pounding. I reached for her hand. "Hey. Are you feeling okay? Like, actually okay?"

Emilia didn't answer right away. Just stared down at her blanket like it might tell her who she was.

Watson rose without a sound, his tail flicking once in quiet judgment, and padded across the cushions to curl against my thigh. His warmth seeped into me like comfort. Or warning. I wasn't sure which.

Emilia glared at her cat. "Traitor. Though I guess I can't blame him." She poked my leg with her toe. "You're always stealing my heat sources. Remember when you used to wedge your feet under me during movie nights? You're like a lizard, needing external heat." She smiled distantly. "Last weekend at the skating rink..." She scrunched her face in confusion.

"Em, that was years ago. The skating rink is all boarded up now."

"Oh." She blinked slowly. "Right. Of course." She reached for her Kung Pao, then hesitated, chopsticks hovering over the container like she couldn't quite remember ordering it. "So, what did you find out at The Purple Pantry?"

My stomach tightened fully now. I told her again about how COWW has been buying raw elderberries for years.

"Let's add this to the murder board." Emilia stood, tossing her blanket aside.

That's when I smelled it.

It hit in a wave—sharp, green, almost bitter. Clary sage? No. Mugwort. And something else. Wormwood. The scent tangled in my lungs, familiar but elusive, stirring something deep in my memory.

My stomach twisted as I followed my little sister into the kitchen.

A cold weight settled in my stomach as Emilia paused in front of the murder board. She touched her fingertips to her temple like she was trying to hold something in place. "Anna? What was I ... I came in here for something."

My sister stared at her murder board as if she'd never seen it before.

She lifted a photograph, tilting her head. "Oh, look at this," she said, her voice light with curiosity. "I don't remember this one."

She smiled, tracing the edges. "It must've been a party or something. You and me, right?" She tapped the two girls in the foreground. "But ... who's this?"

She pointed to the third girl standing beside them.

I looked at the photo. My stomach dipped. It was the photograph of mom, Marianne, and Tabitha as kids.

Emilia frowned, shaking her head. "I don't remember other kids coming over much. But there she is, plain as day." Her finger hovered over the background. "And them, too. At the swings."

I leaned in. Two more figures were in the background, at the big elm tree. A girl was pushing a younger boy on the swing, frozen mid-motion, a moment of childhood joy captured in time.

The air in the room felt heavier. Like someone had shut a door.

"I swear, I've never seen this before in my life." Emilia let out a soft, confused laugh and ran a hand through her hair.

That sharp herbal scent hit me again, stronger now. I *knew* this smell. I'd smelled it before.

I sat up straighter. "Hey, Em?" I kept my voice calm. Gentle. Like I was approaching a spooked animal or a toddler holding scissors.

She didn't answer at first. Then, "You're gonna be late, you know."

I frowned. "Late for what?"

She gave me a look, half teasing, half *are you serious?* "Mom's making waffles. But you never get up on time. You're gonna have to run to catch the bus."

My stomach dropped. I reached out and touched her arm. "Emilia. Look at me."

Everything Susan had taught me about memory loss came rushing back. Meet them where they are. Don't push. Don't panic. But Emilia wasn't eighty, she was *twenty-six*, and just this morning she was buttering up Lisa Marconi and quoting zoning laws like she moonlighted as a municipal attorney.

"Em." I gave her arm a light squeeze. "You're in your house. It's Monday night. You're watching Netflix. *No one is making waffles.*"

Her brow furrowed, just for a second. A tiny crack in the surface. Then she blinked and smiled again, too bright. "Okay, okay. Chill. I was just messing with you."

I didn't let go. "No, you weren't."

She opened her mouth to argue, but nothing came out.

I kept my grip steady. "What's going on with you?"

She looked at me then. Really looked. "You're going to be late for school."

"I'll be ready in a minute," I said finally, unsticking my throat.

The scent on her. I knew I had smelled it somewhere before. "By the way, you smell amazing. Is that a new perfume?"

Emilia lit up. "What? The master perfumer doesn't recognize her latest creation? I hope you don't mind. I just wanted to try it."

My stomach clenched. "What latest creation?"

"I found it on the kitchen table," she said, like that was a normal sentence. "It had a little bow on it. I figured you left it for me."

I stared at her. "You just put on a mystery perfume someone left on the table?"

"Well, yeah. It smelled good." She shrugged, then jumped up from the couch and disappeared into the bathroom. A moment later, she returned with a small, unmarked bottle nestled in her palm.

"See?" She held it out proudly, like she'd just dug up buried treasure in the backyard.

I took it from her carefully. It was still warm. Too warm. Not body heat. More like it had been resting on a sunlit altar. Or microwaved. Either possibility felt equally cursed.

I uncapped it and waved a bit of the scent toward my face. That same sharp, bitter herbal undertow unfolded. Something green and ancient, like walking through a garden that didn't want you there. It curled into my lungs.

And then I realized how stupid I was. What if I'd just signed myself up for my own round of psychological time travel?

But nothing happened. No confusion. No flashbacks. I didn't suddenly want waffles or think I had third-period French. Maybe it wasn't the smell that caused this reaction. Maybe it worked through skin contact.

I recapped the bottle and looked at Emilia. "Where exactly on the kitchen table did you find this?"

She blinked. "Right in the middle. Like... *placed* there."

No note. No box. No idea who it came from.

And she'd just sprayed it on her neck like it was a Sephora sample. Of course she had.

"Em, let's get you cleaned up. This might be what's making you feel weird."

She rubbed her forehead. "I think something is wrong with me. We should call Helen. She takes care of Gran at Golden Pines. Or better yet," she added, with a snap of her fingers, "Let's just go straight to the top. Susan's the head nurse there. You should meet her. She's so great with Gran."

The words barely registered. I knew where I'd smelled that sharp, bitter bite before. I'd smelled it on Gran. Faint, but unmistakable, both times I'd visited.

Helen had mentioned Golden Pines had a no-perfume policy. But Gran always smelled like this. Just weak enough that only I, with my trained nose, noticed.

Someone was sneaking this perfume in and dousing her. Regularly.

And now they're doing the same to Emilia.

My stomach clenched. Golden Pines wasn't safe. Doctors couldn't help, anyway. This was magical, not medical.

"Em," I said carefully, trying to sound steady, normal, like everything wasn't tipping sideways, "I don't think we should call Golden Pines."

Emilia stilled. Her eyes darkened, lips pressing into a thin line.

And then she exploded.

"This is just like you, Anna." The words exploded out of her, raw and jagged. "You come waltzing back and think you can fix everything, but you don't even see what's broken!"

The photo of mom with her childhood friends slipped from Emilia's fingers, landing face-up between us like a truth neither of us wanted to hold. I stared at Mom's young face grinning up at us, unaware of all that would come. All that would break.

"What are you talking about?" I asked, though part of me already knew. Some wounds never really heal; they just wait for moments like this to split open again.

"You're always running off!" Emilia's voice cracked. "You left for college without looking back, and now you're home for spring break, and you think you know what's best for me? You don't! Danny died and you left."

My heart sank. In the harsh kitchen light, I could see tears streaming down her face. "That's not ... I'm here now because I lost my job, remember?"

My own voice sounded distant, like it belonged to someone else. A memory surfaced. Gran at Mom's funeral, staring at an empty chair and insisting Grandpa would be arriving any minute.

Emilia's breath hitched. She swiped at her eyes, looking lost. "The pieces ... I was holding them. They were important, but I can't..." Her voice dropped to a whisper. "I can't remember what they are."

"You're scaring me," I whispered.

She looked at me then, really looked at me, her eyes glassy but present. "I'm scaring myself."

We had unresolved issues. I knew that. I'd left Emilia when she needed me most. Though she hid it well, she'd never really forgiven me for that. But that could wait. First, I needed to get my sister back. "Let's wash this stuff off you, okay?"

She followed me to the restroom, humming some weird little melody that hit me with middle school dread.

I ran warm water and helped her scrub her hands, her neck, her arms. Soap, water, friction, the whole basic human maintenance routine. She giggled when I used too much soap, and for a second, it felt almost normal.

But her eyes stayed foggy. The bitter scent clung to her skin like whatever spell she was under didn't care about my lavender hand soap.

I stared at the suds circling the drain and made a snap decision. "Okay. Shower. We're escalating."

Emilia blinked at me, unfazed. "Will there be more glitter dolphins?"

"No," I said, already guiding her toward the tub. "There will be shampoo. And actual hot water. And scrubbing like we're exorcising a demon, because maybe we are."

She went along with it, docile and humming again. I turned on the water and coaxed her into the stream like I was washing a possessed cat.

I shut the bathroom door behind her and immediately pulled out my phone and searched *magical detox spell mind perfume.*

Google gave me a list of crystals, three Etsy shops, and an article on mold poisoning.

I tried again: *how to undo magical perfume mind control homemade ingredients*

One Reddit thread suggested bathing in saltwater and smudging with sage. Another said pickle juice. Someone named *Shadow_Gremlin13* recommended "grounding through bone marrow extraction," and I had to physically put the phone down before I rage-threw it into the wall.

I paced the hallway. My brain was short-circuiting from panic and internet nonsense.

Emilia's humming drifted from behind the door. Still tuneless. Still wrong.

We needed something stronger. I went into the kitchen like I had a plan. Ethanol would break down the compounds, but the police confiscated all my supplies.

I started rifling through cabinets, then called out to Emilia, "Do we have any vodka?"

From the bathroom, her song-songy voice floated out. "Mom would kill us if we got into the liquor cabinet."

I froze. Hand on the cabinet door, heart suddenly thudding. And then it hit me—Evoko. When we'd used it on Gran, there'd been a moment of perfect clarity. Maybe, just maybe, it could do the same here.

But I had no Evoko left. And no perfume supplies. And no recipe. The weight of that loss sat on my chest like a stone. If only I could remember what I'd done that first time. What had changed? What had made it work?

I stared blankly at the spice rack like it might whisper a secret recipe.

Unless...

Charm & Petal. Maybe there were still ingredients there. And perhaps another copy of the formula buried in Gran's old office.

It was a long shot. But it was the best lead I had.

The bathroom door creaked open. I turned, foolish hope rising.

Emilia stepped out in a bathrobe, her wet hair plastered to her cheeks. The glitter tattoo had mostly melted off, just a faint shimmer across her forearm.

She looked worse. Pale and glassy-eyed, like the hot water had rinsed away whatever fragments were holding her together.

Then she walked into the living room, dropped onto the floor, and pulled a stack of old DVDs out from under the TV stand.

"Movie night," she said, like we were sixteen again and Mom had just left to host a perfume party. "We'll start with *The Fault in Our Stars.* You always cried at the part with the swing set."

She smiled, like she was flipping through a yearbook only she could see. Then she started rearranging the DVD cases by color.

The bitter scent still clung to her skin. Stronger now. Like it was blooming.

I stepped carefully around the stack of alphabetized teen trauma. "Wait here. I need to ... I'll be right back, okay, Em?"

She didn't answer. Just kept moving the DVDs around, still smiling faintly. Completely unaware of the fact that we no longer have a DVD player.

Chapter Twenty-Four

THE SCENT OF DECEPTION

The rain showed no signs of stopping as I gripped the steering wheel of Emilia's hatchback. The windshield wipers struggled against the relentless downpour as water streamed down the glass in twisting, erratic paths, blurring the world outside and mirroring the tangle of fear and desperation in my mind.

I pressed harder on the gas.

I had no idea if I could recreate Evoko, but I had to try. If Charm & Petal still held anything usable, it was my last chance.

Emilia was slipping. Just like Gran.

I clenched my jaw, my hands tightening around the wheel as I turned onto Pearl Street. My heart lurched at the sight of the shop. Even through the rain-streaked glass, Charm & Petal's familiar façade stood out. The ginkgo tree swayed out front, its fan-shaped leaves shimmering with raindrops. But the windows were covered with butcher paper, smudged and streaked with dust and rain.

I drove past and turned into the alley.. The car's headlights cast jagged shadows on the brick walls, distorting everything. I parked behind the shop, killing the engine. The only sound was the rhyth-mic drumming of rain against the roof.

Taking a shaky breath, I grabbed the hammer I'd brought with me and stepped out into the cold.

The back door loomed ahead, its peeling paint and grimy window made all the more dismal by the rain dripping from the roof above. My heart pounded as I approached.

I had broken into exactly zero places before. But this wasn't some stranger's store, it was ours. My family's.

Still, that didn't make it easier.

I tightened my grip on the hammer, lifted it, and whispered, "Sorry," to the window.

Then I froze. I couldn't do it. Even now, after everything, I couldn't bring myself to smash the glass. I couldn't hurt the shop.

I lowered the hammer, rain slipping down my neck as I stood there, breath fogging up the air in front of me.

And then it hit me.

The key.

Gran used to keep a spare up here somewhere, just in case. Perhaps it would still be there.

I stood on my tiptoes and felt along the ledge above the door-frame. My fingers brushed something small and cold. A sharp pang of nostalgia cut through me. Gran had shown me this hiding spot when I was eight and obsessed with secrets. I swallowed and fit the key into the lock.

A click.

The door creaked open.

I stepped inside, and jumped as music hit me, loud and bizarrely cheerful.

"Call Me Maybe" blared from somewhere up front, Carly Rae Jepsen's voice echoing off the shelves like we were about to break into an aggressively upbeat dance number. The air smelled of sawdust and varnish, and the floor was dusted in a fine coat of pale gold, and covered in boot tracks.

A fluorescent light buzzed overhead, casting uneven yellow light into the back hallway. And beneath it all, wood scraping against wood. Rhythmic. Repetitive.

What the heck?

I crept forward, hammer still in hand, boots muffled against drop cloths and stray cardboard. A ladder leaned against the far wall. A coil of extension cord snaked across the floor, half-tucked under a crate labeled "DO NOT TRASH" in Sharpie.

I rounded the edge of the shelf and froze.

Parker stood in the middle of the shop, hunched over two sawhorses with a plank of wood clamped between them, sanding with slow, methodical strokes. He had his sleeves pushed up and sawdust in his hair, like this was just what he did on a rainy Monday night. He was humming along.

To *Call Me Maybe*.

My brain short-circuited.

"Parker?" My voice cracked.

He startled, eyes wide, the sandpaper flying from his hand.

I just stood there in shock, dripping wet and gripping my hammer like I might reenact a Viking raid at any moment.

"Anna? What are you—" He spun toward the phone on a nearby stool and hit pause, plunging the shop into awkward silence. "Uh, sorry. Renovation playlist."

I blinked. "Really?"

"I don't have to justify my pop nostalgia." His gaze dropped to the hammer in my hand, then back to my face. "Did you just break in?"

"Did you?" I shot back.

He hesitated.

It was just long enough for my brain to catch up. Every weird moment, half-answer, and deflection clicked into place. Parker's cagey answer about what brought him to town a year ago. Running into him Saturday night, toolbox in hand, brushing off where he'd just been. Not asking for details when I mentioned I'd missed our date because Emilia was arrested.

"You work for COWW," I said.

His head jerked back like I'd slapped him. For a second, he just stared at me.

"What do you know about COWW?" His voice was careful now. Too careful.

I scoffed. "Well, for starters, they're the ones who bought this building last year. Outright, in cash, when Lawrence was scheming to get it. And now here you are, sneaking around, working on renovations. Coincidence? I don't think so."

Parker hesitated before answering. "That's ... not for me to explain."

"What does that even mean?" My fingers curled into fists around my hammer.

His gaze flickered toward the floor, his expression shifting. Like he wanted to say something, but couldn't.

I should call the cops. I should scream. But Emilia didn't have time for that. And after the last time—their gloved hands bagging my bottles like evidence—I wasn't giving them another chance to ruin what little I had left.

I stepped forward. My clothes clung to me like shrink-wrap, rainwater dripping from my sleeves. The hammer was slick in my hand. Heavy.

"I don't have time for this,. I need ingredients. Real ones. I need Evoko. Emilia—" My voice cracked. "She's forgetting things."

His face shifted. Surprise. Concern. Maybe guilt. Or maybe he was just good at pretending.

I didn't wait to find out. I marched toward the fragrance bar, heart pounding, hammer still in one hand as I yanked open the first drawer with the other. It was about as graceful as you'd expect. Metal clanged against wood as I fumbled with the handle, nearly dropping the darned thing. I ended up wedging it awkwardly under one arm like some unhinged suburban warlock.

The drawer was empty. My breath hitched.

The next one was a sprinkle of dried bay and a feathered ribbon that disintegrated in my fingers. I clawed through it anyway, frantic and clumsy. A single glass vial rolled to the edge.

Behind me, I heard his footsteps. A careful step forward. "Anna—"

"There has to be something left," I snapped, not looking at him. I fumbled open another drawer. Another puff of dust. Panic was a weight on my chest now, thick and suffocating. "I need to make a counterblend. I need to fix this. She's slipping. Emilia's, she's..."

My throat closed, and the rest stuck somewhere behind my ribs.

Parker crouched beside me, his presence quiet, steady. "Anna, what's happening?"

I hesitated. I could lie. Brush him off. Accuse him. But I needed to know if I was wrong about him. Desperately. Maybe it was foolish. Maybe it was reckless. But I wanted to see his face when I said it.

I pressed the heels of my hands to my eyes. "She was poisoned," I said, barely more than a whisper. "Through a perfume. I think it's memory magic. She's forgetting things. Fast. She's not herself." I drew a ragged breath. "It's just like Gran."

And that's when his face changed. The guarded look fell away.

"Anna," he said again, softer. "I'm so sorry."

I exhaled, still digging through the remnants of the perfume bar like I could will the ingredients into existence. "I thought I could make Evoko again. I have to. But this place is empty."

Parker hesitated, then said carefully, "Not entirely."

I froze.

Slowly, I turned to face him. The hammer was still wedged under my arm, absurd and comforting all at once.

"What?"

He ran a hand through his hair, fingers dusted with sawdust. "There's a box of old stock in the basement."

A box of old stock.

Hope flared in my chest, bright and sudden. But it warred almost instantly with something colder.

The basement.

A cold, cavernous space lined with stone walls that had been standing longer than any of us. It was damp, drafty, and filled with the scent of forgotten things. Emilia and I used to call it the murder basement.

And Parker wanted me to follow him down there.

Parker was watching me carefully, like he could sense the war going on inside my head. "I promise you, I'd tell you everything if I could," he said. "But I can say that if there's any chance that box has what you need, you don't have time to second-guess me."

I swallowed hard. The silence stretched between us. Rain drummed against the papered-over windows, filling the shop with a restless, uneven rhythm.

Parker stood a few feet away, waiting. He wasn't making excuses or dodging questions. He'd offered a solution. He wasn't running from me, or attacking.

But that didn't mean I could trust him.

What if he was a murderer?

He was either part of COWW or hired by them. Either way, he was connected to the very corporation that had swept in with a briefcase full of cash and taken Gran's shop right out from under us. A corporation that was also, coincidentally, buying up bulk orders of raw elderberries, the same ingredient that had poisoned Lawrence Riviera.

And now Lawrence was in the hospital, fighting for his life. Had they taken out Lawrence, too? Maybe they were still in litigation over the deed to this shop. If they were, it would explain why it has been sitting empty. Maybe Emilia was right. The Attars hadn't been the targets at all. Maybe we'd just been caught in the wake of something much bigger.

Then Emilia's face flashed in my mind. Still pale, still humming some forgotten middle school tune, her smile tilted at the wrong angle. And if there was even a sliver of a chance that box had what I needed...

She didn't have time for my spirals.

I didn't know what to do. I stared at the darkened doorway that led to the basement.

"Fine." I tightened my grip on the hammer and nodded for Parker to go first. No way I was having him behind me.

I followed Parker through the back storage room. The basement door groaned as he pushed it open, revealing a steep, narrow staircase that looked even more ominous than I remembered. Cold, damp air curled around my ankles, thick with the scent of earth and old stone.

Parker descended first, his footsteps careful but unhurried. I hesitated at the top step, shifting the hammer in my hand. It felt heavier now. Or maybe that was just my spiraling.

Whatever. Down we go.

The stairs creaked with every step. The air grew colder, heavier. Damp stone and rotting wood pressed in around me. And beneath it all, that strange, lingering herbal scent. Like lavender that had died in captivity.

I hit the bottom step and stopped short.

The basement stretched out in front of us, stone walls curving around in a soft, ominous arc. And along the entire far wall, floor to ceiling, stacked in neat rows, were green plastic storage totes.

Dozens of them.

Maybe hundreds.

All labeled in Gran's tight, slanted handwriting.

My stomach dropped. "You said there was *a* box."

"There is," Parker said, already moving toward the shelves. "That one has finished perfumes. Thought that might be the most useful place to start."

I didn't move.

Couldn't.

I was too busy staring at the sheer *amount* of inventory boxed up and gathering dust. All of Charm & Petal, packed away like old tax records.

My voice came out low and sharp. "Are you kidding me?"

Parker turned halfway, cautious. "What?"

"I've been scouring for decent ingredients and placing orders online for mass-market trash, and meanwhile *this* has been down here?"

He opened his mouth. Closed it. "That's ... I would have ... it's not really something I'm allowed to—"

"Oh no. No no no." I stepped forward, finger pointing like I was about to cast a hex. "Don't give me that corporate NDA crap. I want a name. Someone at COWW. Anyone. You want me to trust you? Then tell me *who* made the decision to hoard my family's work like this."

Parker's gaze dropped to the ground like it might open up and save him. "That's not how it works."

"So help me, Parker."

"Anna." He nodded toward the middle shelf. "That one is labeled 'finished perfumes.' Evoko may be in there, or even something close."

It was the world's most obvious subject change.

And yes, I should've called him on it.

But my heart stuttered at the words *finished perfumes*, and everything else dropped away.

I moved toward the nearest tote on the wall of shelves, simmering with outrage.

How long had all of this been sitting here? Months? A year?

COWW hadn't even bothered to *tell* me they had the inventory. Hadn't offered to return so much as a bottle cap. And Parker, standing here with his flashlight and his tragic eyes, had the nerve to act like this was some generous reveal?

I clenched my jaw and reached for a mid-level tote, the label faded but still legible: *finished perfumes.*

But before my fingers closed around it, I saw something else. Sitting on top of another bin, half-buried beneath a couple of loose labels and a dried sprig of rosemary, was a book.

A thick, leather-bound, spine-worn book.

I didn't breathe.

It was *the* book. Gran's scent grimoire.

The one that vanished the same night as the Evoko. The same night someone trashed Emilia's murder board. And here it was, sitting innocently on a shelf like it hadn't been at the heart of everything that had gone wrong.

I didn't look directly at it, just kept my body angled like I hadn't seen a thing. But my brain went full hamster wheel.

Did Parker take it? Because if he did, that meant he'd *lied* to my face on our date. When I told him it was stolen, he'd looked shocked. Genuinely shocked.

So either he was the best actor I'd ever met, or he didn't know it was down here.

Or he *did* know, and this was some elaborate ploy to make me find it on my own, to make me *think* he didn't know—

"Anna?" Parker's voice cut through the spinning. He was a few feet away, wiping off a battered old table with a dust rag he must've found somewhere. The overhead bulb buzzed above us, casting light across the room as Parker wiped down the table. "You can bring the tote over here. I cleared a spot."

I pulled the tote that said *finished perfumes* out and handed it to him, careful not to look at the grimoire again. "Here, check this one. I'll see if there's anything else worth grabbing."

He took the tote and turned toward the worktable.

Then, moving fast and quiet, I reached for the grimoire. It was warm under my fingers, the leather soft and familiar and humming with the weight of years. I slid it off the tote it rested on and crouched down, scanning the label on the cardboard container beneath it: *Fragrance Materials—Blending Stock / Inventory Backlog.*

Yes! I removed the lid. Inside were rows of tiny vials and crumpled waxed paper, each labeled in careful script. Dried resins, powdered roots, corked bottles of essential oils, some ambered with age, others still bright and biting. The scent that hit me was rich and heady, like creativity in exile. But I only had seconds.

I shoved the grimoire inside, wedging it beneath a bundle of dried orris root, then secured the lid and stood up like nothing had happened.

"Hey," Parker called from the worktable, holding up a small bottle. "This one's unlabeled, but it's got that sharp citrus thing going on. Kind of reminds me of Evoko?"

I moved toward him, hope flaring. Then fading as soon as I took a whiff. It was close, but not quite right. Too bitter, no hint of the warm finish Gran always layered in. Not Evoko.

I scanned the rest of the table, picking up one bottle after another. Some were newer blends, others old enough to have handwritten tags curling at the corners. But none of them were it. No Evoko.

I swallowed my disappointment and nodded toward the tote of ingredients I'd hidden the grimoire inside. "That's okay. I'll take this one instead. I can work with this at home."

Parker raised a brow but didn't question it. "Sure."

I cradled the tote in my arms and offered a tight smile. "Thanks. I've got to get back to Emilia."

"Everything okay?"

"Yeah. Just... need to check on her." I was already moving toward the door, heart drumming with urgency that had nothing to do with perfume.

"Anna—"

But I was already climbing the stairs, tote in my arms, adrenaline in my bloodstream.

He didn't stop me.

I didn't look back.

I pushed into the hall, into the dim light of the storm, and out the door before my spiraling brain could talk me into doing something stupid, like trusting him.

The wind slammed into me the second I stepped outside. Rain poured in sheets, cold and punishing. I clutched the tote to my chest and sprinted for the car, the alley narrowing around me.

And then I saw it.

A figure.

Standing by my car, raincoat drawn tight and an umbrella angled low enough to shadow their face.

My heart stuttered. It couldn't be Parker; I had just left him behind in the basement. And definitely not Lawrence.

A spike of panic shot through me, quick and electric. My muscles coiled, every instinct screaming at me to run.

Move. NOW.

I turned and sprinted for the door. The rain blurred everything, my breath loud in my ears, mixing with the steady drumming of water on pavement. The tote thudded against my ribs as I held it close.

My foot hit a slick patch.

Too fast. No traction.

My body pitched forward.

Instinct took over. I curled around the tote, shielding it with my arms as I hit the ground hard. My knee slammed into the asphalt. Pain flared white-hot in my elbow where it scraped and twisted beneath me.

But the tote stayed in my grasp, lid still secured.

I lay there for a second, stunned, the rain soaking through my clothes, the ache spreading. My knee throbbed. My elbow burned.

Relief surged through me, chased immediately by dread.

Footsteps.

Steady. Unhurried. Getting closer.

I forced myself up to my knees, the pain sharp enough to blur the edges of my vision. My hands slipped on the wet pavement, palm slicing on something. I hissed through my teeth.

Somewhere in the rain, the figure moved, half-shadowed beneath a too-large umbrella.

There was something about the posture.

My heart stuttered.

Get up. Move. *Move.*

I tried to stand. My knee buckled.

Too late.

A shadow loomed over me. And a smell. Bergamot.

Then, a voice. Soft. Familiar.

"Oh, Anna. You really shouldn't be out here all alone."

Chapter Twenty-Five

SECRETS

Rain slithered down my neck and into my collar, chilling me to the bone. The alley's cobblestones beneath me were slick, uneven, digging into my knees where I'd fallen. Dim light from the shop's back window cast fractured reflections in the puddles, flickering each time the wind rattled the hanging bulb above the door.

My knee throbbed, sharp and insistent. Then when I tried to grab onto the storage tote full of perfume ingredients and push myself upright, pain lanced through my elbow and up my arm. I gasped and stilled, the cold sinking deeper.

And a shadowy, bergamot-scented figure loomed over me.

"Anna, what happened?" The voice cut through the storm. It was gentle, almost chiding, like I'd been caught sneaking cookies before dinner.

I blinked against the rain, my pulse a roar in my ears.

Tabitha Root.

Her braid was plastered to her shoulder, soaked through. Her long coat clung to her frame, darkened by rain. And in her hand was a ridiculous, charming, utterly useless umbrella, now turned inside out by the wind. She didn't look like a villain. She looked like someone who'd just stepped out of an indie folk album cover. And yet, every hair on my neck stood on end.

"Let me help you," she said, already reaching for me.

I scrambled backward on the slick pavement, pain flaring from what seemed like every part of my body. I clutched the perfume ingredients to my chest. "Stay back."

Tabitha blinked, but didn't move.

My heart thundered as the pieces clattered into place. How she'd hovered by Gran's grimoire that first day at the farmers market, her fingers trailing the edge of the worn leather cover like it meant something to her. The way she'd wrapped me in a hug afterward, warm and familiar, her shawl perfumed with bergamot. And later, that same sharp and citrusy scent lingering in the foyer of our house after someone broke in and stole the very grimoire Tabitha had been eyeing.

"You were in our house," I said, my voice hoarse. "You stole the grimoire."

My chest tightened, but I stayed upright with the tote clutched in my arms, wobbling slightly as the wind picked up again.

Something flickered in her eyes. Alarm? Regret? Too slippery to name.

Did I really think she'd killed Mom? They'd been best friends since childhood. And if the grimoire was her motive, why wait a year to take it?

Still, I couldn't ignore how conveniently trained she was, with her pharmaceutical background and her deep herbal knowledge.

"And Lawrence," I said slowly, watching her face. "Did you poison him? Like you poisoned my mom?"

Tabitha stepped forward, then caught herself. Her arms fluttered at her sides, settling against her chest like she didn't trust herself to touch me. Her shawl, soaked through, dripped steadily onto the cobblestones.

"Oh, honey," she said, voice husky with rain and something deeper. "None of this is what you think."

"Try me," I snapped.

She exhaled through her nose, the breath fogging slightly in the cold. "I did steal the grimoire. I won't lie to you."

"And my Evoko," I said. "And you destroyed Emilia's murder board."

Tabitha blinked. The wind howled through the alley. "I didn't touch the Evoko. When I took the book, it was still there. And I don't know what murder board you're talking about."

A lie? No. Her confusion seemed real. Too raw to be rehearsed.

"I didn't break in. Not really," she added, brushing wet hair off her face with the back of her wrist. "I used the spare key. It was still above the porch door. Just like Margaret used to keep it, tucked under that chipped bit of wood."

That hit me harder than I expected. A memory unspooled of Gran's hands pressing the little wooden sliver back into place, telling us it was "just in case."

And then I remembered something else. I'd only smelled the bergamot in the foyer and dining room. Not the kitchen or upstairs

Maybe Tabitha was telling the truth. She hadn't gone through the whole house.

My thoughts spun, colliding.

"You're not making sense."

"Because none of this is simple." Her voice caught, rough as dried sage. "Because I loved your mother. I would've done anything to protect her."

The rain blurred her face, streaking over the freckles on her cheeks, over the silver threads at her temples. Her expression wavered, something old and aching rising up.

She stepped back, giving me a full arm's length of space. "You're bleeding. You're freezing." Her tone was gently coaxing. "Please.

Come inside. Let me clean those wounds and explain everything. You can leave after, if you still want to."

The rain beat against my shoulders. My legs trembled, not from fear, but cold, exhaustion, loss.

I wanted to run. But curiosity was a stubborn thing. It curled into your bones and kept your feet planted when they should flee.

Still gripping the tote, I stood and took one step. Then another. And followed her inside.

Charm & Petal was warm and golden when we entered the shop, the lights casting a honeyed glow that made everything feel unreal. The storm still howled beyond the windows, but in here, it was quiet.

Parker sat perched on one of the tall workstools near the counter, one boot hooked on the lower rung, fingers tapping a restless rhythm against his knee. At the sound of the door, he stood so fast the stool wobbled behind him. His eyes locked onto mine first, wide with worry, then dropped to the state of me soaked, shivering, and hobbling.

"Anna, what happened?"

I didn't answer. Couldn't. My breath was coming in shallow gasps, adrenaline still racing, the pain in my knee, elbow, and hand a dull throb that echoed up my arm. Rainwater dripped from my fingertips, streaking rust-colored trails down my wrist where it mingled with blood.

"Come here," Tabitha murmured, her voice soft but certain. Her hand hovered near my elbow.

My knees felt like water, and my pride had already been scraped raw by cobblestones and rain. So I let her lead me.

The small round table beside the register looked exactly the way Gran had left it—scuffed wood, a crooked little drawer, and the faintest stain from a spilled tincture that had always smelled like aniseed. The sight of it nearly undid me.

I collapsed into the chair with a wet squelch. My clothes clung, my hair dripped, and my hand throbbed like it had its own storm brewing inside.

Tabitha crouched beside me, her coat puddling on the floor. She reached into one of those cavernous pockets and pulled out a little round weather-worn tin with a label faded to near nothing.

Of course she had balm on her.

"This'll sting," she said, her voice still that maddening blend of kind and calm. She opened the tin with practiced fingers. A wave of scent rose up—lavender, comfrey, and something else. Something cooler. Older. It hit the back of my throat like silver moonlight.

I flinched when she reached for me, and she paused, her hand hovering in the air.

"You can do it yourself, if you'd rather," she offered.

I didn't take the tin. I didn't move at all.

Maybe it was the exhaustion. Maybe it was the memory of my mother's hands doing this same ritual, cleansing, soothing, mending, always with something homemade and herb-stained.

Or maybe it was that darned scent, weaving its way through my fear.

Slowly, I extended my palm first.

Tabitha's touch was gentle, her fingers cool and certain as she smoothed balm over the gash in my palm. The pain flared once, bright and biting, then began to ebb.

I stared, stunned, as the angry red scrapes softened, pinkened, and then—before my eyes—began to knit together. Not gone entirely. Just ... healing. Faster than it should. Cleaner than it should.

I looked up sharply. "Is that ... magic?"

Tabitha met my eyes. "Yes."

I drew my hand back like it had caught fire.

"You used magic on me," I said.

"I used healing balm on a wound," she replied, voice still maddeningly even. "The magic's just part of the recipe."

She set it on the table, then folded her hands in her lap like she was waiting. For permission to tend my other wounds, maybe. Or forgiveness. Or judgment.

I didn't speak. Not yet.

Because my hand was whole.

Because the scent in the balm reminded me of my mother.

Because my mom's best friend—my Auntie—had also stolen Gran's grimoire, and that kind of contradiction had no easy shape.

Behind me, Parker shifted, his boots creaking faintly on the floorboards.

I still wasn't ready to look at him. To discover what, exactly, his role was in this.

Tabitha sat back on her heels. Her hands, still slick with balm, rested lightly on her thighs.

I looked at her, searching her face for something I couldn't quite name. "Why did you take the grimoire?"

"I just wanted to *see* it," she said. "Your sister's always home, and I didn't want to make a scene. But then I saw you both at the Cozy Cup, and I thought maybe this was my only chance."

"To break into our house and steal from us."

"I wasn't going to *take* it," Tabitha went on. "I only meant to read a few pages. Just to be near it again." She hesitated, her voice thinning. "But while I was there, someone else came in through the office window. I panicked. Grabbed the book and ran."

She lifted her head, rain-slick strands of hair clinging to her cheek. "I'm sorry. I didn't see who it was."

Her tone held that simple, aching note that comes with regret that's been sitting too long in the chest.

I stared at her. "Why didn't you bring it back? Or go to the police?"

Tabitha blinked, like the idea had never even occurred to her. "What, ring up the police and tell them that while I was breaking into a house, I saw someone else breaking in?" She gave a short, breathless laugh. "They'd have locked me up first."

I didn't laugh. "Still. You had the book for a week."

Her eyes dropped, her fingers tightening slightly around the tin in her hands. "I was embarrassed," she admitted. "And ... curious. To have that much time with the book was more than I ever thought I'd get. I kept telling myself I'd give it back. I was going to. When we..." She stopped, lips pressing into a line. "I didn't mean for it to get this far."

I didn't answer right away. My thoughts were still a snarl of fear and fury, wrapped tight in the bitter aftertaste of magic.

"You could've asked."

The silence that followed stretched, thick as smoke. Parker hadn't moved from where he stood, still a step behind the counter, still staring at me like I might vanish if he blinked. His eyes dropped to my healed hand, then back to my face.

"Are you okay?" he asked.

"No," I said, voice flat. I didn't have room for him right now, not with everything else crashing in. My elbow throbbed. My knee ached. And the words I wanted to hurl at Parker were too tangled to come out clean.

Then, as if summoned by tension itself, the bell over the shop door jingled.

We all turned.

Marianne swept in, wrapped in a navy cloak that dripped rain across the threshold. She carried two grocery bags.

She took one look at our faces—mine pale and pinched, Tabitha soaked through, Parker stiff as stone—and smiled like we were all just slightly behind schedule for a dinner party.

"Well," she said, with perfect calm, "looks like I walked in just in time."

Chapter Twenty-Six

LEGACY

Marianne set the grocery bags on the nearest counter and shoved back her hood. Her silver-threaded hair sprang out in every direction.

I leaped to standing, and immediately regretted it as my knee throbbed.

Marianne looked at me, then at Parker, then at Tabitha, and smiled like this was just a slightly awkward dinner party.

"Looks like everyone's tense, soaked, and halfway to a hex," she said. "So, we might as well eat."

She pulled a container from the bag and shoved it into Parker's hands. "Heat that on the stove, would you, sweetheart? You know where the knobs are."

He hesitated for half a second, then took the container without a word and disappeared through the doorway into the back room. I heard the creak of the old stove cabinet opening, the clatter of a pot, the hiss of the burner catching.

Marianne turned back to me, taking in my crossed arms, the way I stood half-turned toward the door like I might bolt. "You've got questions. That's good. Questions mean you're still thinking clearly."

"I don't have time for questions," I said, eyeing the storage tote full of perfume supplies on the table next to me. "My sister needs me."

Marianne's expression sharpened, though her voice stayed even. "Then all the more reason not to go off half-prepared."

"She's not just upset," I almost shouted. "Something's wrong with her. Really wrong."

Marianne took a step closer. Her demeanor wasn't at all threatening, but it made me want to back up anyway, and I hated that. I hated that I didn't know if she was on my side.

"You want to help her," she said. "Of course you do. But leaping in blind doesn't make you brave. It makes you reckless."

I flinched. "So what? You want me to sit here and sip tea while she gets worse?"

"I want you to know what you're up against," she said.

Tabitha held out a mug. Her hands were steady, but her face was tight. "Sit. Please."

I didn't move. I stared at the mug, then at her. Then back at the door.

These women had held me when I scraped my knees as a kid. They'd made me rose water cookies and taught me how to bind herbs with twine. They'd loved my mom like a sister.

And yet now we were trading lines like we were on opposite sides of something no one would name out loud.

Finally, I sat, warily, like I was expecting the chair to collapse beneath me. My legs didn't feel totally solid anymore.

Marianne reached into her bag and pulled out a heavy silver thermos. Mugs followed—handmade, chipped, none of them matching. The setup felt too practiced. Too *ceremonial*.

She lined the mugs on the counter, unscrewed the thermos, and started pouring.

"Clove. Lemon balm. Honey. For grounding," she said, as if reading my mind and offering proof of innocence.

I took the mug she handed me, both hands wrapped tight around it. It was warm and slightly sticky at the rim. Comforting. Familiar.

I watched them. But I didn't sip. Not yet. The worn little table, the mismatched mugs, the scent of lemon balm and honey curling through the room didn't feel casual. It felt like a gathering before a battle. I just didn't know if I was having tea with comrades or enemies.

I didn't know who was lying.

I just knew someone had to be.

"We're part of something called the "Council of Wise Women," Marianne said, folding her hands atop the table. "COWW, if you like acronyms. We use what you'd probably call herbalism, aromatherapy, and sometimes a little ... extra. We help where we can. Quietly."

My grip on the mug tightened. "Like a secret society."

"A benevolent one," Tabitha added. "And very disorganized. We're better at tea than treason."

Marianne grinned. "That's true. The closest thing to world domination we've done is reorganize the farmer's market booth chart."

Something inside me shifted. I was finally getting the answers I've been seeking, but it still wasn't making sense.

"*You're* COWW? *You* bought Charm & Petal?" I asked.

Marianne nodded. "Lawrence was trying to turn it into a Green-Mart. We stepped in through COWW. Bought it outright."

"Then left it to rot? Didn't tell my family? Me?"

"We preserved it," Tabitha reached across the table, resting her hand on mine. "Anna your mom passed before we could surprise her with the deed. Then Margaret got sick. Everything happened so fast. It wasn't the time."

I swallowed hard, the mug heavy in my hands.

"We kept it in the hopes you would come back," Tabitha continued, her voice soft but steady. "And when you did, and started selling perfumes at the farmers market, we knew it was time to get Charm & Petal ready for its next owner. So, we hired Parker to help get the shop ready for you."

"It was supposed to be a surprise," grumbled Tabitha.

My throat felt thick, my heart tighter still. I let my gaze drift away from their kind, patient faces and over the bones of the shop. The front counter still had that same notch where Gran used to slam down her big ledger book, swearing under her breath when her reading glasses slipped down her nose. The old hanging shelves were empty now, but I could still picture the rows of tiny vials lined up like soldiers, each labeled in her neat, looping script. A tarp was folded in the corner, and the walls wore fresh patches of plaster where someone had clearly been mid-renovation.

Charm & Petal wasn't abandoned. It was waiting.

All this time, I thought we'd lost the shop. Thought Gran's legacy was gone. But it hadn't been sold out from under us. It had been saved.

"I don't get it," I said, though my voice lacked the sharp edges it might've held before. "Why me?"

Tabitha's smile was tinged with something like nostalgia. She leaned back, her fingers tracing the rim of her mug, eyes distant, as if she were seeing not just me, but the little girl who used to play with empty bottles behind the counter.

"We always knew it was you," she said. "You were the one who inherited the family talent. Emilia has her own strengths, her own kind of magic. But perfume? That's always been yours."

Marianne reached into the satchel slung over the back of her chair and pulled out a weathered envelope, thick with old photographs. She handed it to me without a word.

I slid the contents out. The scent of aged paper arose. On the top was a photo of six girls, shoulder to shoulder, smiling for the camera. Each wore a small sprig of rosemary pinned to their collar. The photo was faded and curled, but their expressions were lit with anticipation and nerves.

In the front row, beaming with one dimple deep in her cheek, was my mother.

Marianne tapped the picture. "This was our induction ceremony. We were thirteen. Your mom was so nervous she spilled chamomile tea down her skirt just before the photo." Her smile softened with the memory. "You're part of it, Anna. Even if no one told you."

Her eyes met mine. "We hope you'll want to be. But it's your choice. We're not here to force anything."

I blinked at her. "So, you what? Just hovered in the background? Followed me at markets? Left weird gaps in booth assignments?"

"Yes," they said in unison, grinning like Cheshire cats.

I stared, half-exasperated. "Why not just tell me?"

Marianne's smile dimmed, touched with solemnity. "Because you weren't ready. Not to see what this place really is. Not to believe."

They weren't wrong. Until recently, I hadn't even believed my perfume held real magic. I looked down at the mug in my hands, steam curling upward. "I thought I was alone."

Tabitha reached across the table, her fingers brushing mine. "You never were."

I set the mug down. My hands were trembling. The warmth wasn't enough anymore. My world had just shifted on its axis, and I was still catching up.

Tabitha and Marianne watched me, patient and calm, like they'd seen this moment unfold before. Like this was how it always went—the disbelief, the wonder, the grief.

I looked back at the induction photo. My mom, thirteen and glowing, stepping into something sacred. No one had ever handed me rosemary. No one had invited me in.

Why?

Before I could ask, Marianne spoke, her voice quieter now. "That was the last public induction ceremony. The flood came through later that day. We had to go deeper underground after that. Quiet circles. No more open gatherings."

She glanced at Tabitha, then back at me. "Everything changed after that year."

I held the photograph tighter. I hadn't been excluded because I wasn't worthy. I'd been left out because the world cracked open.

Somehow, that made it hurt less. And more.

I sifted through the rest of the photos. One after another. A group at a picnic, all gingham blankets and lemonade jars. A bonfire on the riverside, faces lit with flame and laughter.

Then one I recognized from Emilia's murder board: my mom, younger and radiant in a red swimsuit, arms around Tabitha and Marianne, all three of them grinning like they'd just pulled off something mischievous. That must have been taken the day of their induction.

The next photo was two girls, barefoot on the riverbank, arms looped around each other, faces bright with summer joy. One wore a round silver necklace, a tree captured inside a circle. Tucked into the background, almost out of frame, was a crooked elm.

My crooked elm.

Its twin trunks wrapped around each other like dancers mid-spin. Emilia and I used to climb it every summer, our legs streaked with sap and our fingers sticky-green.

That tree stood just behind the garden wall of the Attar property. Our backyard.

The induction ceremony took place at our house? How deep did the Attar COWW connections go? And what happened to COWW after the flood?

"So, COWW hasn't had any inductions for fifty years?"

Marianne and Tabitha exchanged a glance that said more than words could.

"Well," Tabitha said delicately, "not *public* ones."

"We moved the ceremonies underground," Marianne added. "Quiet. Secret. After the flood, there was too much attention on the group. Too many questions. So, we changed the initiation age to eighteen. And only for those who showed aptitude, resilience, and..." Her gaze held mine. "Readiness. That last part matters more than anything."

Tabitha gave a small nod, her smile a little wistful. "Or, as we like to say—magic, mettle, and maturity."

A slow ache settled behind my ribs.

By the time I turned eighteen, I'd been clawing to get out of Serenity Falls like the town itself was suffocating me. College was my escape. Reinvention. A chance to become someone who didn't flinch every time the whispers started or carry the weight of a last name everyone had an opinion about.

And as much as I loved those long afternoons blending scents with Gran, I'd already started pulling away. Little by little, visit by visit, until the shop became just a place I used to belong.

So no, I couldn't blame them for not inviting me into COWW.

I'd already started leaving before they ever had the chance.

And Emilia was in her wild girl phase then. Half fire, half heartbreak, still raw from Danny's death and determined to outrun the ache with noise and rebellion.

We were both flailing in our own ways. Neither of us would've been ready.

Not then.

But now? Seeing that tree—*our* tree—in the corner of the frame of that photo made everything real in a way nothing else had. Even more than seeing mom in the induction class photo. This wasn't some abstract legacy. It wasn't distant or theoretical.

It was *home*.

I took one last look at the photo before tucking them back into the envelope and holding it out to Marianne. "I understand now. Why I wasn't inducted. I wasn't ready."

Tabitha's smile was soft, proud. "No shame in that."

Marianne waved the envelope away. "You keep them."

I held the envelope. The weight of the photographs settled into my hands like something sacred. Then, carefully, I tucked it into the inner pocket of my jacket—close to my heart, and safe from the rain. Only then did I reach for my tea again, the mug still warm between my palms.

And this time, when I drank, I didn't hesitate. The honey clung to the rim. The herbs settled low in my chest.

And something else—something older, deeper—unfurled quietly beneath my ribs.

Like trust.

Like knowing.

The storm still raged outside, wind howling against the windows like it had a bone to pick. Rain lashed in heavy sheets, turning the glass panes to shifting watercolor.

Parker entered the room, balancing a tray with four steaming bowls of soup and a small plate stacked with golden, fragrant rosemary rolls. He moved carefully, almost reverently, setting the tray down on the table like it might break under the weight of everything we weren't saying.

For a moment, none of us moved.

Then Marianne reached for a bowl, handed it to me. "Now, I think there's one more truth that needs clearing."

Parker stood near the counter, arms folded, expression shuttered. His gaze flicked to Tabitha.

Tabitha fidgeted with her spoon, stirring a soup that didn't need stirring. She didn't meet my eyes.

Parker sighed, a low, resigned sound. Then he looked at me directly. "Could I have a moment with Anna? Alone."

Tabitha set her spoon down with a clink and gave a rueful smile. "Sweetheart, you're about as likely to get rid of us as you are to stop that storm with a hairdryer."

Parker didn't even try to argue.

Marianne let out a theatrical sigh. "Tabs, maybe we should give them a little space."

Tabitha opened her mouth to protest, but Marianne cut her off with a look.

With a grumble and a reluctant scrape of her chair, Tabitha stood. She patted my hand. "Just hear him out. He's good people."

Marianne winked at me. "We'll be in the back. Definitely not with our ears pressed to the door."

They bustled toward the rear hallway. Before they disappeared, they both turned and smiled at me with mischief and auntie-level concern. And oddly, the ridiculousness of it all—their nosiness, their complete, unshakeable loyalty—settled something inside me. It was like being wrapped in a crocheted blanket made of sarcasm and love.

The door clicked shut. And just like that, it was me and Parker.

He stood motionless, hands loose at his sides, his expression unreadable. That same quiet concern flickered across his face. The one I used to trust. The one I'd let in.

And maybe that was what made the betrayal worse.

"You knew," I said to him. My voice cracked. "You sat across from me and listened while I talked about my mom. About perfume. About magic. And you just, what? Took notes?"

Parker shifted his weight, mouth parting like he wanted to speak, but didn't.

"Was any of it real? The date, the way you looked at me?" I pushed to my feet, heat rising beneath my skin. "Or was it just part of the job?"

"It wasn't like that," he said, too quickly.

"Then what was it like?" My voice climbed. "Were you spying on me? Trying to figure out if the Attar girl had powers too?"

He didn't answer, but his silence said enough.

I took a step forward, fury sharpening every word. "You were in on this from the beginning, weren't you? Fixing up the shop, pretending not to know what COWW was, lurking in the basement like some undercover—"

"I wasn't pretending," he cut in. "Not all of it. I didn't know everything, not at first. But yes, I was sent here."

The words hit harder than I expected. "You were *sent* here?"

"By my mother." His jaw tightened. "Monica Morgan-Wells."

Morgan. The name curled around me like smoke.

He hesitated. "Carolyne Morgan was my aunt."

I blinked. "Wait. *The* Carolyne Morgan? The one who—"

"Drowned."

I crossed my arms, heart pounding so hard it hurt. "So your mom sent you here. What, to report back if we started chanting in Latin and stirring up whirlpools in the backyard?"

He exhaled, rubbing the back of his neck. "She said I was just supposed to observe. Keep an eye on things around the fifty-year mark. Make sure nothing ... flared up. Her words. She thought it might be some kind of magical cycle. That something bad could happen again, and that your family might be behind it, whether you knew it or not."

"Because clearly, the perfume makers might be a threat."

"Mom always believed there was more to it," Parker said. "She told me Evelyn was reckless, doing spells she didn't understand. That Carolyne got caught in the flood Evelyn started."

I stared. My lungs forgot how to breathe.

"She doesn't think Evelyn meant to hurt anyone," he added quickly, like that might soften it. "But in her eyes, that doesn't matter. It was still her fault. And when no one was held responsible ... well, the grudge kind of calcified."

I studied the set of his jaw, the way his eyes wouldn't quite meet mine now. My brain was spinning, trying to line up the dates, the moments, the strange timing.

"You came here a year ago," I said slowly. "Right around when my mom was murdered."

The air froze between us.

I took a step forward. "Was it before or after?"

Parker looked away, then back. "About two weeks before."

It took a moment for the meaning to sink in. "So you were already in place. Watching my family."

He winced. "I didn't kill your mom, Anna. I swear to you, I would *never*. I didn't even know what was happening until it was too late. I inherited this whole stupid family feud like a bad family heirloom. I didn't ask for any of it. Would I have stuck around this long if I had something to hide?"

I stared at him, anger and confusion warring inside me. "Then why *did* you stick around?"

And then it hit me. The way he talked about his family on our date, calling himself a lone wolf. The look on his face when I asked if he had family here. I could tell then he had some sort of falling out with them, but I hadn't pressed at the time.

"You thought it was them," I ventured. "You thought your family murdered my mom."

"They swear to me they didn't," he said, voice cracking now. "But I was scared they might've. And if they did, I had to know."

The silence that followed was thick with everything unsaid—grief, guilt, something dangerously close to understanding.

"But there's one thing I still don't get. Why would anyone think the Attars could even cause a flood? We're perfumers. We're not—"

"Not what?" said a voice behind me.

I turned to find Marianne leaning casually in the doorway, arms crossed, one eyebrow arched like she hadn't just been eavesdropping on every word.

Beside her, Tabitha cradled her mug of tea with both hands, the picture of innocence. If innocence came with a smug smile.

"Not weather witches," I muttered, feeling heat crawl up the back of my neck.

Tabitha's lips quirked. "You'd be surprised how much influence scent and storm share."

I looked back at Parker. "So, you came here thinking my family was dangerous?"

"I only knew what my mom's family always said about the Attars." He hesitated. "But I didn't know what to think. I didn't even want to come. And somewhere along the line, I stopped reporting back."

"Why?" I asked, flatly.

He met my eyes. "Because I started caring about *you* more than the stories they told me."

I looked away first. My chest ached in too many directions. I didn't trust him. Not fully. But some stubborn, grieving spark in me believed that part of him was real.

Maybe the most important part.

Marianne refilled my tea like we hadn't just unearthed fifty years of inter-family curses and storm-scented suspicion. "Well," she said cheerfully, "this is going better than I expected."

The air in Charm & Petal was thick with secrets, the scent of rosemary rolls, and a lifetime of memories. I sat at the table that had once belonged to Gran, wrapped in an oversized sweater Tabitha had conjured from some forgotten drawer, sipping tea made by women who claimed to be part of a coven.

A real one.

Magic was real.

And so, apparently, was everything I'd never been told.

Tabitha, Marianne, and Parker had each pulled back the veil in different ways. And maybe it wasn't everything, but they weren't hiding anymore. Not from me.

I stared at my tea, watching the flecks of herbs swirl and settle, the way they used to in Mom's kitchen. Lemon balm and chamomile. The comfort blend.

"I need help with Emilia," I said softly.

Marianne looked up, one brow arched. "You have it."

And I did. For the first time in perhaps ever, I knew I wasn't carrying it all alone. I told them everything. About Emilia's symptoms, the surprise perfume, my theory that Evoko might save her. And when I finished, they got to work helping me recreate Evoko.

Marianne scribbled notes like a woman preparing for battle. Tabitha unpacked the ingredients, setting vials and bottles down with practiced care. Parker stayed by the window, watching the street. But when our eyes met, he nodded.

And sure, I was still scared. But the weight of it didn't crush me like it had before.

Chapter Twenty-Seven

MAGIC

"This time, your ratios are leaning floral," Marianne said, her voice low and observational. She sipped from a ceramic mug, legs tucked beneath her on the worktable's bench like some kind of crystal-slinging cat.

"I know." My focus stayed on the bottle in my hand, the blend blooming beneath my nose. "It's what Mom used to wear. Rose and Jasmine. It always made the attic smell like spring."

Marianne smiled at that, said nothing more.

I stood behind the blending table—the same worn oak slab my mother had used, and her mother before her, and her mother before that. The surface was scarred and ringed with oil marks, dusted with powdered resin and the pink flecks of crushed rose petals. My sleeves were rolled to the elbows, fingers smudged. The grimoire lay open beside me, Gran's handwriting looping in faded ink through the margins, but I wasn't really reading anymore.

Not today.

I wasn't measuring down to the tenth of a gram or checking pH levels against an old perfumer's log. I didn't double-check the drop count or recalibrate the scale. I just ... listened. To the scent. To the space between ingredients. To the way my chest tightened when something was off and loosened again when it clicked into place.

And somewhere in the middle of it, I felt it.

Magic.

Steady. Sure. Like it had finally decided I was safe.

I wasn't denying it anymore. Or disparaging it. Or pushing it away like an unwanted heirloom. I had come to embrace it, and in doing so, I think magic had begun to embrace me back.

Tabitha was at the side table, grinding frankincense in a small stone bowl with methodical care. The scent was warm and earthy, heavy with something ancient. A comfort.

Parker stood by the stovetop distiller, coaxing steam through the tangle of glass pipes and copper coils. He looked utterly out of place in his flannel work shirt and sawdust-flecked curls, and yet completely at home. The petals and citrus rinds inside the distiller began to yield their secrets one breath at a time.

The shop was still a construction zone. Trim unfinished. Boxes stacked in the corners. But the air hummed with quiet purpose. Magic stirred in the corners, subtle and steady. As if the act of making perfume here again had woken something old and patient.

I closed my eyes and breathed in. I couldn't afford to screw this up. And I couldn't afford to rush it either. If I pushed the blend too soon, it would fall apart. But if let my fear slow me down, we might lose Emilia for good.

So I sat in the center of the half-renovated chaos, sleeves rolled, heart pounding, listening to the scent, and hoped it was listening back.

I picked up a vanilla bean infusion and pulled the stopper free. The scent rose soft and golden, like warm sugar and sunlit wood. The gentle, familiar fragrance wrapped around me. For a moment, I swore I could hear my mother humming.

That lullaby. The one Emilia had sung to herself the night after the funeral, trying to fall asleep.

I added three drops, because that felt right.

"You're not checking your notes," Parker said.

"I don't need to. I remember." And I did.

I remembered the way my mother's perfume used to smell after a rainstorm. The way Gran's hands smelled of myrrh and mint and a hint of something piney after hours at the shop. The way Emilia had once begged me to bottle the scent of toasted marshmallows on Christmas Eve.

Scent was memory.

And memory was magic.

I swirled the ingredients together in a glass bottle etched with a sigil I hadn't consciously chosen. One my hand had drawn before my brain caught up. It was a small spiral wrapped around a drop. Evoko's true form—a call to memory. A tether.

I held it up to the light. The liquid shimmered, soft gold and pale pink, like sunrise through fog.

"This is it," I said. "It's ready."

The scent in the air shifted. Even the rain at the windows softened, like it knew not to interrupt.

I looked down at the bottle again, my hand trembling just a little.

Please work. Please bring my sister back to me.

Tabitha wiped her hands and stepped forward. She nodded once, solemn as a priestess preparing for ritual.

"Then it's time."

I didn't remember walking upstairs. The familiar creak of the third step must've happened. I just hadn't registered it. A soft lamplight glowed from the hallway sconce, catching on the gallery wall of old family photos. Generations of Attars watching silently as I passed.

The bottle of Evoko was still warm in my hand, cradled like something living. The sigil etched in the glass pulsed faintly in the low light, echoing the rhythm of my heart—which had decided, now of all times, was the perfect moment to remember how to panic.

I paused outside Emilia's door.

Downstairs, Marianne and Tabitha's voices rose in murmurs from the living room, low and steady. I hadn't needed to ask them to come. They just had. Marianne carried her stones, her soft spells, her fierce protectiveness tucked beneath silk scarves and sharp eyeliner. Tabitha had a bundle of herbs in one hand and an unreadable expression that seemed only to indicate things were about to get serious.

Parker was posted on the porch. Quiet, steady, the weight of his presence as certain as the weather. He didn't come inside. Not tonight. Not with everything between us.

The truth still sat heavy in my chest, too big and jagged to swallow. He was a Morgan. He'd come to spy on my family. And yet here he was, standing guard like he'd always belonged. I didn't have the space to unpack it. Not when my sister was unraveling thread by thread right in front of me. So, I opened Emilia's bedroom door.

Emilia was sitting cross-legged on her bed, surrounded by an explosion of clothing, glittery eyeshadow palettes, and a tangle of earrings she'd dumped out from the little jewelry dish on her nightstand. Wearing the expression of someone on the verge of a major life decision, she looked at me and held up a silver hoop in one hand, and an earring shaped like a dangling star in the other.

"Okay," she said, turning her whole body toward me. "Be honest. Danny's totally a 'dangly stars' guy, right? I mean, the leather jacket is cool, but he has a poetic soul. You can tell."

I blinked. "Danny?"

Emilia nodded. "Danny Vance. Remember? Tall, quiet, eyes like storm clouds, rides a motorcycle he's definitely not allowed to have?" She tossed her hair and grinned. "We're going to the old art house theater and then get root beer floats. It's gonna be epic."

My throat tightened. Danny Vance had died on that very motorcycle one year into what had been the happiest, most fiercely protected relationship of my sister's life. But in this potion-twisted, time-slipped version of Emilia's mind, he was still alive, waiting for her outside in the rain with a helmet under one arm and that wry smile that had once undone her completely.

She twisted one glitter-coated wrist toward me. "Can you help me with my bracelet? I want the one with the tiny heart charm. The one he gave me."

I knelt beside her on the bed, heart aching, smile trembling at the edges. "Sure, Em. Of course."

She leaned in conspiratorially, lowering her voice. "Do you think he'll try to kiss me tonight?"

"Oh, I'd count on it," I said, fastening the bracelet and blinking fast.

For a moment, I let her have it. The fantasy. The dress-up. The nerves. It was so vivid in her eyes. So real. And maybe, in some strange way, the magic would honor that. Maybe the echo of that love could lead her back.

Because love like that didn't vanish. It just got buried. And I was about to help her dig it up.

Emilia turned back to the dresser, sifting through the clutter until her hand paused over a small bottle nestled beside her tangled bracelets and a lopsided ceramic cat. She picked it up with a pleased little gasp. "Ooh! This one's pretty. I don't think I've ever noticed it before."

My breath stopped.

Joy.

It looked just as I remembered it. The delicate script I'd handwritten on the label was now smudged at the edges. The teardrop-shaped glass was dusted with a shimmer that had settled like powdered moonlight. I hadn't seen it in years. I didn't even know she still had it, let alone kept it out where she could see it every day.

My heart gripped. *She kept it.* But I couldn't let her wear it. Not tonight. Not with the spell still sunk deep into her bones.

I reached out and curled my fingers around her wrist before she could uncap it. "Try this one instead."

Then I pressed the warm bottle of Evoko into her palm. As soon as she touched it, the sigil etched in the glass shimmered brighter, like it recognized her. "This one's new. I made it just for tonight."

She looked at me, eyes wide. "Wait, really? You made me a custom perfume for my first date with Danny?"

"Of course I did," I said, as lightly as I could, though my voice snagged a little on the words. "Only the best for my little sister."

Emilia let out an exaggerated swoon and collapsed backward onto the pillows for a moment before popping back up again. "You're the *best*. Seriously. The *actual* best. I don't tell you that enough."

"You don't," I teased. "But I'll allow it."

She grinned, then looked down at the bottle in her hand. Her expression softened just a touch. She held it out to me. "You do the honors?" she asked, like it was a secret ritual. Like we were kids again, sitting cross-legged on my bedroom floor, pretending we were queens preparing for a royal ball.

"Yeah." A lump rose in my throat. "Of course."

She beamed at me, then tilted her head, thoughtful. "Hey ... I should probably say I'm sorry, too."

I arched a brow. "For what?"

"For sneaking into your room and borrowing your green lace top without asking. The one you were saving for the Spring Fling? I got mustard on it, and I panicked and stuffed it behind the dryer."

My jaw dropped. "*You* ruined that top?"

"I meant to tell you, but you thought it was Lisa Marconi and she was so mad at the accusation and it kind of snowballed." She winced. "Sorry?"

For half a second, I felt that old, familiar flare of outrage rise up, hot and sharp and completely ridiculous. I *loved* that top.

And then I remembered.

That top had lived and died *ten years ago*.

I laughed. It burst out of me before I could stop it. "Em," I said, shaking my head, "you're lucky you're magically regressing right now, or I'd be making you scrub laundry by hand in penance."

She giggled. "I deserve that. But also, I smelled *amazing* that night. So ... worth it?"

"Unbelievable," I muttered, but there was no anger in it. Just love. So much love I could barely breathe around it.

I gave a breathy little laugh. "Trust me," I murmured, uncorking the bottle. "This is better."

I dabbed the perfume on her wrists first, then her temples in feather-light touches, each one a prayer. Finally, just above her heart.

The scent began to unfurl. Rosemary, jasmine, a whisper of vanilla. But there was something else, too. Something warm and golden. The way the air smells in late August, when the heat has finally broken and the first cool breeze carries the scent of ripe fruit and old wood.

Magic stirred.

The candle on the bedside table flickered, then flared brighter, casting golden halos across the walls. A stillness fell over the room.

Watson, curled at the foot of the bed, lifted his head. His ears swiveled, alert, eyes gone wide and glassy in the glow. He let out a single, questioning *mrrrp*, then tucked his chin back down, as if deciding whatever magic had stirred wasn't worth the trouble of investigating.

Somewhere overhead, the old beams gave a soft creak, like the house itself was settling in for whatever came next.

Emilia blinked, eyes going soft around the edges. "You smell that?"

"I do," I said, even though my throat was too tight.

The bottle in my hand gave one last glint of light, then stilled.

Something had begun.

Emilia blinked, slow and dreamlike. Her gaze drifted around the room, taking in the fairy lights, the papasan, the piles of clothes like she was seeing it all through glass.

"Did I..." Her brow knit, soft confusion settling across her features. "Did I already go on the date?"

Her voice was barely more than a breath. Small. Lost.

I opened my mouth to answer—to lie, maybe, or reassure—but she didn't wait. Her body swayed, then slumped backward onto the bed. One hand curled over her stomach. The other slipped down onto the comforter, fingers still glitter-dusted.

"Emilia?" My voice cracked. "Em. Hey. No, no, no. Don't—"

The perfume bottle slipped from my hand. I didn't hear it hit the floor. Didn't hear anything over the sudden rush in my ears. I was already leaning over her, brushing hair from her forehead, pressing my fingers to her wrist, then to her throat, desperate for proof of breath, of pulse, of *anything*.

"Em. Come on. Don't do this." My breath hitched, sharp and shallow. "Don't leave me, okay? Not like this."

Her eyelids didn't flutter. Her chest rose and fell, but slowly, so slowly. Too slowly.

Panic scraped raw against my ribs.

"Help!" I shouted, voice cracking under the weight of it. "Tabitha! Marianne!"

The footsteps were distant at first, muffled by the roaring in my ears. Then clearer, quicker, climbing the stairs.

I folded Emilia's hand into mine and pressed it against my heart, trying to will something back into her. Something real. Something remembered.

"Please," I whispered. "You have to come back. You *have* to."

She didn't move.

I gripped Emilia's hand like I could anchor her here by sheer force of will, heart thudding against my ribs like a warning bell. Her skin was warm, her eyes closed.

I didn't realize I was shaking until another pair of hands closed over mine.

Tabitha knelt beside me without a sound, her presence so calm and steady it felt like the ground itself had remembered how to hold me. She didn't speak right away, just let the quiet settle, like she was listening to something beneath the surface of the world.

There was a glow about her. A soft shimmer where her skin met the air, like she was catching the light from somewhere no one else could see. Her hand closed over mine, warm and solid, steadying my shaking grip around Emilia's fingers.

Behind her, Marianne stepped into the room with a small velvet pouch in one hand. She moved without speaking, and began placing crystals in a slow circle around the bed. Moonstone, black tourmaline, rose quartz. Each one clicked softly against the wood like punctuation marks in a spell.

Then Tabitha whispered, "It's working."

I turned toward her, heart caught somewhere between hope and fury. "How can you possibly know that?"

Her gaze didn't waver. Her hand stayed wrapped over mine, grounding. "Because magic is like memory. It doesn't always arrive all at once. It unfolds. And for that..." Her eyes flicked toward Emilia's still face. "She has to rest."

I looked back at Emilia. Her face was peaceful now, heartbreakingly so. Like someone who'd finally been allowed to sleep after too many nights afraid to close her eyes.

"But what if she forgets even more?" I whispered. "What if she doesn't come back at all?"

A soft clinking sound drew my eyes to the edge of the bed. Marianne had finished her circle of stones. She placed the final piece, a rough chunk of rose quartz, above Emilia's head.

"She won't forget," Marianne said. "Not with all this holding her."

Tabitha's expression softened. She reached up and brushed a strand of hair from Emilia's brow, tucking it behind her ear with the reverence of a priestess anointing a sacred vessel.

"She will come back," she said. "But you have to let her do it in her own time."

I stayed there, still kneeling, her hand cradled in both of mine. I looked at my sister. Her face, smoothed by sleep, seemed impossibly young. Like the girl she used to be before the world got loud and sharp. Before grief sank its teeth in. Before I learned how it felt to lose her in pieces.

Maybe that's what made it so hard to let go now. Because this was the closest she'd looked to herself in weeks. Years. And the idea of waiting—of not knowing what she'd wake up remembering or forgetting—felt like stepping out over the edge of a cliff with no promise of a net.

But I couldn't trust the magic and fight it at the same time.

I exhaled, the breath shaky but whole, and squeezed her hand.

"Okay," I whispered. "I trust you."

My thumb brushed her knuckles. I leaned in close, just enough that only she could hear.

"Come back to me."

I picked up the Evoko and sat it quietly on the nightstand, next to Joy. The etched sigil along its glass caught the lamplight and shimmered once, faint but steady.

Like a heartbeat.

CHAPTER TWENTY-EIGHT

SCIENCE

At some point, the sun had risen, but the kitchen still felt dim, as if the storm that had rolled in overnight had wrung all the color out of the world. Weak light pooled across the floorboards, just enough to make the glittery notes on the murder board sparkle.

I stood in front of it, arms crossed, eyes dry and burning. Pins, yarn, scribbled notes. Photos of Lawrence, of our mother, of Emilia beaming beside Danny. Half of it was color-coded, the other half looked like a migraine waiting to happen. The longer I stared at Emilia's murder board, the less any of it made sense.

How did detectives use these things? What were they supposed to *do* with them?

Watson rubbed against my ankle and let out a plaintive *mrrrp*, like he, too, was unimpressed by the lack of answers. I reached down to scratch behind his ears, then kept staring at the board, willing it to arrange itself into something useful.

Marianne and Tabitha had left last night, but Parker was asleep on the couch. I'd heard him settle in sometime around four. I still wasn't speaking to him. Not because I didn't believe him. I did. That was half the problem. He may have come into our lives under false pretenses, but what he was doing now was unmistakably real.

He'd stood guard over Emilia and me all night, and part of me hated how much comfort I took from that.

Because he was a Morgan, and I was an Attar. Capulet and Montague. Lancaster and York. Oil and water and whatever metaphor you wanted to slap on half a century of inherited hostility.

And yet.

My gaze dragged back to the chaotic board Emilia had left in her wake—beautiful, frenetic, all heart and instinct. She'd been the one driving this investigation, chasing leads, always two steps ahead.

But Emilia hadn't woken up yet. And her arraignment was tomorrow. If we didn't figure out who poisoned Lawrence and our mother, Emilia was going to open her eyes just in time to find herself in prison.

My hands clenched, then released. The murder board was a mess. But it wasn't *just* a mess. It was data points, waiting to be arranged. And somewhere in that wall of glitter and heartbreak, the truth was hiding.

Then it hit me. I didn't have to choose between magic and science.

I didn't have to stop being the woman who once lost entire weekends to data sets and p-values, and found solace in patterns and probabilities. That woman wasn't a rejection of my past. She was *born* of it. A girl shunned for magic, who fled into the arms of logic because it felt safer than spells.

I spun on my heel, grabbed my laptop from the counter, and opened a blank spreadsheet like I was summoning a spell of my own. Names. Dates. Evidence types. Interview notes. Potential magical anomalies. Known connections. Columns bloomed across the screen as my fingers flew, heart pounding with the force of something sacred.

The board may have been beautiful chaos, but data was something I could wield like a blade.

The clack of keys was the only sound in the kitchen now. Well, that and the low purring of Watson curled on the windowsill. My spreadsheet began to fill quickly. Clue after clue, lead after lead. I wasn't thinking like a perfumer anymore, or a grieving daughter, or a terrified sister. I was thinking like a researcher.

Emilia's notes were half chaos, half brilliance, but I knew how to translate them. I created tags, filters, conditional highlights. I linked timelines and cross-referenced witness statements. I pulled up historical weather data, text messages, info about the Purple Pantry.

My fingers flew. And slowly, a pattern began to emerge from the chaos.

Tabitha had confessed to taking the grimoire. She'd admitted it without flinching. But she'd also said someone else came in through the window and scared her off. She didn't even see the murder board, and she didn't take the Evoko.

So who had? And how did they know we weren't home?

I stared at Emilia's last notes from our visit to the Cozy Cup, my stomach tightening. Lawrence's hands. They'd trembled that day. I'd brushed it off at the time, chalking it up to age or nerves. But they'd trembled again on the bridge, just before the lightening.

My cursor blinked beside the words *bitter almond scent.*

I froze, staring at the screen. I remembered it now. That smell had clung to Lawrence at the Cozy Cup.

Bitter almond.

Cyanide.

My breath caught. Lawrence had smelled of cyanide *before* he was supposedly poisoned.

I pulled out Gran's old herbal alchemy texts, fingers moving faster now. And there it was, in a chapter on binding potions. Trace cyanide, naturally-derived, if used in minuscule amounts to root spells deep into the body, will keep someone bound.

Dangerous in the wrong hands, but not inherently malicious.

Unless the patient had built up a tolerance due to years of exposure.

Fifty-one years of exposure.

But why? I had to be sure.

I leaned back in my chair, breath shallow, pulse drumming a nervous rhythm against my ribs. Then I opened a new tab on my laptop. I entered everything I knew—ingredient purchases, theft dates, known magical signatures. Tiny fragments of data that, until now, had refused to speak the same language.

Then I added a new column: connections to Carolyne Morgan.

I hesitated, then reached for the photographs Marianne had given me. One in particular—the induction ceremony from fifty-one years ago. The paper was soft at the edges, worn from time and handling. I turned it over, careful not to smudge the faded ink. On the back was a list of names, handwritten in looping script. I started typing them into my spreadsheet, one by one.

As the names filtered in, something shifted. Not in the room, not in any obvious way. No candles flickered. No ghostly whispers curled beneath the floorboards. But the air got heavier. Denser. Like the truth itself had entered the room and sat down beside me.

The cursor blinked in the console, waiting.

My fingers hovered, then danced—*dplyr, lubridate, stringr*—like old friends greeting me after a long absence. I filtered, grouped, joined. Ran scripts I hadn't touched in weeks. I didn't need pins and yarn. I needed structure. Logic. A dataframe I could manipulate until the truth fell out like loose change.

And then, deep in the lines of code, the algorithm responded. A single name surfaced at the top of the output. Highlighted. Statistically significant. Anomaly turned anchor.

A cold breath caught in my throat. It had been there all along, woven through the timelines, magical residues, and social links. I just hadn't seen it until now.

Lawrence wasn't the murderer. But Emilia had been right to focus on him. He was the axis. Everything orbited around him.

I stared at the glowing name, a whisper of code still flickering in the console. Then, with a reverence that surprised me, I closed the laptop.

Watson let out a low, throaty *mrrrow*, his green eyes locked on mine, unblinking.

"Yeah," I said, heart still thudding. "I know."

The rain, which had been nothing more than a steady whisper against the kitchen windows, turned violent in an instant, like someone had flipped a switch. It came down in sheets, slamming the roof with a force that rattled the walls. The sky outside turned the color of bruises. Wind howled down the chimney, and the trees groaned under its weight.

Then came the weather sirens. That eerie, rising wail sliced through the storm and made the hair on my arms lift. The town's sirens weren't subtle. And they didn't sing unless something bad was coming.

Something *was* coming, and it had everything and nothing to do with my mother's murder. I could feel the truth trying to settle in my bones, but there was one puzzle piece I was still missing. I still didn't know who killed my mom. My fingers itched to return to my computer, but there wasn't time for justice. Not yet. That would have to wait.

Because this storm was more pressing. *This* was fifty-one years in the making.

I bolted for the box of supplies I had brought home last night, pulling it open with the precision of someone who had been raised to prepare for magical emergencies, even if I hadn't known it until recently. Jars clinked together. I grabbed what I needed by feel: pink grapefruit, cypress, geranium. My brain was already assembling the formula as I moved. Not a perfume for memory this time. This was something different.

I closed the door just as a crack of thunder split the sky directly overhead. The lights flickered. Something massive crashed outside—wood against wood, the splintering sound of a tree limb shattering on impact.

A clap of thunder cracked overhead, so loud the windows rattled in their panes.

"Anna?" Parker's voice came from the living room, groggy and alarmed. "Are you okay?"

"I'm fine!" I called back, heart pounding, half-wild with adrenaline and certainty. "Actually, fantastic."

A moment later, he appeared in the dining room doorway, blinking at me like I'd grown wings.

"I know what to do." I held up the bundle of ingredients. "I need to make a perfume. Now."

I dropped the ingredients on the dining room table with a clatter. My hands moved on instinct, already sorting them into piles, mentally sketching a blend sharp enough to cut through magic. Strong enough to stop what was coming.

But then I stopped.

My palms went flat against the table's surface. The wood was scarred, pitted with heat rings and candle wax. And something colder. This was where I'd worked when I'd blended the first trial version of Evoko. And where I'd left it, unguarded, only to return and find it stolen. Gran's grimoire too.

I'd told myself at the time it didn't matter. That the dining room was convenient. That I didn't *need* Gran's perfume organ. But that wasn't the truth.

The truth was, I hadn't felt worthy of it.

Gran's organ was a legacy. A cathedral of scent, built with decades of love and painstaking precision. Sitting at it felt like playing priestess in someone else's temple. But I wasn't that girl anymore. I needed all the help I could get. And more than that, I needed *her*. Gran had taught me how to blend with purpose. And right now, I needed every tool in my arsenal.

Behind me, I heard Parker step into the room. He stood there quietly, like an emotionally complicated houseplant. I didn't turn to look at him. "I need to use the organ," I said.

"Do you want help carrying things?"

I hesitated, the weight of everything unsaid pressing at my throat. I needed all the help I could get. But I had to do this part on my own.

I turned to face him. "Actually, I need you to go up. Sit with my sister. Let me know if anything changes."

He gave a small nod and went upstairs.

The moment I stepped into Gran's atelier, something in me stilled. Outside, the storm was still having its dramatic breakdown, but in here, it was like the universe hit pause.

The perfume organ stood at the center, curved and golden. Labels in Gran's precise script peeked out at me, some still wearing a dusting of petal powder like vintage makeup. The drawers were stuffed with dried herbs, parchment curls, and ribbon-tied bundles that looked like little secrets.

I moved toward it slowly and sat on the velvet stool. I set down the ingredients, unsure and slightly shaky.

I took one of those dramatic, grounding breathes you're supposed to do in yoga but that usually just makes me dizzy, and started working. Bergamot first. Then pink grapefruit. The bottles made a soft music as I moved. The scent of citrus and herbs started to rise.

I added galbanum next. Its scent was warm and strange, like standing in the eye of a storm and realizing you still don't trust the quiet.

I reached for the final notes. Vetiver, dark and earthy, grounding like roots sunk deep in rain-soaked soil. Then amber, thick and golden. A resinous prayer.

I swirled the mixture in the blending vial, and the scent rose in a slow, spiraling bloom. It shimmered in the air, unfolding in layers.

It smelled like awareness.

Like awakening.

A shimmer clung to the bottle as I sealed it. The sigil on the glass pulsed with a light not entirely from this world. I cradled it in both hands, feeling the warmth of it soak into my skin and steadying me from the inside out.

Mentis.

The first intentionally magical perfume I had ever designed entirely on my own.

And it was perfect.

I stood, bottle in hand, heart steadier than it had been in days.

But then the wind rose again, higher and wilder. The windows rattled in their frames, and thunder rolled so loudly it felt like it cracked through the floorboards. Lightning split the sky outside in a blinding flash.

And for one breathless second, I saw a figure in the yard, standing just beyond the rosemary hedge. Still. Watching. A silhouette backlit by the storm. My blood turned to ice.

Then another flash. Brighter, closer.

And the figure was gone.

I stumbled back from the window, clutching the bottle of Mentis like it could shield me. My mind spun.

Was I too late?

Chapter Twenty-Nine
Sibling Bonds

The wind shrieked, unhinged and furious as I stood frozen by Gran's window, clutching the vial of Mentis so tight it nearly cracked. Storm sirens wailed in the distance, and rain hammered the glass like it was trying to break in.

I focused on the figure hunched against the storm, brown hair plastered to her face, arms raised like she was trying to be seen. Or heard. Or maybe warn.

Susan.

I turned to call for Parker, then stopped myself. I'd rather have his protective instincts focused on keeping Emilia safe right now. Besides, I could handle this.

Lightning cracked across the yard, low and close and weirdly horizontal, like a whip made of electricity. I blinked.

She was gone.

"What the—" I muttered, heart thudding hard enough to hurt. The yard was empty. Just wind, rain, and garden shadows.

Then I heard raised voices and footsteps on the front porch. Something heavy clattered against the siding. I spun and bolted down the hallway. When I threw open the front door, the storm slapped me in the face.

Marianne stood at the steps, her cloak hood pulled low, hands trembling around a bundle of sage and rowan wrapped in red thread. Ash streaked her fingers. The charm smoldered, barely holding on. Tabitha was beside her, gripping her umbrella like she was preparing to duel the storm itself. Which, to be honest, might've been the plan. The umbrella inverted with a loud snap—again—and she cursed, before going back to her chanting. Voice hoarse, soaked to the bone, arms outstretched like she was holding back the weather with sheer will.

Susan stumbled backwards against the siding, arms raised. "Wait! Please wait! I'm not—"

"Anna!" Marianne aimed her smoldering charm at Susan. "She's been circling the house like she's checking on her *experiment*!"

"Leave her alone!" I stepped fully onto the porch. "She's not the bad guy."

Everyone turned to stare at me. Marianne's brow furrowed. Her fingers gripped the charm tighter. "You're sure?"

"She's not here to hurt us," I said. "She's here because she needs our help."

Tabitha's arms dropped a few inches, but her jaw stayed tight, her whole body coiled. Like she was two seconds away from launching an attack with her umbrella, just to be safe.

Marianne's charm sparked once, then sputtered out. Smoke curled up and vanished into the night. Silence. For a moment, everything went still.

Then Susan looked at me. Her eyes were terrified and hollow. "I can't find him," she said, voice cracking. "He's gone."

"Who's gone?" asked Marianne.

But I already knew. "Lawrence."

Susan nodded, her face crumpling. "He disappeared from the hospital last night. The storm knocked out the power. The cameras.

Everything. No one even noticed until this morning. I haven't given him his dose."

My stomach dropped. "He's unbound."

"For the first time in fifty-one years," said Susan.

Everything stilled. The storm sirens were still wailing, but they felt far away now. Or maybe my brain had just hit capacity.

A gust of wind blew the rain sideways onto the porch. I wiped my face, shivering. "We can't stay out here. Come inside. We need to talk."

Tabitha hesitated, still eyeing Susan like she might grow horns.

Marianne looked down at the soggy and dead charm in her hand. Her jaw worked once. Then she muttered, "Fine. But if she even blinks wrong, I hex first, ask questions never."

"Same," said Tabitha, shifting her grip on the umbrella handle.

Susan didn't flinch. "I wouldn't blame you."

We turned and filed inside, boots squelching, coats dripping. The storm howled behind us, rattling the windows as the door slammed shut on its own.

Parker was in the entryway, halfway to the door, eyes wide. "I was coming to find you. Everything okay?"

"No," I said. "But we're trying."

We moved into the dining room. Everyone found a seat, damp and tense. Susan hovered by the doorway until I nodded at an empty chair. She sat last.

"Tea?" Marianne asked, because of course she had a dented thermos ready like it was a potion she'd brewed in her sleep. She unscrewed the lid with ceremony. "I brought enough even for *her*," she added, with the tone of someone extending an olive branch wrapped in barbed wire.

Susan didn't respond. She looked ... wrecked. Smaller, somehow. Like she'd been carrying the storm around inside her for years, and it was finally breaking loose.

"We need mugs," I said, already heading to the kitchen.

It felt wrong in there without Emilia. No sarcastic commentary. No dramatic huffs. No sister perched on the counter like a gremlin watching chaos unfold. Just the low hum of the fridge and the steady pounding of rain above.

And still there, hanging over the table, was her murder board. The mess of theories that used to make me roll my eyes now practically thrummed with energy. My gaze drifted over the tangle of notes and photos, stopping at one near the center, pinned with a bright pink pushpin.

Three girls in swimsuits, bellies sticking out on purpose, grins wide and wild. My mother in the middle, hair in fiery pigtails, streaked with mud, looking absurdly happy. Tabitha with blonde braids on one side. Marianne, tall and watchful, on the other.

But it was the background that mattered. A boy mid-swing, legs blurred with motion, and a teenage girl pushing him.

Susan and Lawrence.

I unpinned the photo and slid it into my pocket before grabbing mugs and heading back.

At the table, I handed out the mugs to Marianne, Tabitha, Parker, and Susan. My hand hovered before placing the last one in the empty space beside me.

Just in case Emilia woke up.

Silence stretched out between us, broken only by the quiet clink of Marianne's impromptu tea service and the wind battering the windows. Susan's hands trembled around her mug.

"I know you've been drugging your brother," I said, watching her carefully. "Not to hurt him, but to keep him bound."

Marianne straightened, fingers twitching toward her charm. Tabitha sipped her tea, eyes narrowed. Parker leaned forward, brows knit. But Susan just sat there, head bowed.

"Cyanide," I continued. "In small doses. Just enough to suppress his magic. Hidden in a potion. Family recipe?"

Susan closed her eyes. Something in her face broke. Like resignation had been sitting in her lungs for years, just waiting for permission to settle in.

I continued to press. "Your family name—Riviera. *River*. You're water witches, right?"

Susan's fingers curled tighter around the mug. "How did you figure it out?"

I shrugged. "You're his sister. Head nurse at Golden Pines. Regular at The Purple Pantry. You had access, knowledge, and most importantly, history. But it didn't fully click until I realized you and Lawrence were at the last induction ceremony. The one right before the flood."

I pulled the photo from my pocket and slid it across the table. Susan picked it up with both hands, like it might crumble. She blinked once. Then again. Her fingers tightened on the edges.

"I forgot this existed," she said finally, voice rough. "God, look at us. We thought we were invincible."

No one spoke.

"That day was the last time I saw him happy," she said. "Before the flood. Before the binding. Before our parents made him into something ... manageable."

"Because he wasn't manageable before, was he?"

Susan shook her head, eyes glassy. "He caused the flood. He killed Carolyne Morgan and destroyed nearly half the town. And he didn't even know it was him."

Marianne looked stunned, like someone had pulled the ground out from under her. "And he never figured it out?"

"Our parents bound him afterwards." Susan hung her head. "When they died, it became my responsibility."

Parker stared at her, stunned. "You've been poisoning your brother for fifty-one years?"

"To protect people," she snapped, then softened. "To protect *him* from himself, too."

Tabitha looked appalled. "That's not protection. That's a leash."

She ran a thumb over her brother's face in the picture. "They told me I had to help. That it was the only way to keep everyone safe. That Lawrence wanted it. I believed them."

The storm slammed a gust against the house. A collective shiver ran through us.

"I didn't realize until years later that the spell wasn't just suppressing his magic," she said. "It was suppressing him. His memory. His joy. I didn't know."

Parker opened his mouth, then closed it again. Tabitha shifted like she wanted to cross the room. Marianne stayed still as stone.

"After the flood ... after Carolyne ... The Morgans left, packed up and never came back. But the Rivieras," Susan drew in a breath, sharp and shallow, "we stayed."

Tabitha crossed her arms. "Yeah, we all know that part."

"What you *don't* know is why." Susan glanced down at the photo again, her thumb brushing over the edge like it might anchor her. "COWW knew what really happened."

Marianne straightened in her chair. Tabitha froze mid-eye-roll.

"What do you mean *knew*?" Tabitha asked, voice low.

Susan turned to me. "Your great-grandmother, Agnes Attar, was head of COWW at the time. Formidable woman. Ran the whole coven out of her sunroom with a cat that never blinked."

She gave a humorless smile. "And Margaret was her second-in-command. Both were instrumental in helping stop Lawrence and quiet the storms. Even Evelyn did what she could to help, young as she was. So yes, your family knew. And they offered us a deal."

The air in the room pulled taut.

"They told my parents we could leave quietly or stay under their watch, bound and silent. Lawrence would never use magic again. The rest of us would be stripped of our place in the magical community."

Parker swore under his breath. Tabitha looked like someone had flipped her upside down.

"A quiet exile in plain sight," Susan said. Her voice didn't shake, but something in her posture did. "My parents agreed. Said it was mercy."

Marianne's face softened. "He was only eleven."

Tabitha sat upright. Affront laced her voice. "That's not fair. It wasn't your whole family's fault."

"He was our responsibility. My parents' and mine. I helped cast the binding. I didn't fight it. I should have." Susan shook her head. "Somewhere along the way, I stopped being his sister and started being his warden."

She set the photo down in front of her and didn't look at it again. "He hated magic after that day. I think part of him remembered what he lost. He always hated the Attars after that, too; he just didn't fully understand why."

Her voice dropped to a whisper. "Lawrence got into a huge fight with your mom the day she died. I always assumed it was a heart attack, but when Margaret said someone killed your mom ... I knew it had to be Lawrence."

"So, you increased Gran's medication, in case she remembered more."

Susan flinched. "I was trying to keep her calm. I didn't want Lawrence to notice. I thought if I kept her quiet, he'd be safe. *She'd* be safe."

"Then you broke into our house. Destroyed Emilia's murder board. Stole all the Evoko, just to make sure Gran stayed quiet."

Susan looked up sharply. Her eyes locked with mine, wide and unsteady, the mug in her hands trembling slightly against the lip of the saucer. For a heartbeat, she didn't speak. Just stared, like I'd knocked the wind out of her with words alone.

"Anna..." Her voice was barely there. "Evoko would only work if Margaret didn't actually have dementia."

I didn't answer right away. Instead, I let her sit with it. See how she responded.

She blinked, once. Twice. A crack of wind hit the window hard enough to rattle the glass.

"Are you saying that her state is..." Her voice caught, staggered under the weight of the thought. "Magically induced?"

Tabitha lowered her teacup slowly, brows knit. Parker straightened in his chair, jaw tight. Marianne continued tracking Susan's reactions with her watchful eye.

"I think so," I said finally. "Yeah."

Susan reeled back like she'd been slapped. "But that means..."

"Someone else has been using magic to keep her silent," I said.

Susan opened her mouth. Closed it. Then tried again, voice rising with panic. "But I would've known. I would've *seen* something. She's under my care. Nothing gets past my staff."

"I know," I said. "I've already had a bottle of Evoko confiscated while I was there. But whatever spell is being used on Gran leaves a scent residue. It's almost like someone else is doing perfume magic. But this magic is topical, whereas mine is airborne. I smelled it on her both times I visited. I just didn't piece it together right away."

Susan's face twisted. "I *did* destroy the murder board. Emilia was getting too close. I was afraid she'd trigger something in Lawrence. I wanted to protect all of you. But I didn't touch the Evoko. I swear."

I blinked. "Wait. You didn't take it?"

She shook her head. "Didn't even *see* any."

I groaned and dropped my head to the table. "We were gone for *one* afternoon. *One.* And in that time, *three* people broke into our house?"

Marianne raised a finger like she was doing roll call. "Okay. Susan destroyed the board. Tabitha took the grimoire—"

Parker cut in, grim. "But the Evoko's still unaccounted for."

The room stilled. Cold. Heavy.

I looked at the empty mug in front of Emilia's chair. Whoever took the Evoko had to be the one who murdered Mom. But could Susan be right? Could it have been Lawrence? He left at the same time as Tabitha, and she came straight to the house. Wouldn't they have run into each other?

Something still wasn't clicking.

Before the silence could settle too long, a voice cut through the air. "The whispers on the water. They know. Always knew."

I turned, and there she was. Emilia. Pale as dawn, leaning hard against the doorframe, but awake. *Gloriously* awake. Her hair was a wild tangle, and she had Gran's old robe wrapped tight around her shoulders, but it was her eyes that stopped me. Glassy. Far-off. Like she was seeing something the rest of us couldn't.

I rushed to her. "Em? Are you okay?"

Everyone else stood, forming a loose semicircle. Marianne edged against the wall. Tabitha lingered close to Parker. Susan stood in the middle, her eyes flicking between Emilia and the rest of us, tense.

Emilia didn't seem to see me. Her gaze slid past like I was made of smoke. "The bridge couldn't hold it all." She sucked in a breath, sharp and sudden, like she'd just been struck. "The bridge. They were on the bridge. Great-Gran, Gran, and Mom. Throwing bottles into the flood. Not to cause it ... to *stop* it."

And just like that, it all snapped into place.

Why everyone blamed the Attars for the flood.

Because it happened during the COWW induction ceremony, and the ceremony was held at the Attar house.

Because when people get scared, they get stupid. And paranoid.

They saw witches tossing potions into a raging river, and minutes later, the water rose and swept away Carolyne Morgan.

Of course they thought my family caused it. But correlation doesn't mean causation. That was one of the first things I learned in stats class. My family didn't *cause* the flood. We just failed to stop it.

Emilia swayed, still staring at something only she could see. "The whispers on the water remember everything."

I cupped her face, still streaked in eyeliner from a date twelve years ago. My heart raced. She was in there. I just had to reach her.

"Scent," I whispered, turning to Parker. "Scent's the strongest tie to memory."

Parker nodded and brought me the bottle of Evoko. I uncapped it and waved it under her nose.

"Em, come back. Follow the scent back. It's me. Anna."

Her eyes didn't change, but her fingers twitched. Like she was reaching for something just out of reach. Not enough.

I looked around the room, frantic, and then it hit me. Not *my* scent. Hers.

I ran. In her room, the bottle was still there. Right where I'd seen it earlier, tucked beside the ceramic cat and the clutter of bracelets, quiet and patient as a heartbeat.

Joy. The last perfume I made before I left for college. The one I made after Danny died. I had poured into it every trace of love, thread of desperation, and note of memory I could coax from my aching heart. I thought if I got the magic right, I could bring my sister back from the edge.

When it didn't work, I quit. I told myself that if magic couldn't save the person I loved most, it wasn't worth anything at all.

But now I understood. She never needed saving. She needed space to break, to heal, to become. She needed time.

Magic doesn't overwrite grief. It walks beside it.

Magic isn't the fix. It's the witness.

Magic can't change nature. Magic *is* nature.

"Hold her steady," I called, rushing back into the room.

Parker caught Emilia gently by the waist. I uncapped the bottle and waved it under her nose.

"Come back to us, Em."

For a moment, nothing. Just rain pounding the roof. Thunder in the distance. Then, like a wave breaking, Emilia gasped. Her eyes widened. Focused. And locked onto mine.

"Anna?" Her voice cracked.

I grabbed her hands. "I'm here. You're back."

She clutched my arm, urgent now. "I saw Lawrence in my vision. Or whatever that was."

"You saw my brother?" Susan stepped forward, voice trembling.

Emilia nodded. Her eyes were clearing fast now, her grip tightening. "He's at Whisperwind Bridge."

"Why would he go there?" Parker asked.

"Because that's where it all started," I said. "He's confused. Angry. And now he knows the truth."

Susan's face crumpled. "Yesterday I finally told him I'd been binding his magic since he was eleven years old."

No one spoke. Outside, thunder cracked, rattling the windows.

Emilia pushed herself upright. She swayed but didn't fall. "We don't have much time."

Parker opened the door. The wind howled like something alive. Rain came down in silvery sheets. Water creeped over curbs, pooled across pavement.

As we stepped out, I felt it. That wrongness in the air. Something bitter, old and personal.

"Whisperwind Bridge," I said, pulling my coat tight around me. "And hurry."

The clock was ticking. The water was rising. And somewhere in the darkness, a man with fifty years of bottled rage was unleashing his fury on everything we loved.

CHAPTER THIRTY

RISING WATERS

The storm had swallowed the sun hours ago, but Whisperwind Bridge gleamed like a mirage in the gloom. Strings of rainbow lights blinked against the dark, their glow flickering in odd, arrhythmic bursts. Classical music floated through the air, warped and waterlogged. The notes stretched and sagged like they'd been submerged. What might have once been Vivaldi now sounded like it was clawing its way out of a nightmare.

I tightened my grip on the bottle of Mentis tucked into my jacket pocket. As Emilia, Marianne, Tabitha, Susan, Parker and I stepped onto the bridge, our boots splashed through puddles that shimmered in unnatural hues. The wind hissed through the trees, a low, whispering murmur that seemed to carry voices just beyond the edge of hearing.

Lawrence stood alone at the center of the bridge, rain swirling in strange spirals around him. It didn't fall on him so much as move with him, like he was the eye of the storm, and the storm loved him for it. The air pulsed with tension. Each gust of wind carried water, anger, and grief.

"He's in pain." Susan's voice broke as she stepped forward, reaching toward him. "I need to go to him. He needs someone he trusts."

Emilia caught her by the arm. "No."

The lights above shifted to a jaundiced green, then a stuttering violet. The music on the speakers bent in and out of tune, twisted by the current of Lawrence's unraveling magic.

"He's scared," Susan pleaded, trying to shake her off. "He's not a threat, he just doesn't understand what's happening to him."

"He *is* a threat," Emilia said. "The whispers on the river told me. He's angry. Out of control. And if you get close right now, he could hurt you without even meaning to."

Susan faltered, blinking rain from her lashes. She looked at her brother with horror and heartbreak written across her face.

A surge of wind shoved across the bridge, rattling the railings and sending a spray of river mist into our faces. I had to brace myself to stay upright. Behind me, Parker shifted closer, steadying both himself and Marianne, who had grabbed the edge of the railing with white-knuckled fingers.

Lawrence looked as if he were trying to hold himself together with sheer force of will. And failing.

"This isn't like before," Susan whispered. "It's happening again, but worse."

Tabitha stepped closer, her voice barely audible over the wind. "What do we do?"

"We snap him out of it." I took the bottle of Mentis from my pocket and turned toward Susan. "We go together. Slowly."

She nodded, her face pale and drawn. Her eyes never left Lawrence.

As we stepped forward, one cautious foot at a time, Parker moved behind us, scanning the bridge for weak spots like he might patch them with sheer focus. Tabitha followed a few paces behind, fingers reaching for the pouch at her belt. Marianne stayed near Emilia.

Lawrence didn't notice us at first. Then his head jerked up and his eyes locked on Susan.

"No," he barked, his voice raw and unsteady. "Not you. Don't pretend you care."

Susan flinched. "Lawrence, please! Listen to me."

"You *lied* to me!" He staggered a step backward, and the rain pulsed harder around him, the lights above flaring erratic green and blue. "You kept this from me—this *curse*—for fifty years!"

"It wasn't a curse," Susan pleaded, stepping forward.

But I could see the moment his gaze found me. His face twisted.

"You," he spat. "Stay back!"

I froze.

"You and your sister. You did this, didn't you? You Attars. You put this *on* me. That potion, your spells. It's all from *you*."

"Lawrence—" I began.

"No! Don't talk to me like I'm some poor, confused man. You're the witches, not me."

Susan tried again. "You've always had magic, Lawrence. You were born with it. I never wanted to hurt you. I was trying to protect you. We bound you because you couldn't control your magic. It was hurting you, and others. You remember the flood. What happened to Carolyne."

"Don't," he whispered. "Don't bring her up."

Susan's voice trembled, but she pressed on. "I'm sorry. I should have told you the truth. I should have helped you learn instead of hiding it. But I was scared."

Lawrence's breath hitched. The storm around him faltered for the briefest second. The lights dimmed.

He turned toward us again, soaked through and trembling. "Then take it back."

"What?" I asked.

"Take it back," he begged. "Please. I don't want it. I don't want this. I don't want to feel everything all the time. I can't breathe, I can't think. It's like I'm drowning from the inside."

Susan reached out. "We can help you."

"No!" he cried. "Take it *away!*"

The wind howled through the bridge. The lights above flickered violently, then one by one they popped, plunging us into the darkness of a storm that was grief, shame, and panic given shape.

Behind us, Parker and Tabitha stood at the mouth of the bridge, flanking either side like stone lions. Marianne still hovered near Emilia, her arms outstretched, lips moving in whispered incantations.

The storm quieted, barely. The music still played, warbled and wrong. Lawrence's shoulders shook under the weight of it all.

Susan and I exchanged a glance. Then, slowly, we took another step forward—me with Mentis still in hand, her with nothing but bare truth and a heart cracked wide open.

Lawrence crumpled. He sank to his knees with a choked sob. Susan ran and dropped beside him, arms wrapping around his frame. For a moment, they were just two siblings in the rain, clinging to each other in the middle of a bridge built for wishes and secrets.

"I didn't mean to," he whispered. "I never meant to hurt anyone."

"I know," Susan murmured, brushing a wet strand of hair from his face.

After a few moments, they pulled apart. Susan's hand lingered on his shoulder, grounding him.

"Lawrence." I took a tentative step toward him, holding out the perfume. "I made this. It's a clarity perfume. I call it Mentis."

He looked at me, hollowed out and blinking. "You think a perfume's going to fix me?"

"No," I said. "But I think your magic is tied to how you're feeling. And if we can clear your mind, maybe we can quiet the storm."

His eyes flicked to the bottle. For a moment, I thought he might refuse. But instead, he straightened, rising to his feet in slow, theatrical defiance.

He walked to the very center of the bridge, spread his arms wide like he was about to be crucified, and looked me dead in the eye.

"Then drench me."

The rain paused. I uncorked the Mentis. The scent of bergamot, geranium, a hint of pink grapefruit released instantly. It cut through the damp and the fear like a soft breath of summer. I held the bottle close, letting the fragrance cling to the air around me. I walked towards Lawrence.

Then came a shout. "*Get away from him!*"

We all turned.

Helen Hevel stood at the edge of the bridge, her eyes wild, soaked to the bone, one arm outstretched like she could physically stop the moment with sheer will.

Her gaze locked on the bottle in my hand.

"You're trying to poison him!"

And with those words, the storm snapped awake.

A fresh gust howled across the river, as if her fury had summoned it. Rain came sideways, harder, colder. The wind screamed between the slats of the bridge, drowning out the fading music and muffling Susan's gasp.

Helen stormed forward, each step stiff with purpose, her ponytail plastered to her jacket.

"She's trying to kill him!" she shouted again, pointing at me like I'd pulled a knife.

Susan stepped forward. "Helen, it's perfume. It's meant to help."

"Help?" Helen's voice cracked like thunder. "Don't you see what they're doing to him? Messing with his head again! Twisting him up with their potions and secrets. This," she pointed to the perfume in my hand, "This is how it starts!"

Before we could react, the air blasted us. It was as though the earth exhaled wrong, straight into our chests.

I flew backward and landed flat on my back, knocking the breath out of me. Lights strobed wildly, fractured by wind and rain, casting everything in surreal carnival hues.

Behind me, Tabitha cried out. Parker lunged, catching her as she stumbled.

Marianne dropped low, shielding Emilia, who'd collapsed by the railing. With one hand pressed to the wood, she whispered a protective spell, her voice barely audible over the shrieking wind and the warped strains of classical music still drifting from the hidden speakers.

Parker shouted. I twisted, pain lighting up my spine, just in time to see Tabitha tottering at the edge of the bridge. The railing had snapped, and one of her feet hovering over open air.

"Tabs!" Marianne and Parker launched forward, and Parker caught her wrist just as her heel slipped. He and Marianne both held fast, teeth clenched, dragging Tabitha back onto solid ground.

Another blast. Susan reached for Lawrence, trying to shield him, but Helen thrust out a hand. The wind shoved Susan like she weighed nothing. She collapsed by the bridge entrance, gasping, hair whipping across her face. Parker and Tabitha sprinted to help her.

"Helen, stop!" I shouted, struggling to sit. My coat twisted around me, heavy with rain. I forced my arms beneath me, searching for footing.

"I told the council this would happen," Helen roared, voice carrying over the storm. "That it was a mistake to let Margaret keep her grimoire. The Attar line can't be trusted. But no one listened."

I stared at her, disoriented, trying to piece it together. Which council? What mistake? Then something glinted around her neck.

A pendant. Silver. Familiar.

I blinked.

A tree. Encircled by a ring of tiny symbols.

The Tree of Life. I'd seen it yesterday, cataloging symbols for my database. Listed under Common Magical Glyphs—Wiccan, Celtic, Hermetic. A marker of power. Of lineage. Of witches.

Witches like Helen. Of course Helen was a witch. An air witch, from the looks of it. And a powerful one. I mean, she'd just tossed half of us around like dandelion fluff. This was hardly a groundbreaking deduction.

But I'd seen it in one other place, too—the photographs Marianne gave me.

My stomach dropped, as if the river itself had surged up and pulled me under. Cold swept through me, sharper than the rain. My breath hitched enough to make my chest ache. I tried to speak, but the words lodged in my throat like stones. I hadn't made the connection before. Different hair, different last name. But now I saw it. This woman had taken everything from us.

Helen stole Evoko. Helen murdered our mom.

And then tried to erase the rest of us, piece by piece.

A surge of heat rushed to my face. I didn't know if it was fury or grief or some twisted combination of both. My hands trembled. I rose to my feet, boots squelching on the soaked wood, my knees trembling with each step. The rain blurred my vision, but I didn't blink it away. Let it sting. Let it cut. I welcomed the pain—anything to keep me from collapsing.

"You're wrong, you know," I said, voice shaking, but not breaking. "The Attars were never responsible for the flood."

Helen's lip curled. "You expect me to believe that?" Her voice rose with the wind. "After everything your family has done? After what you did to Carolyne?"

She lunged toward me, fury radiating off her.

Marianne caught her arm. Tabitha rushed in, grabbing the other.

"Stop protecting them!" Helen shrieked at the women, trying to twist free. "You don't know what they are!"

"Anna is telling the truth." Susan stepped forward, partially propped up by Parker. Her movements were slow and deliberate. Blood dripping down her pale face. "It's not them. It's Lawrence. My brother. He's the one doing this."

Helen froze. "No. He couldn't have. He was just a boy. I saw Evelyn with my own eyes."

I reached into my inside jacket pocket, fingers closing around the envelope that was still there from last night. I found the photograph and held it out to Helen.

Two girls on a riverbank, arms looped around each other, faces bright with summer joy. Carolyne Morgan on the right. The barefoot and beaming girl beside her wore a silver Tree of Life pendant around her neck.

I turned the photo. *Carolyne Morgan & Helen Fairchild, Summer, 1984.*

Fairchild. Helen's maiden name. I extended the photo toward her. "You were her best friend."

Helen's eyes lingered on the photograph. Her fingers trembled. She looked up.

She looked at Susan first. Susan stood straight despite the wind. Her eyes were full of something unspoken—regret, maybe, or guilt.

Then Lawrence. He wasn't really *there*. Not fully. His eyes were glazed, caught in some unseen current, the magic in him still seeping out like smoke from a cracked lantern. The storm bent around him, tugging at his coat, his hair, as if drawn to its source. He swayed slightly, oblivious to it all, the center of a chaos he didn't seem to recognize.

Then Tabitha, holding tight to Marianne's arm. Parker just behind them. Emilia kneeling by the railing. Each of them still, wind-lashed and waiting. All of us bearing witness.

Something inside Helen gave way. I saw it in the soft collapse of her shoulders, the shimmer in her eyes.

"You don't know what it was like, watching her drown." Her fingers clutched her pendant like it might anchor her in place. "She was my best friend. I loved her. And I saw Evelyn out on that bridge, tossing potions into the storm. I thought she caused it, and that Margaret and the others came to stop her. When Carolyne died, I believed they covered it up, to protect their own."

She blinked hard. "But I was wrong, wasn't I?"

Marianne stepped forward. "You were right about the cover-up. But wrong about who they were protecting."

Helen's knees buckled, and she sank to the boards.

"They weren't starting the storm," she murmured. "They were trying to stop it. Evelyn was just a frightened and reckless kid. Her mother and grandmother were trying to pull her back."

"They weren't the cause," Marianne said gently. "They were the shield."

Helen's breath hitched. Her shoulders sagged.

My pulse thundered in my ears. I couldn't look away from this woman whose actions had carved holes in our family. I wanted to scream. To shake her. To demand *why*. But there was nothing left in her face now but ruin.

I thought I'd feel the satisfaction of justice when I'd found my mom's killer, but all I felt was ... hollow.

Silence. Then the bridge groaned beneath us. Lightning split the sky. The storm surged.

My voice came low, almost too quiet to hear over the wind. But I couldn't keep it in. "You killed our mom. And when Gran started to suspect, you hexed her too."

Helen flinched. "I never meant to ... It wasn't supposed to go that far."

"And Emilia?" I asked. "She got too close?"

My sister took a defiant step towards Helen, chin lifted.

Marianne's voice broke through it, barely a whisper. "Tell me it's not true."

Helen didn't answer. She just clutched her pendant tighter, like it might rewrite everything.

"I didn't know what else to do. The rains were starting up again. Just like fifty years ago. I thought I was saving the town." Helen's mouth opened to say more, but no sound came. Her eyes shimmered.

Her knees buckled. Marianne caught her before she hit the ground. Tabitha moved to help, her touch cautious and tentative. The way you'd handle something that might still bite.

Helen's fingers slipped from the pendant. It swung loose around her neck, the silver catching the light in a sudden, sharp glint.

I wanted to hate her. I *should* have hated her. But all I could feel in that moment was exhaustion. The ache of too many losses.

And then the bridge emitted a long, low groan, like the river itself was mourning.

We all looked down.

Then—*crack*. Lightning split the sky above us. The wind shrieked like a banshee let loose. The rain came down so hard it stung our skin.

Arms extended and palms open to the sky, Lawrence stood at the center of it all. His eyes were wide open but unseeing. Rain spun around him like a whirlpool, caught in a vortex of raw, unfiltered power.

"He's not in control," Susan whispered, voice tight.

"He's not *here*," I said. "He's somewhere inside himself. And if we don't pull him out—"

Another crack jolted the bridge, and several of us stumbled.

Parker dropped to one knee, then pressed his bare palm to the soaked planks beneath us. His eyes fluttered closed. For a moment, the storm quieted around us, just a little.

"I can't stop the storm," Parker said, opening his eyes, "but if the rest of you handle him, I can keep the bridge together."

I stared at him. "You're magic?"

"Not really." Parker shrugged. "Just a bit of earth magic. Grounding. Stability. Useful at times like this."

"Oh, we are talking about this later."

With the next gust of wind, Marianne's shawl whipped loose from her shoulders, and she caught it with a flick of her fingers, face already determined.

The wind tore at my jacket, cold and insistent, but I held my ground.

"We need to work together," I said, pitching my voice above the chaos, turning slowly to face each of them. "Marianne, your crystals. Tabitha, your balms and castings."

I hesitated. My gaze fell on Helen, who stood just off-center from the group. Her face was pale, eyes shadowed with guilt and fury and fear. But she hadn't run.

I took a step toward her. "Even you, Helen."

She blinked. "What?"

"Whatever power you have left—air, wards, grounding spells—I don't care. Anything that can help."

She stared at me like I'd slapped her. Or forgiven her. Maybe both.

"You want *me* to help?" Her voice was ragged. "After everything I've done?"

"Yes." I nodded. "You can't fix the past. But you can help him, and our town, have a future."

She swallowed hard, fingers twitching at her sides like she didn't trust herself to move forward. Or didn't believe she deserved to.

"Helen. You can still do what you came here to do. Save the town."

She stepped forward, drawing the pendant from her chest and lifting it in one hand. Wind shifted around her like a sigh. Her face was tight, lips pressed into a hard line, but her eyes had cleared. Helen nodded once, then stepped past me into the worst of the storm, her hair whipping like ribbons around her face. She lifted both hands—one clutching the pendant, the other palm open to the sky—and drew in a deep breath. For a moment, it seemed like nothing happened.

Then the wind around us *reversed*.

The air directly surrounding our circle on the bridge began to still, folding outward in a dome. Rain curved as it hit the invisible wall, sliding harmlessly to the sides. The howling died down to a murmur, muffled outside the barrier she'd cast. Inside the bubble, the world grew quiet.

Helen looked back at us. "Do what you need to do, and quick! I can't hold this for long."

Marianne was already in motion. She pulled a handful of stones from her pouch and lay them around Lawrence in a careful circle before dropping to the boards in a cross-legged pose. Her eyes fluttered shut as she chanted low and steady. Each stone gave off a pulse, like they were syncing to the rhythm of Lawrence's breath.

Tabitha followed, whispering a stream of words. Her breathe shimmered in the air before dissolving into mist. She smeared a thick balm across her palms and temples. Rosemary and camphor filled the space, sharp and clearing. Her hands glowed as she traced sigils in the air, weaving them into the invisible shell around Lawrence.

I drenched Lawrence in Mentis. "Come back," I whispered in his ear. "You're not alone anymore."

The wind slowed. Lawrence's shoulders dropped. His fingers twitched. The rain spiral above his head began to unravel, the wild energy losing its grip.

Marianne's stones glowed brighter. Tabitha chanted faster, her eyes locked on his face.

And finally, Lawrence *breathed*.

One deep inhale. Then another. His eyes fluttered. Focused.

And the storm broke. The spiral collapsed into nothing, the wind stopped short, and outside the bubble, the rain softened to a drizzle.

But before anyone could speak, a different sound pierced the calm. The low, warbling wail of sirens. Red and blue lights flashed across the mist like fire and ice.

Footsteps echoed on the bridge, fast and heavy. Then came the unmistakable voice, sharp and commanding. "All of you! Hands where I can see them!"

I turned, heart stalling.

David. Just like that, magic made way for the law. He and two other officers advanced toward us, hands on holsters, eyes wide as they took in the scene.

Lawrence collapsed into Susan's arms just as the rain outside the bubble gave way to police lights and chaos. And that was how the night ended. Not in fire or fury, but in the quiet, red-blue hush of consequences.

CHAPTER THIRTY-ONE

CHARM & PETAL

"Are you ready?" Emilia appeared at my side.

The morning sun had just begun to spill across the fresh-painted facade of Charm & Petal, warming the cobblestones under our feet and casting long, golden shafts of light across the street.

Above us, the shop's old sign swung gently in the breeze, its elegant, swirling font and faded pastel colors freshly restored to their former beauty. The edges were still worn, but the imperfections only made it feel more like *ours*. Rooted, real, and full of history.

The scent of vanilla and rose—my own blend, subtle and steady—hung in the air, woven into the silk of my dress and the folds of memory.

Two weeks had passed since the storm. Since Lawrence's unbound magic had nearly swept Serenity Falls away for the second time in fifty years. Two weeks since Helen's confession and arrest. Two weeks of rebuilding, remembering, and for me, reconnecting with a side of myself I'd spent years running from.

The town was finally starting to breathe again. Even Lawrence.

After a long, overdue conversation with Susan, he'd agreed it was time to stop hiding behind the binding potion and learn who he was without it. With surprising clarity (and a bit of Susan's stern nudging), he'd checked himself into The Briar Path, a remote magical rehabilitation center nestled somewhere deep in the Appalachian Mountains. No cell service or other such distractions. Just mist, magic, and a team of cranky old witches determined to break him down and build him back up.

He even sent me and Emilia a postcard. He was doing well. Healing, finally.

Emilia's recovery had been nothing short of remarkable. Once the tainted perfume had been flushed from her system, her memories had returned in slow, deliberate waves. Emilia still sometimes heard whispers in the wind. She didn't talk about them much, but when the breeze went still and her gaze drifted into the distance, I knew she was listening.

I nodded, my fingers brushing down the front of my dress—a soft green number that had once belonged to our mother. Marianne had unearthed it from an old cedar chest, its fabric scented with cedar sachets and sealed with a protection charm that still held a quiet pulse of warmth. Wearing it felt right. Like an invocation. Like armor.

"As I'll ever be," I replied.

A small crowd had already gathered for the grand reopening. Marianne and Tabitha stood with Parker, front and center, radiant with pride. Vivian held court by the coffee table with a pot of Cozy Cup's finest. Beside her, Sophia bounced on her toes with barely contained excitement, already talking about the book club meeting where we planned to discuss aromatherapy next month. Tom Kline passed out pastries while Juniper Martinez buzzed from group to group like the social butterfly she was always destined to be.

David Miller stood at the edge of the gathering, his police uniform crisp and professional as he directed traffic around the blocked-off section of sidewalk. He caught my eye and gave a small, supportive nod that made my chest tighten in the best way. My heart warmed with his presence, and the knowledge that we had a friendship built on mutual respect and shared history.

And then there was Lisa Marconi—polished, poised, with a "Lisa for Mayor" button gleaming. Our eyes met across the gathering, and her smile, though coolly professional, carried something else. Something I couldn't quite name.

"Well, if it isn't Antenna Anna." Her voice was teasing, but gentler than I remembered.

"I go by Anna these days," I replied, half-smiling.

Lisa chuckled. "I suppose we've both outgrown our high school selves. Believe it or not, I've always found your family's ... mystique fascinating. All those rumors about magic and moonlight recipes. I used to think they were silly." Her eyes gleamed. "Now I think there might've been more truth in them than we gave you credit for."

I tilted my head, unsure how to respond. Was this genuine reflection? A compliment wrapped in camouflage? With Lisa, it was always hard to tell.

Before I could dig deeper, she gestured toward the makeshift stage where the mayor usually stood. "The Mayor had to head to a state conference last minute. Asked me to fill in. I hope you don't mind."

I blinked. Lisa Marconi, giving the opening speech at *my* family's shop?

She must've read my expression, because she added with a smirk, "Don't worry, I'll keep it tasteful."

And to my surprise, she did.

Lisa stepped up to the podium with the ease of someone born to command attention. She cleared her throat, and the crowd fell into a respectful hush.

"Citizens of Serenity Falls," she began, her voice smooth as satin, "we stand here not just to reopen a business, but to celebrate something deeper—resilience, renewal, and the quiet power of believing in things that others might overlook."

She glanced in my direction, her gaze lingering a beat too long to be accidental.

"For decades, the Charm & Petal shop was a cornerstone of our town's identity. A place where perfume came with a promise. When it closed, something intangible left with it. But today, we welcome it back. And with it, a new era for Serenity Falls."

Applause rippled through the gathering. I caught sight of Vivian giving me a thumbs-up, and Juniper nodding appreciatively.

Lisa continued, "Thanks to the brave testimony of Helen Hevel and Susan Eldridge, and the truth brought to light by Anna and Emilia Attar, we can finally put to rest the shadows that have haunted this place. The charges against Emilia have been dismissed, and the Attar name restored to its rightful place in our community."

Another round of applause. Emilia reached for my hand, squeezing it tight.

"And now," Lisa said, stepping aside, "I'll let the true heart of this story cut the ribbon."

Taking a deep breath, I stepped forward to the royal blue ribbon stretched across the doorway of Charm & Petal. The ginkgo tree outside rustled its fan-shaped leaves, as if in anticipation.

"Thank you all for coming," I began, my voice steadier than I expected. "This shop has been in my family for generations. For over a year, it stood empty, a victim of misunderstandings and missed opportunities."

I glanced at Emilia, who gave me an encouraging nod.

"But today marks a new chapter." I lifted the scissors. "Charm & Petal was always meant to be a place of healing, of connection. A bridge between science and something ... a little more magical."

A knowing chuckle rippled through the crowd—louder from the COWW members present.

"So without further ado…" I positioned the scissors at the ribbon and cut cleanly through. "Charm & Petal is officially open for business!"

Cheers erupted as the ribbon fluttered to the cobblestones. As if of its own accord, the door swung open, releasing the complex symphony of herbs and flowers that had defined my childhood.

People streamed inside, exclaiming over the renovated interior. Parker had done most of the woodwork himself. The curved counter, the floor-to-ceiling shelves, the ornate perfumer's organ that now stood as the centerpiece of the main room were each crafted with care, love, and a respect for what had come before.

"He did a beautiful job," Emilia murmured, following my gaze to where Parker stood by one of the display tables, fielding questions about the craftsmanship.

"He did," I agreed, watching as he demonstrated the smooth glide of a drawer to an elderly woman whose eyes had gone wide with delight.

Things between Parker and me were … complicated. The revelation of his Morgan heritage had been a shock, but in the aftermath of the storm, with the truth finally laid bare, I was ready to begin the tentative work of building something new. Something that acknowledged the past, but wasn't defined by it.

"Well, go talk to him," Emilia nudged me, rolling her eyes. "You've been dancing around each other for weeks."

"We have not been—"

"Anna." She fixed me with her most exasperated look. "You both stare when you think the other isn't looking. It's nauseating."

I felt my cheeks warm. "I'll talk to him when I'm ready."

"Fine, be stubborn." Emilia grinned, then glanced toward the door where Juniper had just entered, her violet curls bouncing as she scanned the room. "I'm going to say hi to Juniper."

She squeezed my arm and drifted away, leaving me to navigate the crowd of well-wishers alone. I made my way toward the back of the shop, where a small gathering had formed around the refreshment table. Marianne was holding court, her silver-streaked hair pulled into an elegant twist, her hands gesturing animatedly as she recounted some story that had her audience in stitches.

"Anna!" she called when she spotted me. "Come here, darling. We were just talking about the meeting tonight."

I approached, smiling at the small circle of women—all members of COWW, though most people in the room wouldn't have known it. They blended in seamlessly: the bookstore owner with her cat-eye glasses, the retired seamstress who still carried a tape measure in her pocket out of habit.

"Are you nervous?" asked the owner of the bookstore across the street from me, who I belatedly realized was Juniper's mother.

"A little," I admitted. "It's been a long time since there was a formal induction."

"You'll be wonderful," Marianne assured me, patting my hand. "The Council has unanimously agreed. You're ready."

The words sent a thrill through me. After fifty years of secrecy, of underground meetings and whispered initiations, COWW was stepping back into the light. Tonight, in the same garden where my mother had once stood, I would join their ranks officially.

"Speaking of ready," Tabitha said, appearing at my elbow, "there's someone here to see you."

I turned, expecting another well-wisher, perhaps another apology from a town council member. Instead, I found myself face to face with Gran.

She stood in the doorway to the back room, supported by Susan's careful arm. Her silver curls were neatly arranged, her blue eyes clear and sharp. She wore a pale yellow dress with tiny embroidered flowers along the collar that I recognized from my childhood.

"Gran?" I whispered, hardly daring to believe.

"Hello, my dear," she said, her voice strong. "I hear you've been making quite the stir."

I crossed the room in three quick strides and wrapped my arms around her, breathing in the scent of her, now blessedly free of the poison that had held her prisoner for the last year. "You're here," I murmured into her shoulder. "You're really here."

She patted my back, her touch as gentle as I remembered. "Of course I am. Did you think I'd miss my granddaughter's big day?"

I pulled back, wiping at my eyes. "But how are you..."

"Lucid?" Gran smiled, a knowing twinkle in her eye. "Let's just say Evoko was even more effective than we realized. It took time, but with Susan's help..." She glanced at the woman beside her, who managed a tentative smile.

I looked between them, understanding dawning. "You've been working together."

Susan nodded. "After everything that happened with Lawrence, I needed to make amends somehow." She hesitated. "When I realized what Helen had been doing to your grandmother, I knew I had to help undo the damage."

"Susan has been giving me special treatments," Gran explained. "A little Evoko every day, plus some other remedies we've been experimenting with."

I shook my head in wonder. "I can't believe it. I thought—"

"That I was gone for good?" Gran's smile was gentle. "Not quite yet, dear. Though I must admit, it comes and goes. Today is a good day."

The shop had quieted. People were watching our reunion with curious, misty-eyed expressions. From the crowd, I caught a glimpse of Emilia weaving her way toward us, her movements hesitant, almost disbelieving.

The moment Gran spotted her, her whole face lit up. "Emilia," she said, opening her arms.

Emilia's breath hitched, her hand flying to her mouth. For a heartbeat she stood frozen, and then she rushed forward, colliding into Gran's embrace so hard it made both of them laugh.

Gran cradled Emilia's head against her shoulder, her hands smoothing her hair the way she must have done when we were small. "My girl," Gran murmured, her voice thick with emotion. "My fierce, stubborn girl."

Emilia clung to her, tears streaming freely now, her whole body shaking with silent sobs. "I missed you," she choked out. "I missed you so much."

"And I missed you," Gran whispered back. "Every single day, even when I couldn't say it."

I blinked hard against my own tears, my heart aching in the sweetest way.

Gran surveyed the room with sharp, discerning eyes, then turned to me. "Well," she said, adjusting her shawl, "show me what you've done with my shop."

We wove through the aisles, her hand light on my arm as I pointed out the changes—Parker's woodworking, the reorganized herb drawers, the sigil etched into the threshold for protection. I showed her the new blends I'd crafted, the ones that had emerged during the storm and after, born of intuition and necessity.

Gran sniffed each bottle with reverence, her eyes narrowing thoughtfully. "Too much clary sage, dear," she murmured at one, then smiled at another. "Now *that's* balance."

She didn't need to say much. Her approval lived in the nods, in the way her fingers brushed the labeled jars with affection, in the small exhale of satisfaction when she looked at the reclaimed altar shelf beneath the ginkgo painting.

And then she squeezed my hand. "You've honored this place. And you've made it yours."

Around us, the grand opening picked up again. Vivian and Ms. Hattie passed out sweet potato hand pies, someone turned the music back up, and Emilia rang up a customer. Gran drifted back toward a chair near the window, settling in with a cup of tea like the matriarch she was, content to observe the new rhythm of a legacy continuing.

The crowd gradually thinned as afternoon stretched toward evening. Soon only a handful of people remained—the COWW members, lingering to discuss the night's ceremony; Parker, methodically checking each shelf and drawer one last time; Emilia and Juniper, deep in conversation by the window.

I found myself by the perfume bar, hands tracing the lines of the wood, when I sensed someone approaching.

"Hey," said David, a little awkwardly. "Before you disappear into another mystery or potion experiment, I wanted to give you something."

He held out a small, box, neatly wrapped in kraft paper and tied with a lavender ribbon.

I blinked. "What's this?"

"Open it," he said, shifting his weight like he wasn't sure if this was a good idea.

Inside was a silver pendant, shaped like a single drop of water, encased in a spiral. Just like the symbol on Evoko. It glinted in the light, delicate but precise.

"I ... wow." I ran a thumb over it. "Where did you even find this?"

"I didn't. I had it made," he said. "You always liked weird jewelry."

I laughed, but something about it caught in my throat. Before I could respond, he stepped forward and pulled me into a hug. And not the kind of hug you give an old friend.

It lasted just a beat too long for that.

When he pulled back, his hands lingered at my elbows. His eyes met mine, and for a split second, the world narrowed.

Oh.

I felt it.

That shift. That quiet weight of something unspoken.

I swallowed hard and looked down at the necklace. "It's beautiful. Thank you."

"Anytime," he said, voice soft.

He stepped away, and I exhaled.

A minute later, Parker came up beside me, holding two glasses of cider. "So ... David, huh?"

I didn't look at him. "Old friend from high school."

"Mmhmm." He handed me a glass.

"We dissected frogs together," I added, probably too quickly.

Parker's brow lifted. He took a sip of cider, eyes still on me.

I glanced up at him, taking in the soft curve of his smile, the hint of jealousy in his eyes. "Thank you. For all of this." I gestured around us. "You saved it."

He shook his head. "I just did the woodwork. You're the one who brought it back to life."

We stood in silence for a moment, the air between us charged with all the things we hadn't said. Finally, I took a breath. "Parker, about us—"

"You don't have to explain," he interrupted. "I understand why you were angry. Why you still might be."

"I'm not," I said, surprising myself with the truth of it. "Not anymore. We were both caught in something bigger than ourselves. Something that started before we were even born."

He nodded, his gaze steady on mine. "And now?"

I reached for his hand. His fingers curled around mine without hesitation, warm and solid. We stayed like that for a moment.

I was aware of his closeness, the way he looked at me like he actually saw me. But David was not far behind in my thoughts. It was a strange and unfamiliar feeling, being noticed. Wanted.

Since when did I become the center of a low-key love triangle?

I wasn't sure what to do with that, but maybe I didn't have to decide. Not yet.

"For now," I said, "maybe we just try things without the family feuds and magical disasters hanging over our heads. See what normal feels like."

His smile widened.

"There you are!" Tabitha appeared around the corner, eyes locking on our joined hands with shameless delight. "Sorry to interrupt, but we need to get going if we're going to set up for tonight."

Parker gave my hand a final, gentle squeeze before letting go. "I'll finish up here," he said. "You go get ready for your big induction."

I nodded, nerves fluttering again. "You'll be there?"

"Wouldn't miss it."

As I followed Tabitha toward the door where the other COWW members were gathering, I caught sight of Emilia saying goodbye to Juniper. My sister's smile was wider than I'd seen in ages.

"Making plans?" I asked, as she joined me.

Emilia replied with an enthusiastic grin. "Juniper runs the Serenity Falls Murder Club. They meet every Thursday to discuss true crime cases and solve mystery puzzles. She's inviting me to be a guest speaker next week!"

I smiled, happy to see my sister reconnecting with old friends and sharing her passion. "From amateur detective to featured expert. That's quite a promotion."

"I know, right?" Emilia's eyes practically sparkled. "They've been analyzing that cold case from Millfield County. The one with the mysterious garden clues? I have theories."

I raised an eyebrow, amused by her excitement. "I bet you do."

Together, we stepped out into the golden light of late afternoon. The street was quiet now that the festivities were over, but the air still buzzed with possibility. I glanced back at the newly restored sign swinging above the door: Charm & Petal, the letters painted in the same graceful script my grandmother had chosen decades ago.

This was my legacy. One I was finally ready to embrace.

As we walked toward home, toward the garden where my journey would officially begin, I felt a sense of rightness settle over me. The path ahead wasn't clear yet, but for the first time in years, I wasn't afraid of the unknown.

I was an Attar. A perfumer. A witch.

And I was finally home.

Chapter Thirty-Two

COMING HOME

The sun had begun its slow descent by the time we got home. The garden behind our house had been transformed in the past two weeks. Dead branches were cleared away, overgrown paths neatly trimmed, and in the center, a circle of twelve white stones gleamed in the golden light.

Watson prowled along the edge of the stone circle, his gray fur catching the last rays of sunlight as he inspected the proceedings with a grave little frown, like an official garden inspector.

COWW members moved with quiet purpose, arranging herbs and candles in a pattern only they understood. Marianne directed the setup with graceful precision, while Tabitha double-checked each element with scientific care. But at the heart of it all, seated in her weathered wicker chair, was Gran, her chin lifted with quiet authority.

Her eyes found mine across the gathering, bright as ever, and she gave me a slow, approving nod. The kind that said: *You're exactly where you're meant to be.* And just like that, the fluttering in my chest steadied.

"I'm going to change," I told Emilia, gesturing to my green dress.

She nodded, her eyes still scanning the garden with wonder. "I'll wait here."

Watson leapt up onto the bench beside her, giving a theatrical little *mrrrp* as if demanding an update on the ceremony preparations. Emilia absentmindedly scratched behind his ears.

When I returned wearing the simple white linen ceremonial robe that Marianne had prepared, Emilia was sitting on the old stone bench beneath our old climbing tree. She patted the space beside her.

"Nervous?" she asked as I settled next to her.

"Terrified," I admitted. "But in a good way."

Emilia chuckled. "Never thought I'd see the day when my hyper-rational sister would be joining a coven."

"You know," I said, studying my sister's face in the lantern light, "there's room for you in COWW too, if you wanted. They'd value your talent for research and pattern recognition. It doesn't always have to be about spells and potions."

Emilia gave a short laugh, shaking her head. "Thanks, but after my own special experience with being magically hexed into remembering my awkward teenage years? I think I'll stick to true crime." She gestured toward the gathering of witches. "Besides, one magical Attar sister is enough for this town. I've seen what happens when people mess with forces beyond their understanding—both in my documentaries and, you know, literally last month when I almost drowned in mud."

The honesty in her voice was unmistakable beneath the humor. She wasn't afraid, exactly, just realistic about where her strengths lay. And maybe a little wary after everything she'd been through.

My smile turned wry. "Sure, I'll handle the magic and you handle the murder boards. Probably safer that way. For everyone."

We sat in comfortable silence for a moment, watching as more COWW members arrived. Parker was among them, hanging back respectfully, still unsure of his place in this house that his family had shunned for generations.

Watson, sensing the shifting mood, abandoned his post by Emilia's side and trotted over to Parker, winding around his ankles before settling nearby with a dignified plop. Apparently, he'd decided Parker could stay.

"So," Emilia said finally, "you're really staying, huh?"

I turned to her, studying the face I knew better than my own. Despite everything we'd been through, there was still so much we hadn't said to each other.

"I am," I said. "If that's okay with you."

"Okay with me?" Emilia's eyebrows shot up. "Anna, it's all I've wanted since you left for college. This house is too big, too empty, with just me rattling around in it."

"I should have visited more. Called more. Been there when Mom died. When Gran got sick. I—"

"Hey." Emilia put her hand over mine. "We both made mistakes. I shut down after Danny died. I pushed everyone away, including you. And then I got so wrapped up in my theories about Mom that I almost got myself arrested."

I laughed despite myself. "You *did* get yourself arrested."

"Details," she said, waving dismissively. "The point is, we've both got stuff to work on."

"We do," I agreed. "And it won't be fixed overnight. But I'm in it for the long haul if you are."

Emilia's smile turned mischievous. "You mean you're committed to us eventually becoming the batty old witch sisters in the creepy house on the edge of the forest?"

I grinned, recalling our conversation from when I'd first arrived. "Complete with floppy hats and mysterious herbal brews that make the neighbors nervous."

"And regular trips to the wishing bridge to terrorize local teenagers with our cryptic prophecies," Emilia added with delight.

Then her tone softened just a notch. "And, hey ... Now you'll be here to help get Gran's suite ready. She's planning to move back in as soon as Susan gives the okay."

"Oh?" I said, surprised and warmed by the news all at once.

"Yeah. And as much as I love her," Emilia said with a dramatic sigh, "I'm very relieved I won't be managing her tea preferences, crystal placement, and moon-calendar meal prep all by myself."

"Don't worry," I said, nudging her playfully. "We'll tag-team the batty old witch triple threat."

"Wouldn't have it any other way," she said, squeezing my hand.

We shared a quiet moment, then three clear notes rang through the evening air.

Parker slid in beside Emilia, offering a small, knowing smile. "Ceremony time?"

"Yep," Emilia said, nudging him with her elbow. "She hasn't levitated yet, but any minute now."

Parker raised an eyebrow at me, amused. "Should I be worried?"

"Only if I start speaking in ancient tongues," I said, rising from the bench. "Then maybe run."

Emilia grinned. "We'll hold the fort from here. Go on, witch-in-training."

As I approached the stone circle, the women of the Council parted, forming an open path. At the center now stood Gran, wrapped in her ceremonial cloak, a circlet of woven flowers and silver threading her hair like starlight.

"Anna Attar," she called, her voice carrying across the garden with surprising strength. "You stand before the Council of Wise Women, seeking to join our circle. Do you come of your own free will?"

"I do," I answered, my voice steady despite the flutter in my chest.

"Do you pledge to use your gifts for healing and protection, never for harm?"

"I do."

"Do you swear to uphold the secrets of our order, to preserve the balance of power, and to mentor those who come after you?"

"I do."

Gran nodded, then turned to Tabitha, who stepped forward with a small silver dish filled with freshly cut herbs—rosemary for remembrance, lavender for peace, mugwort for vision, and clary sage for clarity. Tabitha set the dish on a small stone altar and lit it with a match. Fragrant smoke curled upward, sweet and sharp.

"Breathe deep," Gran instructed. "Let the essence of these plants become part of you."

I inhaled, feeling the smoke fill my lungs, the scents mingling and blooming inside me. My head felt lighter, my senses sharper.

Gran's eyes softened as she reached for a small bowl of shimmering water drawn from the Whisperwind River on a full moon. Its silver glow caught the last of the sun.

"With this water," she said, "I mark you as one of us."

She dipped her finger into the bowl and traced a spiral on my forehead—a symbol of beginnings and endings and the magic that lives in between. The water tingled on my skin, cool then warm.

"Let the waters of memory flow through you," Gran intoned. "Let the wisdom of those who came before guide your hands and your heart."

She stepped back, and the circle of women began to move clockwise around me, each one stopping to place something small in my outstretched palms—a river stone, a dried flower, a feather, a seed. Gifts of the elements, symbols of the power and responsibility I was accepting.

Gran was the last to stand before me. She looked at me, not just as a granddaughter, but as a woman grown into her power. Then pinned a sprig of rosemary over my heart and said the words I would carry with me always.

"By the power vested in me as Head of the Council of Wise Women, and by the blood we share, I welcome you, Anna Attar, into our circle. May your path be blessed, your heart be true, and your magic flow like the river—ever changing, ever constant."

A breeze swept through the garden, stirring the leaves of the trees and sending the smoke from the burning herbs spiraling upward. For a moment, I thought I saw other figures standing among the COWW members, transparent as mist but unmistakable: My mother, her smile radiant; Great-Gran in her prime, straight-backed and proud; and other women I didn't recognize but somehow knew were Attars, stretching back through generations.

Then they were gone, and I was standing in a circle of living women, their faces alight with welcome and pride.

"Welcome home, sister," Tabitha said, stepping forward to embrace me.

As the circle broke and people began to move around the garden, congratulating me and sharing stories of their own inductions, I found myself drifting back to where Emilia and Parker sat under the climbing tree, the two of them deep in conversation that paused when I approached.

"So?" Emilia asked, her eyes wide. "How does it feel to be officially witchy?"

"Like I've always been this way," I said, surprised by the truth of it. "Like I just needed someone to remind me."

Parker's smile was soft, almost shy. "It suits you."

The golden light was fading now, the garden settling into the blue hush of evening. Across the lawn, Council members were lighting lanterns and unpacking baskets of food for the feast that would follow. The air was alive with laughter, conversation, and the promise of new beginnings.

I looked at my sister. In that moment, standing in the garden where generations of Attars had gathered before me, I felt a certainty settle in my bones.

This was where I belonged. With Emilia beside me, and the Council's wisdom to guide me and my own magic finally acknowledged, I was ready for whatever came next.

The sun slipped below the horizon, painting the sky in shades of pink and purple. As darkness fell, the lanterns glowed brighter, casting warm pools of light across the garden. The feast was in full swing now, laughter and the clatter of dishes rising into the twilight a ir.

Watson, clearly deciding my initiation deserved official acknowledgment, sprang into my lap without warning. He turned three slow, deliberate circles, his tail flicking against my robes, before settling with the heavy, satisfied thump of a cat who knew exactly where he belonged.

I looked down at him, amused. "Guess I'm officially approved."

Watson blinked up at me once, slow and solemn, then tucked his paws under his chest.

Emilia snorted into her drink. "Knighted by the house guardian. That's a lifetime appointment, you know."

I smiled, threading my fingers through the thick gray fur at Watson's neck, feeling his rumbling purr against my palm. For a moment, I let myself simply exist there, surrounded by family, food, and laughter.

But a small pull inside me, steady and insistent, reminded me I wasn't done yet. There was one more thing I needed to do.

"I'll be back before they cut the cake," I whispered to Emilia, who nodded knowingly.

"The bridge?" she asked.

"One more circle needs closing," I said. "I won't be long."

"Go," Emilia replied with an understanding smile. "We'll be here when you get back."

I slipped away from the celebration, following the familiar path that wound from our backyard, through the trees, and down to the water's edge. The sounds of laughter and conversation faded behind me, replaced by the gentle murmur of the river and the whispering of leaves.

By the time I reached Whisperwind Bridge, the stars had risen.

Calm now, the river flowed steadily beneath me. The storm had passed, leaving only echoes in the mist. Beneath my boots, the bridge stood, weathered and worn, but solid. Rain, smoke, and the scent of wild things still lingered in the air.

I stepped into the center of the bridge. This was where it had all begun. And ended. And begun again. I reached into my coat pocket and pulled out a small bottle of Evoko. I spritzed it once, let the rosemary, rain-soaked petals, and memory rise around me.

Then I stepped up to the railing and looked down at the river.

"I'm a witch," I said. Quietly. Like I wasn't sure if I meant it, or if the bridge would believe me.

The breeze caught the words and carried them, threading them through the trees, over the rooftops of Serenity Falls, across the water.

I took a breath, squared my shoulders, and said it again. This time loud enough to scare a few birds out of the trees.

"I'm a witch!"

It echoed through the hollow of the valley. No lightning. No thunder. No flames or falling stars. Just the wind.

But *something* shifted. The breeze rose, circling me, playful and strange. It tugged at my sleeves, ruffled my hair, wrapped around me, curious.

Like the bridge was listening. And maybe it always had been.

When I was little, I used to come here and make wishes. The rumor was, if you spoke a secret truth aloud—really offered it to the bridge—it would grant you a wish. I must've stood here a dozen times, whispering the same wish over and over.

I wish I could find a place that feels like home.

But I never gave it my truth. Not the real one. Not until now.

I looked out at the water, the forest beyond, the whole little town I used to think I didn't belong in. And I realized I'd been wrong about the story of the bridge.

It wasn't a transaction. It was a *path*.

The bridge didn't *grant* wishes. It showed you how to meet them halfway. But you had to go first. You had to speak the thing you were most afraid to say. Until you do, nowhere feels like home. The truth is, you don't find home by running. You find it by standing still.

The wind gusted one last time, spinning leaves up from the road and dancing them across the wooden planks of the bridge. One brushed against my cheek, soft as a kiss. Then it faded. Gone, but not forgotten.

And then, just to the river. Just to myself.

"I'm a witch," I said again. No fear or hiding this time. Just truth.

I smiled, eyes damp, heart full. The case was closed, the town was at peace.

And my wish?

It had already come true.

GRATITUDE

To the magic-makers.

To my Kick Ass Alpha Team, Isa and Keyna. You are the dream collaborators I never knew I needed until you showed up with wit, wisdom, and just the right amount of chaos. Thank you for your fierce friendship and fearless feedback. You make this ride wild and wonderful.

To the brilliant minds behind Fictionary. Your software may be built on story structure, but its soul is community. Thank you for creating a space where data-loving nerds like me can thrive, and for charting a path through the fog of first drafts.

To my early readers, you polished this story until it shone. Your sharp eyes and generous hearts made this book better than I imagined it could be.

To my Vetiver Aromatics family. Thank you for infusing my life with perfume, mischief, and moments of pure sparkle. Who knew chaos could smell so good?

And finally, to every reader who picked up my first book and asked for more. This story exists because you believed. May you always follow your nose, trust your instincts, and find the magic waiting in unexpected places.

ABOUT THE AUTHOR

I'm Iris Applewood, your friendly neighborhood magical realist, cooking up worlds of wonder from my quaint home in Southern Indiana. I've always believed that the boundaries between the mundane and the magical are just waiting to be blurred. And boy howdy, do I love blurring them!

In my spare time, you'll find me tinkering in the kitchen, where I channel my creativity into concocting delightful dishes and perfumes that could almost pass for potions. When I'm not busy mixing spices or stirring tales, I cherish my sleep. It's like pressing the reset button on my imagination. Dreamland is often where I stumble upon my next big story idea, so you bet I take my bedtime seriously!

Writing is my way of stitching a little more enchantment into the fabric of our lives. And as you dive into my stories, I hope you find that magic can bloom in the most unexpected of places. Perhaps even in your own backyard.

Want to know more about me? Scan the QR code below to sign up for my newsletter. Or go to www.irisapplewood.com

CHARM & PETAL PERFUMES

(Notes from Gran's Grimoire)

Perfume is patience in liquid form. In the world beyond this book, a true perfume requires time—weeks, often months—to macerate. The essences must mingle and marry, their sharp edges softened by time's slow alchemy. But time is a luxury not always afforded to the brokenhearted, the forgetful, or the urgently enchanted.

Here, in this book, you will find a different path. These blends were not made for mass production or idle vanity. They are tonics, each with a purpose and a pulse. They do not wait. With the right intent (and the proper ritual), they can be ready in a day.

The Ritual of the Quickened Steep

At moonrise, place the sealed bottle in a bowl of saltwater (a pinch of sea salt stirred into spring water will do). Light a white candle beside it. Speak thrice aloud the name of the tonic. Then breathe slowly and steadily over the bottle while imagining the scent unfurling its magic. Let it rest until the candle burns down.

Once done, the perfume will be bound to its intention. Use wisely.

And remember: scent is a key. Once turned, some doors do not easily close again.

Evoko

A Tonic for Lost Things

For when the past slips through your fingers like mist, and names sit heavy on the tip of the tongue. To awaken what's been tucked away.

Instructions:
Apply one spritz to pulse points while thinking of what you wish to remember. Close your eyes. Inhale deeply. Let the scent guide you.

Notes & Properties:

- **Sun-orange (blooded and sweet):** For brightness of mind and warm recollection

- **Wild mint & rosemary:** To stir the senses and open the inner gate

- **Pear & jasmine:** For the sweetness of long-lost moments and dreams almost remembered

- **Tea rose & sage (twice blessed):** Clarity, wisdom, and the courage to know

- **Rose & frankincense smoke:** Anchors the vision in truth

- **Sandalwood & vanilla (absolute):** Softness, comfort, and a trail that lingers

Side Effects:

May evoke déjà vu, forgotten birthdays, the scent of an old love letter, or the feeling that someone you miss just passed by.

Storage:

Keep sealed when not in use. Memories, once stirred, can be difficult to return to sleep.

Solamen

A Tonic for Troubled Hearts and Restless Spirits

Brewed for the weary, the frayed, the quietly undone. Solamen is not to be rushed. It is a hush in a bottle, a fragrant hand on your shoulder, a lullaby for the soul.

To Use:

Apply gently to wrists, neck, or over your heart. Best used after tears, before sleep, or when the world is just a little too loud. Sip a cup of something warm. Light a candle, if you like. Breathe in.

Infused With:

- **Melissa & green tea:** For stillness, renewal, and thoughts that no longer clamor

- **Litsea cubeba & orange blossom:** To lift what is heavy and soften sharp corners

- **Lavender & chamomile:** Classic comforts; faithful herbs of hearth and healing

- **Clary sage (a third part only):** To clear the mind without stirring too deep

- **Blue tansy:** The rarest calm; deep, floral, and a little otherworldly

- **White musk & patchouli:** A grounding embrace, steady and quiet

- **Myrrh:** The echo of silence in a sacred space

Warning:

Extended use may result in sighs of relief, unplanned naps, and spontaneous poetry. May also attract cats.

Storage:

Keep in a cool, dim drawer beside your softest things. Do not lend it lightly. Peace is personal, and this potion knows its keeper.

Mentis

A Tonic for Storm Minds and Tempest Hearts

When the winds rise and thoughts scatter like leaves, Mentis is the breath between thunderclaps. A draught of lucidity, conjured for moments when clarity is not a luxury, but a lifeline.

To Use:

Inhale at the first sign of emotional squalls. Apply to temples, throat, or the inside of your wrists. Best used in silence, or with the faintest hum of wind chimes. For stubborn storms (emotional or meteorological), use in combination with deep breathing and firm intentions.

Blended With:

- **Bergamot & pink grapefruit:** To cut through mental fog and call back focus with bright urgency

- **Bay laurel & blue cypress:** For clear thought and calm command in the face of chaos

- **Fresh water accord:** A memory of stillness; the lake before the ripple

- **Geranium (absolute & African):** To balance the storm within and temper extremes

- **Cardamom (cold-captured):** A sharp snap of insight, clean and quick

- **ISO E Super:** For unseen structure. What holds when all else wavers

- **Cypress, balsam fir & cedarwood:** Roots and resin, ancient strength to anchor the moment

- **Oakmoss (real & mimic):** The wisdom of forests in full quiet

- **Vetiver & white musk:** The final exhale: grounded, cool, resolved

Note:
Do not underestimate its strength. Mentis is a truth-teller. Use only when you are ready to see clearly. Not recommended during full moons, family arguments, or before impulsive love letters.

Storage:
Wrap in dark cloth and keep near your journals or maps. The bottle may hum slightly during lightning storms—this is normal. It is listening.